THE FIRST MO
PREACHERS
ASSAULT

THE FIRST MOUNTAIN MAN
PREACHER'S ASSAULT

WILLIAM W. JOHNSTONE
with J. A. Johnstone

PINNACLE BOOKS
Kensington Publishing Corp.
www.kensingtonbooks.com

PINNACLE BOOKS are published by

Kensington Publishing Corp.
119 West 40th Street
New York, NY 10018

PUBLISHER'S NOTE
Following the death of William W. Johnstone, the Johnstone family is working with a carefully selected writer to organize and complete Mr. Johnstone's outlines and many unfinished manuscripts to create additional novels in all of his series like The Last Gunfighter, Mountain Man, and Eagles, among others. This novel was inspired by Mr. Johnstone's superb storytelling.

All Kensington titles, imprints, and distributed lines are available at special quantity discounts for bulk purchases for sales promotions, premiums, fund-raising, educational, or institutional use. Special book excerpts or customized printings can also be created to fit specific needs. For details, write or phone the office of the Kensington special sales manager: Kensington Publishing Corp., 119 West 40th Street, New York, NY 10018, attn: Special Sales Department; phone 1-800-221-2647.

PINNACLE BOOKS and the Pinnacle logo are Reg. U.S. Pat. & TM Off.
The WWJ steer head logo is a trademark of Kensington Publishing Corp.

ISBN-13: 978-0-7860-2342-4
ISBN-10: 0-7860-2342-2

First printing: January 2011

10 9 8 7 6 5 4 3

Printed in the United States of America

CHAPTER 1

Independence, Missouri, was a place most folks visited solely in order to leave. The route people had recently started to call the Oregon Trail began there, and already hundreds of wagons carrying immigrants had traversed it, heading to the Pacific Northwest where those settlers would make their new homes.

Independence was also where the Santa Fe Trail began, but the wagons that followed that path weren't loaded down with immigrants. Instead, they were packed with trade goods bound for the markets of Santa Fe, in Mexican territory. A few settlers made that trip, too, but the Mexican government discouraged immigration in favor of commerce. When the wagons made their return journey to the States, they would be filled with Mexican gold and silver.

Like most people who went to Independence, the man called Preacher didn't intend to stay long. But as he stared down the barrel of a pistol, he wondered if he was going to be staying in Independence from now on, probably in an unmarked grave. "Take it easy there, hoss," he drawled in his gravelly voice. "I ain't lookin' for trouble."

"I ain't either," replied the man pointing the gun at him. "I'm lookin' for money, and I'll take what you got."

Preacher couldn't help but chuckle. "Well, you are smack-dab out of luck, friend, because I don't have a single coin in my pocket."

It was true. Earlier that evening, Preacher had spent the last of his money on supplies for him and his two companions, Lorenzo and Casey. He'd cached the goods in the stable where they had their horses, and he was on his way to the tavern where he knew he would find them.

Lorenzo had a small stake, and he planned to try running it into a bigger one if he could find a suitable poker game. Preacher had decided to cut through the alley to reach the tavern, and it was looking like a questionable decision. A man had stepped out of the shadows and accosted him at gunpoint, and Preacher's keen ears had picked up a scuff of boot leather on hard-packed ground behind him, as well. There were two of the scoundrels.

But Preacher wasn't exactly alone. Standing tensely beside him was the big, shaggy, wolflike cur known only as Dog.

"No money?" the would-be robber in front of Preacher said. "You're a liar! You got to have some money!"

Until then, Preacher might have been willing to turn out his pockets to prove he was penniless, since he'd been in an unusually peaceable mood.

He didn't cotton to being called a liar and his back stiffened in anger.

"You'd best put away that pistol and step aside, mister," he said harshly. "Else I won't be responsible for what happens."

The man laughed. "Are you crazy? There are two of us and only one of you. If you don't have any money, gimme your guns and anything else you got that's worth anything."

"Seems to me like the odds are against you," Preacher said.

"You talkin' about that mutt? You think he's the equal of one of us?"

"Hell, no," Preacher said. "I think he's worth a dozen no-account scum like you. Probably more."

The robber grated a curse.

Preacher didn't wait any longer. He had already cut those damn fools a sight more slack than they deserved. He said sharply, "Dog!"

The big cur moved with blinding speed, a gray phantom in the shadows of the alley. He whirled and launched himself at the man behind Preacher, crashing into him just as the man pulled the trigger on his pistol. Dog's weight and strength drove the man backward off his feet, so the shot went well over Preacher's head.

At the same time, Preacher went into action with the same sort of deadly speed. He lashed out with the flintlock rifle in his hands. The long barrel cracked across the wrist of the would-be robber's gun hand, breaking it and knocking the pistol aside as it roared. The two shots came so close together they sounded like one, and the twin muzzle flashes lit up the alley for a split-second, revealing the ugly, unshaven face twisted in pain.

The next instant, Preacher drove the rifle butt into the man's throat. The robber staggered backward, choking and gasping as he tried unsuccessfully to drag a breath through his ruined airways. Preacher could have stopped right there and let him die a slow, suffocating, agonizing death.

Instead, the mountain man's hand went to the sheath on his belt and drew the long, heavy-bladed hunting knife he carried. The knife flashed forward, burying more than a foot of cold steel in the robber's belly. Preacher ripped it back and forth, opening a hideous wound through which the man's steaming entrails spilled as he collapsed on the dirty floor of the alley. His last breath rattled in his throat as Preacher pulled the knife free and stepped back.

The snarling and screaming that had filled the alley behind him were coming to an end. The screams faded away in a gurgling sigh of death, and the big cur fell silent as Preacher said, "Dog."

Preacher bent and wiped his knife clean of blood on the clothes of the man he had killed. As he slid the weapon back in its sheath, he reflected that he wouldn't lose any sleep over either of those deaths. Men such as those who lurked in alleys and robbed folks had almost certainly slashed any number of innocent throats. Preacher knew that was what they'd had in mind for him.

That mistake had cost them their lives.

"Come on, Dog," he said softly. "Let's get out of here. They probably got a constable in this town, and we ain't got time to deal with that foolishness."

Both of them faded into the night with a skill born of long practice. Stealth had saved their lives on many occasions.

A short time later, having taken a longer way around, Preacher entered the tavern where he had told Lorenzo and Casey he would meet them. The smoky lantern light filling the room revealed a tall, lean man in fringed buckskins, a broad-brimmed felt hat, and high-topped boot moccasins. Preacher's face was too craggy to be called handsome, but it possessed a great deal of raw power. A dark mustache drooped over his wide mouth. He was in his mid-thirties, old enough for the rumpled thatch of dark hair under his hat to have a number of gray strands threaded through it. His skin bore the permanent tan of a life lived out in the elements.

He nestled his rifle in his arms, and two flintlock pistols were tucked behind his belt in addition to the knife he carried. A powder horn and a shot pouch were draped over his shoulders, their rawhide thongs crossing on his chest and back. In a frontier full of dangerous men, Preacher was one of the most dangerous, and he looked it.

But the keen eyes under his bushy brows were also filled with intelligence and humor. He had seen and done a great deal since coming west as a young man, and it had taught him to appreciate every minute of his adventurous life.

He looked around the room, spotted Lorenzo at one of the tables playing cards and Casey standing at the bar. A number of hostile stares were being directed at them, and that told Preacher several things.

For one, the other card players didn't like losing. They especially didn't like losing to a black man, even one who had been freed from his former status as a slave.

The angry looks cast Casey's way came from the trollops who worked in the tavern. Even with the scar on her left cheek from a knife wound, Casey was the prettiest woman in there. The fact that several men clustered around her at the bar proved that. The serving wenches didn't like having the competition.

Casey's whoring days were over, though. She shared Preacher's blankets sometimes, but it was out of friendship and good, healthy, animal lust. No money would ever change hands.

The three of them, Preacher, Lorenzo, and Casey, had been traveling together for a couple of weeks, taking their time moseying west after leaving St. Louis. A mission of vengeance had taken Preacher from his beloved Rocky Mountains to the big city, and in the course of that mission, Lorenzo and Casey had become allies of his, as well as friends. When he left and headed west again, they had come with him.

Instead of traveling up the Missouri River to the northern Rockies, Preacher had decided to meander in a more southerly direction for a change, into *Nuevo Mexico*. He hadn't been that way for several years. From there, he and his two companions could work their way north along the rugged mountain ranges. That way, Lorenzo and Casey could see a lot of different country. Since neither of them had ever been west of St. Louis, they were going to be impressed by how vast the American frontier really was.

The plan was to leave in the morning and ride

west along the Santa Fe Trail, but before they could do that, they had to make it through the night. Between thieves in dark alleys, sore losers in a poker game, and jealous whores, Preacher wasn't sure they were going to make it.

Lorenzo laid down his cards at the end of a hand. A grin wrinkled his wizened face as he reached out to rake in the money in the center of the table, adding it to the pile of winnings in front of him. "Luck is with me tonight, gentlemen," he said.

"Somethin's with you, but I ain't sure it's luck," one of the men at the table said with a scowl.

"Fortune favors the bold, or so they say. I always done had a streak of boldness in me. That's why they call it gamblin'."

The hand of the man with the scowl slapped down on the table. "Don't you lecture me, you little coon. Your master wouldn't like it if he knew you were out sassin' white men."

"Ain't got no master," Lorenzo said. "I'm a free man. Fella I used to work for didn't hold with havin' slaves."

"One of those damned do-gooders, eh?"

Lorenzo laughed. "No, sir. If you'd knowed him, you wouldn't ever say that. He never done good in any way, shape, or form."

That was the truth, thought Preacher. Lorenzo's former employer was the man he had gone to St. Louis to kill.

"I still say you're too damn lucky," the poker player went on.

"You wouldn't be hintin' that I'm a cheater, would you?"

"You said it, not me," the man snapped. "But I'm damn sure something fishy is goin' on here."

Preacher saw the old-timer's face grow taut with anger and stepped over to the table. "You about ready to go, Lorenzo?"

Glaring across at the man who had all but accused him of cheating, Lorenzo said, "I reckon so. It ain't feelin' too hospitable in here no more."

He reached for his winnings. The man on the other side of the table suddenly whipped out a knife and plunged the tip of the blade into the wood with a solid *thunk!* The knife pinned some of the bills to the table.

"You just hold on a minute there, darky," he said. "You and your partner ain't gonna waltz off with my money like that."

Preacher put his hand on the butt of one of his pistols. "No, *you* might want to hold on, mister," he warned. "I know Lorenzo, and he ain't a cheater."

The words were barely out of Preacher's mouth when from behind him came Casey's alarmed voice. "Preacher, watch out!" she cried, as the metallic cocking of a gun's hammer sounded.

Preacher glanced over his shoulder and saw a man pointing an old blunderbuss pistol at him. At the same time, Lorenzo grabbed the edge of the table and shoved upward. Despite his age, he was still nimble and strong. The table went up and over with a crash, scattering cards and money across the puncheon floor.

Twisting and whirling, Preacher exploded into action. He drew both pistols and lashed out with the one in his left hand, smashing the barrel against the skull of the man who had accused Lorenzo of cheating.

The blunderbuss pistol went off with a dull boom. It fired a heavy ball, but at low velocity. Preacher ducked aside to avoid it and fired the pistol in his right hand. The ball from it smashed the shoulder of the man who had just shot at him.

Lorenzo was on the floor, scrambling to gather up as much of the money as he could. Preacher told him, "Come on!" and headed for the door, ready to shoot and slug his way out of there if he had to.

And it looked like he might have to. Several men, probably friends of the pair that had started the trouble, were moving to block his path.

Casey was in trouble, too. A couple of the serving girls attacked her, slapping at her and trying to pull her hair. Suddenly, a stranger moved in, grabbing one of the trollops and flinging her aside. The man shoved the other serving girl away, took hold of Casey's hand, and pulled her away from the bar.

"Come with me!" he told her. "I'll get you out of here!"

Six men barred Preacher from the door. He could have waded into them, but there was a simpler way. He let out a piercing whistle, and the door banged open as Dog threw himself against it from outside. The big cur hit the men from behind like a cyclone, scattering them like ninepins.

Preacher stuck his empty pistol behind his belt and reached down to take hold of Lorenzo's arm. He hauled the old-timer to his feet and hustled him toward the entrance.

"I wasn't cheatin', Preacher, I swear it!" Lorenzo

declared. "That fella, he just couldn't play cards worth a fig!"

"I know," Preacher said. "But let's get outta here first, then we can talk about it."

Dog whirled this way and that, snapping and snarling, keeping a path open to the door. One man scooped up a fallen chair and raised it to strike at the dog, but before the blow could fall, the barrel of Preacher's pistol thudded against the back of his head. The man dropped the chair and folded up.

Preacher shouldered another man aside and shoved Lorenzo ahead of him. The old man went through the door right behind Casey and the man who had rescued her at the bar. Preacher turned and backed through the door, holding the loaded pistol in front of him in menacing fashion. When he was clear of the threshold, he called, "Dog!"

The big cur bounded out of the tavern, leaving several shaken and bleeding men behind him. He loped easily alongside Preacher as the mountain man followed the other three.

Preacher had expected their last night in Independence to be a peaceful one. The attempted robbery in the alley and the brawl in the tavern had ruined those plans.

The trouble might not be over yet. As men spilled out of the tavern, a torch flared to life.

"There they go!" a man shouted. "After 'em!"

"We'll tar and feather the bastards!" another man bellowed.

No, thought Preacher as he hurried through the night with an angry mob on his heels, their last night in Independence wasn't going to be a peaceful one at all.

CHAPTER 2

The man who had helped Casey held her arm as he trotted beside her. He turned his head to look back at Preacher and Lorenzo. "Follow me!" he said. "I know a place we can go to get away from them!"

Preacher had gotten only a brief look at the man in the tavern. He was young, with dark hair worn long over his ears and the back of his neck, and was dressed in store-bought duds, but not fancy ones. Preacher had never seen him before.

He seemed to be on their side, although Preacher couldn't discount the possibility the young man was leading them into a trap. But it didn't feel likely.

Besides, with a bunch of howling, angry varmints behind them, what did they have to lose?

"Lead the way, mister!" Preacher told the stranger. "We're right behind you!"

They ran through the streets, around corners, down alleys. More torches had sprung to life behind them, casting long, misshapen shadows that seemed to pursue Preacher and his friends with a life of their own.

Preacher spotted lights ahead of them, and a moment later they came up to a wagon encampment on the western edge of the settlement. Twenty massive freight wagons were ranged in a circle, with the herd of oxen that would pull them penned in the center. A cooking fire burned in a pit outside the wagons. Half a dozen men stood talking near the fire, while others who had already turned in for the night were dark, formless shapes in bedrolls underneath the wagons.

One of the men by the fire heard them coming and stepped forward to meet them. "Roland, what's the meaning of this?" he demanded roughly. "Who are these people?"

"Friends, Pa," the young man replied. "We have to help them."

A curse came from the older man. "What in blazes have you gotten yourself into, boy?"

The youngster called Roland didn't answer. He pushed Casey toward one of the wagons and told her, "Crawl under there and wrap yourself up in the blanket you'll find. Don't come out until I tell you it's all right."

Casey glanced at Preacher. He gave her a curt nod. The mob wasn't far behind them. There wasn't time to question the offer.

"You two get under one of the wagons as well," Roland said to Preacher and Lorenzo. "Take the wolf with you."

Normally, Preacher would have explained that Dog was only part wolf, but he didn't take the time to do that.

"Wait just a minute," Roland's father objected. "Is that a black man?"

"It's all right, Pa," Roland said. "I'll explain it all later. They didn't do anything wrong. I give you my word. But in a minute some men are going to show up looking for them. I want you to say that you haven't seen them."

"You mean you want me to lie?"

"Please, Pa."

The older man looked like he was going to argue. But after a couple seconds, he jerked his head in an angry nod and said, "All right. But when this is over, I'll be expecting a damned good explanation!"

Preacher, Lorenzo, Dog, and Roland crawled into the shadows underneath a couple wagons. With Dog close beside him panting slightly, Preacher waited.

But not for long. The mob arrived less than a minute later, shouting questions, demanding to know where Preacher and the others had gone.

Roland's father strode forward to meet the mob and planted himself squarely in its path. "Who are you men?" he demanded. "What the hell do you want?"

A spokesman stepped out of the torch-wielding group. Preacher could see his face and recognized him as the sore loser from Lorenzo's poker game. "We're lookin' for three men and a girl," he said. "One of the men is an old nigger, and the girl looks like a whore."

"We don't have any slaves here, or any harlots," Roland's father said, the words lashing out.

"The darky claimed to be a freedman, and I just

said the girl looked like a whore. I don't know if she is one or not."

"That doesn't make any difference. They're not here. This is a respectable wagon train."

"I'm not sayin' it ain't, damn it. But those bastards came in this direction. You must've seen 'em or at least heard 'em."

"The only commotion I've seen or heard is the one you're creating," Roland's father insisted. In the darkness under the wagon, Preacher grinned. The fella had struck him as the prickly sort, but he had to admit, Roland's pa was doing a good job playing his part.

The spokesman for the mob rubbed his angular, beard-stubbled jaw. "I don't understand it," he said. "I know good and well they came this way."

"They must have headed off in another direction without you realizing it." Roland's father paused. "Why are you looking for them, anyway?"

"They started a ruckus in a tavern, attacked the folks there, and stole some money."

"Why don't you report that to the law? I know Independence has a constable."

The spokesman made a disgusted face. "My friends and I handle our own troubles. When we catch those varmints, we'll tar and feather 'em and teach 'em they can't get away with things like that around here."

"Well, that's none of my business," Roland's father said, "and since some of my men are trying to sleep, I'll thank you to go on your way and stop disturbing us. We're setting out on a long journey early in the morning."

The spokesman regarded him with a narrow-eyed glare. "I'm thinkin' maybe it'd be a good idea if we took a look around this camp for ourselves."

Roland's father made a curt gesture that brought the men from the fire to his side. They were all brawny, powerful-looking men, and several of them had bullwhips wrapped around their waists. Preacher recognized them as bullwhackers, the men who whipped, prodded, and cursed the ox teams across the long miles of the Santa Fe Trail. Such men were tough as nails, with a reputation for brawling.

The spokesman for the mob seemed to know that, too. He looked a little nervous as he said, "There are more of us than there are of you."

"I have more than a dozen other men here in camp, and all I have to do is call them. That's exactly what I'm going to do if you don't get out of here."

"All right, all right," the spokesman muttered. "No need to get proddy. We're leaving."

"You'll have to find the people you're looking for somewhere else," Roland's father said.

With plenty of frustrated curses, the mob took their torches and started drifting back toward town. Roland's father and his men watched them go.

When the mob was out of earshot and the torches had dwindled to sparks, Roland's father turned and called softly, "All right, you can come out of there now."

Preacher and the others emerged from their hiding places. Running away from trouble rubbed Preacher the wrong way and always had. Hiding from it was even worse. Sometimes, though, it was the only prudent thing to do.

Besides, they had Casey to look out for. Preacher didn't want her to come to any harm, and there was no telling what some of those men might have done to her if they'd gotten their hands on her. She had suffered enough in her life.

"Thanks, Pa," Roland said as he used his hat to knock dust from the ground off his clothes.

His father glared at him. "I'll have that explanation now," he said. "What sort of thieves and scoundrels have you fallen in with?"

Preacher didn't wait for Roland to reply. He said, "Mister, we're obliged to you for your help, but that don't give you leave to call us names. The fella doin' the talkin' for that mob didn't exactly give you the whole story."

The man crossed his arms over his chest. He was a tall, thick-bodied man with graying hair, prominent side-whiskers, and a jaw that jutted out like the prow of a boat. He gave Preacher a cool stare and said, "That's fair enough, I suppose. Why don't you tell me the whole story?"

"That fella accused my friend here of cheatin' at cards," Preacher replied with a nod of his head toward Lorenzo. "It's true the table got knocked over durin' the scuffle and Lorenzo grabbed up some cash, but I reckon he didn't wind up with as much as he won fair and square."

"That's right," Lorenzo put in. "Fact is, I had to leave some of our money there."

"As for Casey here," Preacher went on, "it appeared some of the gals who work in that tavern took a dislike to her on account of how she's so much prettier'n they are. There was some scratchin' and hair-pullin' goin' on when your boy gave her a hand and got her out of there."

As a matter of fact, Roland was still hovering rather attentively around Casey, enough so that if things had been different between her and Preacher, he might have been a little jealous. Neither of them had any claim on the other, though. They were just traveling together and enjoying each other's company from time to time.

"So that's all there was to it? Just a sordid tavern brawl over a card game and a woman?"

Preacher shrugged. "That's one way of lookin' at it, I reckon."

The man shook his head in apparent disgust. He looked at Roland and said, "I thought you had more sense than to get mixed up in something like that, son. You shouldn't have been in one of those squalid dives in the first place, not with our trip to Santa Fe starting in the morning."

Roland returned the look with a defiant gaze of his own. "These people didn't do anything wrong, Pa, and when they stuck up for themselves, the men in that tavern tried to gang up on them. I would think you'd be proud of me for helping them."

His father snorted and turned back to Preacher and his companions. "If anyone asks us, we'll continue to say that we haven't seen you, although it pains me to lie."

"I try to be an honest man, too," Preacher drawled.

"Well, it should be safe for you to go on your way now. That mob seems to be gone."

Roland said, "We can't be sure they're not lurking out there somewhere, waiting for them. Why don't we let these folks stay the night with us, Pa?"

"Absolutely not," the man snapped. "I won't have you associating any longer than you have to with such gutter trash—"

Dog sensed the way Preacher stiffened, and a growl came from deep in the big cur's throat.

Preacher was about to point out to the man that they didn't cotton to being called names, when one of the bullwhackers stepped forward and said, "Beggin' your pardon, Mr. Bartlett, but I think you got it wrong about these folks. I recognize that big fella. Saw him in St. Louis last year. He's the one they call Preacher."

Bartlett, who had been about to snap at his employee for butting in, jerked his head toward Preacher and drew in a deep breath that caused his nostrils to flare. "Preacher," he repeated. "That's who you are?"

"Wasn't the name I was born with," Preacher said, "but it's the one I've answered to for a heap of years now."

"My God. I owe you an apology, sir. My son and I discussed trying to locate you and hire you to accompany us." The man held out a hand. "My name is Leeman Bartlett."

His attitude had undergone a dramatic turn-around in a few seconds. Preacher still thought he was a stiff-necked, judgmental varmint, but Bartlett had offered his hand and an apology. A man couldn't do more than that. Preacher gripped Bartlett's hand and nodded.

"This here's Lorenzo," he said with a nod toward the black man. "He ain't a slave. He's a freedman."

Bartlett shook hands with him as well.

"And the lady's name is Cassandra," Preacher went on.

"But my friends call me Casey," she added.

Bartlett nodded to her. "Miss," he said. "That fellow making a fuss over you is my son Roland, as you've no doubt figured out by now."

"Pa!" Roland said, looking embarrassed. "I'm not making a fuss over anybody."

Bartlett grunted. "Yes, well . . ." He swung back toward Preacher. "Fate has led you to us, sir. Is there any chance you'd consider accepting my proposition?"

"You mean about comin' along with your wagon train to Santa Fe?"

"Indeed. I've heard it said that you probably know more about the country west of the Mississippi than any man alive."

"I ain't so sure about that," Preacher said, "but it's true I've been to see the elephant. You don't really need a guide, though. The trail ain't that hard to follow."

"Call it an advisor, then," Bartlett said. "There are bound to be pitfalls along the way, and circumstances where I could use the counsel of a canny frontiersman."

"Have you made this trip before?" Preacher asked.

"No, this will be the first time, although some of my men have worked on other wagon trains that made the journey."

In that case, it was probably true there would be times when Bartlett could use some advice from a man who knew what he was talking about. It was also true that Preacher, Lorenzo, and Casey had discussed trying to hook up with one of the freight wagon caravans headed west. There was a lot of dangerous country between Independence and Santa Fe, and they would be safer with the wagons than trying to go it alone.

Preacher looked at Lorenzo and Casey.

The old-timer said, "Whatever you want to do is fine with me, Preacher. You know a lot more about this sort of thing than I do."

"That goes for me, too," Casey said.

Preacher saw that Roland was watching and waiting for his decision with barely concealed eagerness. The young man was obviously looking forward to the possibility of spending the next several weeks traveling with Casey.

Since Preacher didn't have a jealous bone in his body, that was all right with him. He turned to Bartlett and nodded. "Sounds like a pretty good idea. You're pullin' out in the mornin', you said?"

Bartlett smiled and replied, "At first light."

"I'll have to go back to the stable and get our horses. But when your wagons are ready to roll, we'll be ready to ride."

CHAPTER 3

Preacher was up before dawn the next morning, intending to return to the stable and collect their horses and gear. He and Lorenzo and Casey had planned to sleep there, but the three of them had actually spent the night under one of the wagons in the freight caravan. Lorenzo and Casey had still been rolled up in their blankets sleeping when Preacher crawled out to fetch the horses.

Leeman Bartlett was already up, stirring the embers of the cook fire back to life. Preacher told him where he was bound, and Bartlett said, "The coffee will be ready by the time you get back. I trust you slept well?"

"Well enough," Preacher said. "I sorta kept one eye open, in case that bunch came back." He shrugged. "I never sleep as well in a town as I do out in the open."

"We'll be in the open soon enough," Bartlett commented. "There's not much between here and Santa Fe *except* open ground, is there?"

"Not much," Preacher agreed. "Other than

scorchin' sun, rattlesnakes, cyclones that come outta nowhere, gangs of highwaymen, and bands of hostile Injuns. But that's all," he added dryly.

Bartlett chuckled. "You make it sound like the wise thing to do would be to turn around and go back to St. Louis."

"There's no profit in turnin' back. And if you *are* lucky enough to make it through, you'll be able to sell those goods for plenty once you get to Santa Fe."

"That's the plan," Bartlett said with a nod as the flames began to crackle. "I've invested a great deal in this venture. I believe the odds of it being successful went up a great deal when you came into our camp last night."

"Reckon we'll see about that," Preacher said.

When Preacher got to the stable the hostler who worked nights was still on duty and didn't question their absence. They had already paid, so that was all that mattered to the man.

True to Bartlett's word, the coffee was ready when Preacher got back with the horses. So were flapjacks and bacon. Lorenzo and Casey were up and already eating. Casey looked mighty cute as she sat on a keg near the fire with a blanket draped around her shoulders. Roland Bartlett hunkered on his heels beside her, obviously ready to fetch her anything she might need.

Preacher picketed the horses, including the pack animal they had brought with them from St. Louis. As he had his breakfast the orange glow in the eastern sky grew brighter. The camp bustled with activity as Bartlett's men hitched up their teams and moved the wagons into a long line.

"Are all your water barrels filled up?" Preacher asked Leeman Bartlett.

"Yes, of course."

"You should fill them every chance you get," Preacher advised. "There'll be some long dry stretches once you get to the Cimarron Cutoff."

"Is that the best way to go? I wasn't sure."

Preacher nodded. "You could take the northern route and go by Bent's Fort, but you'd have a hell of a time gettin' heavy wagons like these through Raton Pass. It's more suited for mule trains. You might lose several wagons if you tried it."

"We certainly don't want that," Bartlett said. "The Cimarron Cutoff it is."

"Don't go thinkin' that route's safe, though. Like I said, there's some stretches where you won't find any water and damn little graze for the oxen. Plus that's where you're most likely to run into trouble from the Comanch'."

"Indians, you mean?"

"Yeah. Durin' the first part of the trip, you'll have to worry about Pawnee and Kiowa, but they're less likely to cause trouble . . . dependin', of course, on what sort of mood their war chiefs are in. The Comanche, though . . . Well, nine times outta ten, they're gonna be a mite proddy."

"Will we have to fight them?" Bartlett asked with a worried look on his lined face.

"We might. Sometimes you can trade with 'em and get through that way. And it could be we won't even run into any of the varmints. Their regular huntin' ground is farther south than we'll be goin', but they wander up into the Cimarron country quite a bit."

"We'll hope for good luck, then," Bartlett said.

"You can always hope," Preacher said, leaving unspoken the fact that hoping often did no good at all.

Roland leaned over to Casey and said, "We can find a place for you to ride in one of the wagons, if you'd like."

She smiled and shook her head. "Thanks, but that's not necessary. I rode horseback from St. Louis, and I can continue to do so. I was raised on a farm, you know."

"No, I didn't know that. I'd like to learn more about you."

"We'll see," she said. Preacher thought Roland's doglike devotion was starting to get on Casey's nerves, but that was her problem, he told himself.

Bartlett had several outriders armed with rifles, and he and his son each had a couple saddle horses, so they could switch back and forth and rest the animals. The big freight wagons weren't equipped with seats for the drivers, so the bullwhackers walked alongside their teams, working their magic with whips and shouted curses. As the sun began to peek over the eastern horizon, Bartlett rode to the front of the wagon train and waved an arm over his head as he shouted the well-known order.

"Wagons . . . *ho!*"

The bullwhackers popped their whips and turned the air around their heads blue with profanity. The oxen, in their stolid way, surged against the singletrees yoked to them, and under that immense power, the heavily loaded wagons rolled slowly forward.

Casey pulled up her dress revealing a pair of

doeskin trousers underneath. She swung up onto her horse and rode astride like a man. From the way she handled the reins, it was clear she was telling the truth about being an experienced rider.

Roland rode up and joined her. Preacher and Lorenzo fell in on horseback on her other side.

Leeman Bartlett turned from leading the caravan and rode past them, calling to his son, "Roland, I want you up front with me!"

Roland looked at Casey, obviously reluctant to leave her. But she smiled at him and said, "Go ahead, Mr. Bartlett, I'll be fine."

"Roland," he said. "I told you to call me Roland."

"All right. I'll see you later, Roland."

With a sigh, the young man heeled his horse into a trot and rode after his father. When he was out of earshot, Lorenzo chuckled and said, "That boy has sure got it bad for you, Miss Casey."

"He's sweet," she said, "but I'm afraid he's going to be disappointed." She looked at Preacher with a smile.

He tried not to frown. He didn't want Casey getting any ideas about him. He had been in love a time or two in his life, but it had never worked out. The first girl he'd ever had real feelings for had been murdered, and a couple of other gals he had been close to had wound up getting themselves killed, too.

He was bound and determined another tragedy like that wasn't going to take place again, even if it meant never letting himself get too involved with a woman. If Casey was starting to think about the two of them settling down together, she was whistling up the wrong tree.

Preacher was too fiddlefooted for that, and he thought Casey knew that.

But it wasn't the time or place to discuss it. The three of them rode alongside the wagons, gradually moving closer to the front of the caravan. They saw Bartlett and Roland up ahead, leading the way along the trail that had been worn into the ground by the wide wheels of hundreds of wagons in the past dozen years. The pops of bullwhips and the curses of the bullwhackers filled the cool, early morning air.

The oxen pulling the wagons never got in any hurry. The massive beasts simply weren't capable of speed. Men on horseback who accompanied wagon trains had to hold their mounts to a slow walk to keep from drawing too far ahead. Preacher knew that creeping along like that was going to chafe at him and make him impatient, but in the long run, it was safer for Lorenzo and Casey to travel with the wagons.

If he had been alone, he would have struck out for *Nuevo Mexico* as fast as the rangy gray horse under him could carry him.

Dog roamed far ahead, but Preacher didn't worry about the big cur getting lost. He and Dog could always find each other. They had been trail partners for many years and an almost supernatural connection existed between them. The same was true of Preacher and Horse. At times it was like they could read each other's minds.

Preacher moved up alongside the Bartletts. The sun was completely above the horizon, an orange ball that cast its garish light over the plains ahead of them.

"We've made a good start, don't you think, Mr. Preacher?" Bartlett asked.

Preacher glanced over his shoulder and said, "Well, considerin' that you can still see Independence back there about half a mile away, it's sort of early to say. And you can forget about that *mister* business. The handle's just Preacher."

"What about Miss Casey?" Roland asked. "What's her last name?"

Preacher ran a thumbnail down his jawline. "You know, I never asked her, and she never offered it," he mused. "I reckon it just never seemed important enough to bother about."

"I'll ask her sometime."

"You do that," Preacher said dryly.

"Tell us more about the journey we're facing," Bartlett urged. "Have you traveled the Santa Fe Trail numerous times?"

"Half a dozen, maybe. Most of my time in the mountains has been spent farther north, up around the Grand Tetons. But I've done some trappin' down in the Sangre de Cristos. Last time I was in Santa Fe was a couple years ago."

He didn't mention the trouble he had run into on that visit. Since trouble seemed to dog his trail just about everywhere he went, it didn't really seem worth going into.

"They say that Santa Fe is quite some town."

Preacher nodded. "It's a nice enough place, I reckon, if you don't mind the fact that the streets are a mite loco and run ever' which way. Folks say it's like they were laid out by a drunk man on a blind mule. Or was it a blind man on a drunk mule? Anyway, once you learn your way around, it ain't bad." He grinned. "Lots of pretty señoritas, that's for sure."

"Yes, well, I'm not interested in that, and my son doesn't have time for such things," Bartlett said.

Preacher thought the old man ought to let his son speak for himself, because from what he had seen so far, Roland had plenty of time to make calf eyes at Casey.

The wagons rolled on through the morning. The flat, grassy prairie was so featureless, it was hard to tell if they were making any progress. For all the difference in the landscape, they might have gone five miles or five hundred yards. It was all the same.

The sun was what marked time, rising higher in the sky until it reached its zenith. When it did, the wagons halted so the teams could rest and the men could eat lunch.

While the caravan was stopped, Bartlett asked Preacher, "Is there any need to send a man ahead to scout the trail?"

"This close to Independence, you're not liable to run into any trouble," Preacher said, "but it never hurts to have a look at where you're goin'. Why don't you let me and Dog do that?"

"You don't mind?"

"Nope." To tell the truth, Preacher was glad for the excuse to get away from the slow-moving wagon train for a while. It would also give Horse a chance to stretch his legs.

Bartlett said, "You know, we agreed to travel together, but we never did discuss the matter of wages."

"You don't have to pay me anything," Preacher

told him. "We'll be usin' some of your supplies. That's enough."

"But I'm taking advantage of your expertise."

"And I'm takin' advantage of the extra guns if we happen to run into trouble," Preacher pointed out. "I reckon we'll come out square enough."

"Well, if that's the way you feel, I won't argue with you."

"It is."

Preacher went to mount up. Casey followed him. "I'll come with you, Preacher."

Preacher saw the frown that suddenly appeared on the face of Roland Bartlett. He shook his head and said, "Naw, you should just stay with the wagons. I'm not gonna be doin' anything all that interestin'."

She frowned, too, but her expression was a little offended. "Preacher . . ."

"Maybe next time," he told her.

He didn't want to hurt Casey's feelings. She was a good-hearted gal, no doubt about it, and smart and brave, too. She had proven that during the trouble back in St. Louis. But he couldn't have her getting ideas in her head about him. Roland seemed like a decent youngster, just wet behind the ears. Casey would be better off with him, or at least someone like him.

Or someone who wasn't Preacher, anyway.

Leaving the wagons to get started when the rest period was over, Preacher mounted up and rode west along the trail. Dog trotted along beside him. He loosened the reins and gave Horse his head, and the big gray stallion responded by tossing his head and breaking into a run. Dog bounded ahead, and Preacher grinned. All three of the old friends were glad to be out on their own again.

A few minutes later Preacher saw riders ahead of him, angling to cut across his path and intercept him. He knew instantly that they were Indians.

CHAPTER 4

Preacher wasn't going to ride right into the middle of that bunch. If they wanted him, they could come to him. He reined Horse to a halt and called, "Dog!" The big cur whirled around and raced back to Preacher's side. He unslung the flintlock rifle and rested it across the saddle in front of him. The rifle was loaded and primed, as were the pistols behind his belt and the second set of pistols he carried in the saddlebags. His thumb was looped over the rifle's hammer, ready to cock it.

The Indians reached the trail. Instead of crossing it and continuing on their way, as he had hoped but not expected, they turned and rode directly toward him. Preacher waited calmly. He knew the worst thing he could do was turn and try to get away from them. That would just encourage them to chase him and get their blood up.

As they came closer, he saw the Indians weren't painted for war. More than likely a hunting party. From the way they wore their hair and the markings on their buckskins, he recognized them as Pawnee. They weren't all that friendly toward white men, but as a rule they didn't go out of their way to be hostile.

There were seven warriors in the group, most of them young along with a couple older, more weathered men. One of those veterans edged his pony ahead as the others came to a stop. The leader raised a hand in greeting.

Solemnly, Preacher returned the gesture. "My friends," he said in the Pawnee tongue. After so many years on the frontier, there weren't many Indian languages and dialects he didn't speak.

"You use our words," the Pawnee warrior said, sounding slightly surprised.

"When a man goes among those who are not his own people, he should learn to speak their tongue."

The warrior nodded slowly. "This is wise. How are you called?"

"I am Preacher."

Recognition flared in the Pawnee's eyes. Preacher was pretty sure he had never met the man before, but clearly the warrior had heard of him.

"The one known to the Blackfeet as Ghost-killer?"

Preacher nodded. He had picked up that name because of the way he had slipped into camps of the Blackfeet and slit the throats of several warriors before crawling away without anyone knowing what had happened.

He and the Blackfeet were old enemies. As a young man, he had been the prisoner of a Blackfoot band. To save his life and make his captors believe he was touched by the spirits, he had begun to preach, like a street minister he had seen back in

St. Louis. All night and all day the words had tumbled from his mouth, and when he could talk no more, the Blackfeet spared him. Once the story spread among his fellow mountain men, they dubbed him Preacher, and the name had stuck.

Luckily, the fact that the Blackfeet hated him wouldn't mean much to those Pawnee. Most of the other tribes didn't get along that well with the Blackfeet. The Pawnee wouldn't try to kill him just because the Blackfeet wanted him dead.

However, the power the warriors might obtain by killing a famous fighting man such as Preacher might be too strong a temptation to withstand. He saw the eagerness in the eyes of the younger men and knew he was on the knife edge of deadly danger.

"Ghost-killer does not come often to the land of the Pawnee," the spokesman said. "Do you travel alone?"

Preacher shook his head. "I have many friends with me." It wouldn't do any good to lie. The caravan would be in sight at any minute. "They take wagons full of goods to Santa Fe, to sell to the Mexicans."

Preacher didn't think there was any chance the small hunting party would attack a large, well-armed group such as the Bartlett wagon train. But they might come back with more warriors from their village, so Preacher knew he would have to be extra watchful until the wagons were through the area.

"This is Pawnee land," the spokesman said with a frown.

Preacher nodded. "I know. That is why we will give gifts to the Pawnee, so we may pass through in peace."

He didn't have any right to commit Bartlett to such an exchange, but on the other hand, Bartlett had wanted him to come along because he knew what he was doing and how to deal with the Indians. If the man had any sense, he would follow Preacher's advice in the matter.

The older warrior nodded gravely. "This is fair," he said. "We will wait here."

"Good. We can talk of places we have been and things we have seen."

Preacher's keen eyes had spotted another warrior sitting on his pony about half a mile away. That Pawnee would watch the coming confrontation, and if there was trouble, he would race back to the village and bring help. Preacher was going to do his best to see to it that there was no trouble.

The wagons lumbered into sight. Preacher saw the outriders moving back to the wagons and knew they had spotted the Indians waiting in the trail. A few minutes later, the wagons lurched to a halt, and one of the men rode forward to find out what was going on.

Preacher waved the man in. The outrider came up wearing a nervous expression. His rifle was across the saddle in front of him. He asked, "What's going on here, Preacher?"

"These are Pawnee," he said with a nod toward the Indians. "They're friendly, but they want gifts in exchange for safe passage across their land. Tell Bartlett I figure that's a good idea. Have him bring up a bolt of the most colorful cloth he's got in those wagons, along with some knives and maybe a handful of whatever bright, sparkly geegaws he's got. That ought to do it."

The outrider nodded. "I'll tell him. I ain't sure he'll go along with it, though."

"He will if he's got any sense."

"Hell, no offense, Preacher, but there's only about half a dozen of these savages."

"There's only half a dozen *right here, right now*," Preacher said meaningfully. "We don't know how many more there could be later on."

"Well, that's true, I reckon." The man turned his horse. "I'll pass the word."

He galloped back toward the wagons. Preacher turned to the Pawnee and said in their tongue, "I have sent word to my chief to bring gifts."

The warrior nodded. Preacher could tell he was pleased, even though the man was careful to keep his face impassive.

Preacher talked with the Pawnee leader for several minutes before three riders set out from the wagon train. As they approached, Preacher recognized one of them as Leeman Bartlett. The other two were outriders, including the one who had talked to Preacher a few minutes earlier.

One of the men was carrying a bolt of bright yellow cloth. Preacher saw the Pawnee leader's eyes light up at the sight of it. Bartlett had a canvas bag that clattered metallically as the men rode up.

"This is robbery, you know," he said as he held out the bag to Preacher.

"Nope, it's just good business," Preacher countered. "Man's got to expect to pay his way in the world."

"I suppose."

"It's a pretty small price to pay to keep your hair," Preacher added.

He swung down from the saddle and spread out the contents of the bag on the ground so the Pawnee could see them. There were three hunting knives, some spoons, a couple sewing thimbles, and a compass. The only items of any practical value to the Indians were the hunting knives, but they showed plenty of interest in the other items, too.

Preacher took the bolt of cloth from the man who held it and offered it to the leader. The warrior took it and passed it along solemnly to one of the other men. He looked at the rest of the offerings and nodded his head in approval.

"It is good," he said. "The white men and their wagons may pass through Pawnee land unharmed."

"You will see that the rest of your people know of this as well?"

"Yes, of course."

"Then the bargain is sealed."

Preacher mounted up and told Bartlett, "You can go back and get the wagons moving again. The Pawnee won't bother you."

"You're certain? They won't come back later and demand more tribute?"

"Nope. Their leader gave his word. They'll abide by it. Wouldn't be honorable not to."

"What about the *next* group of savages?"

"Well, that might be a different story," Preacher allowed. "But like I said, that's just the cost of doin' business."

"They don't actually own this land, you know."

"No Indian *owns* land, at least not in his mind," Preacher said. "They don't believe in it. But they use it as hunting grounds, and they believe in protecting what they use."

The Pawnee gathered up their gifts and raced off on their ponies, taking the warrior they had left behind as a watcher with them. Preacher returned to the wagons with Bartlett and the other two men.

Lorenzo, Casey, and Roland were waiting anxiously for them. "Is it all right?" Roland asked. "Are they going to attack us?"

"Not this group," his father replied. "According to Preacher, we've successfully bought them off."

"That's a relief. I was sure we were going to have to fight."

Preacher said, "Likely you will have to, before you get to Santa Fe. But not today."

"Those were real savages, weren't they?" Lorenzo said. "I never seen any Injuns in St. Louis except tame ones."

"They were plenty real," Preacher said, nodding.

The wagons resumed their journey. The rest of the afternoon passed without incident. The first encounter with Indians had occurred sooner than Preacher expected it to, but maybe that meant they would be lucky the rest of the way.

"How far did we come today, do you think?" Bartlett asked over supper.

Preacher shrugged. "Four, maybe five miles."

"Is that all?" Roland asked.

"You can't expect much more than that out of those oxen, not with the loads they're pullin'. That's why it's gonna take several weeks to get to Santa Fe. It's not like just goin' down the street."

"But as you said, the payoff will be worth it," Bartlett commented.

When they had finished eating, Preacher and Bartlett discussed the need for guards. Preacher suggested they have four men standing watch in four hour shifts.

"Lorenzo and I will take our turns," he said.

"Mighty quick to volunteer me, ain't you?" the old-timer said.

Preacher grinned. "I figured you'd want to do your part to make sure you don't get your hair lifted."

"Well, since you put it like that, I suppose I can give up a little sleep."

"I can stand guard, too," Casey offered.

Quickly, Roland said, "I'm sure that won't be necessary. You need a full night's sleep."

"No more than anybody else, I don't."

"We've got plenty of men to stand guard," Preacher told her. "But if we need you to take a turn, we'll let you know."

"All right," she said. "I'm going to hold you to that."

Except for the men standing the first watch, everyone turned in, crawling under the wagons to get some sleep. Preacher curled up in his bedroll, and with the frontiersman's knack for grabbing any chance he could to sleep, he dropped off as soon as his head hit the saddle he was using for a pillow.

He wasn't sure how long he had been asleep—it seemed like no time at all—when he came instantly awake and knew something had roused him. All his senses were alert. He heard the faint rustle of cloth somewhere nearby and smelled the unmistakable scent of a woman's hair and skin.

He felt the warmth of that skin a moment later when Casey slipped into the blankets with him, naked as the day she was born, and pressed her mouth to his in a hungry kiss.

CHAPTER 5

Preacher was as human as the next man. He couldn't help but respond when he found his arms full of naked, eager female flesh. He tightened his grip on her and returned the kiss.

But after a mighty enjoyable moment, he pulled his head back and asked in a low voice, "Casey, what in blazes do you think you're doin'?"

"What does it *feel* like I'm doing, Preacher?" she whispered as she moved her hand, exploring under the blankets.

"Blast it, gal, there are too many folks around for this sort of carryin' on. Not to mention the fact that I'm too dang old for a youngster like you."

"I'm not all that young, at least when it comes to experience," Casey said. "And you're not that old. You've been doing just fine as far as I can tell."

"Somebody might've seen you crawl under here."

"I wasn't naked. I had a blanket wrapped around me." She gave a defiant toss of her head, which made her blond hair swirl like wings around her face. "Anyway, I don't care who sees me. You think

Lorenzo didn't know we were together all those other nights on the trail?"

"That's different," Preacher insisted. "Lorenzo's not the same as a whole camp full of folks."

Casey sighed in exasperation. "I swear, you're the only man I've ever met who'd argue with a gal in a situation like this. Do you really want me to go back to my own bedroll?"

"I wouldn't go so far as to say I *want* you to," Preacher told her, "but I think it'd be the right thing to do."

"All right," she sniffed. "But don't be surprised if it's a long time before I come crawling into *your* blankets again."

She rolled off him, pulled her blanket around herself, and crawled out from under the wagon. Preacher sighed. Sometimes doing the right thing was damned inconvenient, he thought, and downright frustrating to boot!

Not surprisingly, it was quite a while before he got back to sleep.

Preacher took one of the final turns on guard duty that first night. He wasn't sure yet how reliable Bartlett's men were, and those hours before dawn were the ones when it was the most difficult to stay awake. He didn't want to take a chance on all the sentries dozing off at the same time. He would know that he was awake and alert, at the very least.

The night seemed about as quiet and peaceful as it could be. A gentle breeze blew across the prairie, stirring the grass that grew on both sides of the broad, dusty trail. With his flintlock cradled in his arms and Dog padding along softly beside him, Preacher walked all the way around the camp. Whenever one of the other guards challenged him, he identified himself and asked if there had been any signs of trouble. In each case, he was told that everything was all clear.

He knew that. Dog would have warned him if it were otherwise. It was well nigh impossible for any threat to sneak past the big cur's sharp hearing and phenomenal sense of smell.

The eastern sky lightened to gray. Someone stirred up the fire and got the flames crackling merrily again. Preacher came in and found Bartlett putting the coffee on to boil.

"Early riser, are you?" the mountain man asked.

"That's right," Bartlett replied. "I've found that the older I get, the more difficult it is to sleep. The aches and pains of age, you know. They keep a man awake."

"Yeah, I'm startin' to figure that out myself," Preacher admitted with a grin.

"But you're a young man yet," Bartlett said.

"It ain't so much the years. It's the miles, and everything you see and do along the way. I've been a heap of miles since I came west."

"I suppose you have. What made you leave home in the first place, if you don't mind me asking."

Preacher leaned on his rife. "No, I don't mind, but I sort of don't remember. I was always a mite restless, I reckon. Always wanted to know what was out there, past what I could see."

"By now have you seen it all?" Bartlett asked. He wasn't smiling, and evidently he was serious.

Preacher shook his head. "I don't figure one man could live long enough to see all there is to see out here. The country stretches too far, all the way out to the Pacific and from the Rio Grande in the south to the Milk River in the north. I've seen a heap of it, I reckon, but there are still plenty of places I've never been. I intend to keep lookin' as long as I can."

Casey and Lorenzo came over to the fire a short time later. Casey was rather cool toward Preacher, cool enough that Lorenzo noticed. While they were saddling their horses after breakfast, the old-timer asked, "You do somethin' to make that gal mad at you, Preacher?"

"Nope," Preacher replied. It was more a matter of what he *hadn't* done, he thought wryly, but he didn't see any need to explain that to Lorenzo.

The day was much like the one before, at least as far as the ground they covered. They did a little better because they didn't run into any Indians. The scenery didn't change any and wouldn't for quite a while, Preacher knew. They had a lot of prairie to cover before the mountains came into view in the distance. Once that occurred, it would still be a week or more before they actually reached the higher ground.

During the day, Preacher noticed on several occasions that Roland Bartlett was watching him. The youngster's stare wasn't a friendly one. He always looked away quickly whenever Preacher glanced toward him, but then he would start glaring at the mountain man again.

Preacher wondered if Roland's hostility had something to do with Casey. He could have seen her crawling under the wagon where Preacher was sleeping the night before and made more out of the incident than it really was.

When they made camp that evening, Roland continued casting unfriendly glances toward Preacher from time to time. Preacher was convinced the youngster was jealous. It was the only explanation that made any sense. Roland had been quick to help them two nights earlier in the tavern in Independence, but at that time he hadn't known there was any sort of relationship between Preacher and Casey. Now he had figured it out . . . and he didn't like it. He was attracted to Casey himself.

Even so, Preacher didn't expect any real trouble to come from the situation. It would be fine with him if Casey decided to throw him over in favor of Roland. That would do away with the inevitable unpleasantness when the day came that he told her he was moving on without her.

Casey sat down next to Preacher to eat supper and smiled at him, putting her hand on his arm for a second as she said, "It was a good day today, wasn't it?"

"We covered some ground," he allowed.

"And we didn't run into any more hostiles."

Lorenzo sat down on Preacher's other side in time to hear Casey's comment. "I'll bet there's plenty more out there, ain't they, Preacher?"

"The farther west we go, the more likely we'll be to see them," Preacher replied with a nod.

Roland came over carrying a plate of beans and cornbread. "Mind if I join you?" he asked the three of them in general, but Preacher could tell the question was really directed at Casey.

She smiled up at the young man. "That'll be just fine," she told him.

Roland sat down cross-legged on the ground beside her, close but not too close. He ate in silence for a few moments, then asked, "Did you say you grew up on a farm, Miss Casey?"

"You don't have to call me Miss. Just call me Casey. And yes, I was born and raised on a farm."

"Why did you leave there?"

That was sort of an awkward question to ask a gal, Preacher thought. Casey didn't seem bothered by it, though. She said, "Oh, I wanted to see more of the world than just a barn and a kitchen. That's how I wound up in St. Louis."

At least Roland had the good sense not to press the issue and ask her about what she had done in the city. Instead, he said, "I grew up in Philadelphia, so I always had a city around. I have to say, I like it out here on the frontier. It's not nearly as crowded, and the air smells better."

"You're sure right about that," Lorenzo put in. "I didn't know it was possible for the air not to stink until Preacher and Casey and me rode out of St. Louis."

"It's even better up in the mountains, isn't it, Preacher?" Casey asked. "That's what I've heard."

He nodded. "It's mighty nice country up there. Leastways, it seems like that to me. Some folks can't handle the loneliness, though."

"What about you?"

"I've never minded bein' alone," he said. Maybe that would give her a hint that he didn't intend to travel with her from now on.

"I'm not sure I could stand being completely by

myself like that," she mused. "I'm used to having people around—"

Casey might have said more, but at that moment, Dog lifted his shaggy head from the ground and growled. The sound was a low rumble, deep in his throat. His ears pricked up as he stared into the darkness to the north of the camp.

Preacher knew those signals very well. Dog had smelled something, or maybe heard it, and the big cur regarded whatever it was as a potential threat. Preacher reached over and rested a hand on the thick fur on the back of the dog's neck.

"What is it?" Lorenzo asked.

"Don't know." Preacher looked toward the area where the saddle horses were picketed, and he saw the way the rangy gray stallion's head lifted. Horse sensed whatever it was, too. He wasn't the only one. The other horses stirred nervously.

"Is something wrong?" Roland asked as Preacher reached for the rifle he had placed on the ground beside him.

"The critters think there is, and I trust 'em more'n I trust my own self," Preacher said. He got to his feet. "I'm gonna have a look around."

"Want me to come with you?" Lorenzo asked.

"No, you stay here. Stay alert."

Roland scrambled to his feet. "I'll tell my father. Maybe those Indians have come back."

Preacher made a curt slashing motion with his hand and said, "No, just take it easy for now. Ain't no point in throwin' the whole camp into an uproar if it's nothin'. Might just be a wolf or some-thin' like that lopin' by a mile away. Dog and the horses could've caught its scent. I'll go scout around a mite."

"Be careful, Preacher," Casey urged. "I don't know what any of us would do if anything happened to you."

That comment put a brief frown on Roland's face, but he was too worried they might be in danger again to dwell on being jealous. The youngster clutched his rifle tightly.

Preacher hoped Roland wouldn't get too trigger-happy. Sometimes inexperience made a man's own allies the biggest danger to him. He pulled Lorenzo aside. "Keep an eye on that kid," he told the old-timer. "Don't let him start blazin' away at nothin'. I might be in the way of one of those balls."

Lorenzo nodded, understanding etched on his wizened face.

In an easy lope, Preacher moved away from the camp to the north. Nobody but Casey, Lorenzo, and Roland saw him leave, and within moments he had vanished into the shadows.

Dog trotted alongside Preacher. The mountain man's every sense was alert, but he relied on the big cur's senses even more. Wherever and whatever the danger might be, Dog would lead him to it.

As they put more distance between themselves and the camp, Dog began to hang back a little. Instead of growls, a little whine came from his throat every now and then. Preacher came to a halt, and Dog stopped as well. The powerful, thick-furred body pressed against Preacher's leg.

Preacher dropped to a knee and looped an arm around Dog's neck. "What is it?" he asked in a whisper. "It must be something mighty bad if it's got you spooked, you old varmint."

He felt a slight tremble in Dog's muscles. Preacher knew the reaction wasn't from fear. Dog was anxious to get out there and tangle with whatever it was. At the same time, something more than Preacher's grip held him back. Dog was wary, torn between the desire to attack whatever it was he had sensed and the urge to get the hell away from it as fast as he could.

Dog wouldn't react that way to Indians. The big cur knew their scent quite well and had never been afraid of them. A wolf wouldn't spook him that bad, either. It had to be something else.

Preacher got to his feet and moved forward again, as silent as the night breeze. He didn't have to tell Dog to come with him. Dog wouldn't willingly leave Preacher's side in the face of danger, no matter how scared he was.

A glance over his shoulder told Preacher he was about half a mile north of the camp. He could see the fire, a bright orange dot in the darkness.

Dog stopped short and began to growl. The thing was close. Preacher stopped and waited, reaching out into the darkness with his senses. He didn't hear anything, but he caught a faint whiff of a rank odor, then it was gone as quickly as it had come. Dog stopped growling, and when Preacher reached down to rub him, he found that the fur on the back of the big cur's neck had settled down. Dog was no longer upset.

Whatever had been out there in the shadows was gone. Dog relaxed and let his tongue loll out of his mouth.

Preacher stood and waited several minutes to make sure the thing didn't come back. When he was sure the danger was over, he grunted and said to Dog, "Well, if that don't beat all. I'd sure like to know what it was that got you so spooked."

Dog couldn't tell him, though. The bond between man and animal was almost supernatural, but it still had its limits.

Preacher turned and walked back toward the camp. The sentries were already at their posts for the first shift, and one of them demanded to know who Preacher was.

"Just me, friend," Preacher told the man.

"Something wrong, Preacher?" the bullwhacker asked.

"Nope, just takin' a look around." It didn't make any sense to panic Bartlett's men by telling the truth, especially when Preacher didn't know the whole story yet.

When he rejoined Casey, Lorenzo, and Roland, they all looked at him with wordless curiosity. "I didn't find anything," he told them. "Somethin' was out there, no doubt about that, but whatever it was, left."

"What could it have been?" Roland asked. "Should I tell my father about it?"

Preacher shook his head. "No, we don't know anything. We'll keep quiet about it for now and just keep our eyes open. I'll do some more scoutin' tomorrow and see if I can find any tracks. That might tell us what we're dealin' with."

"I hope we don't have to deal with it," Casey said with a little shiver. "Maybe whatever it was will go on and leave us alone."

"That'd be good," Preacher said. But he wasn't convinced that was the way it would turn out. His instincts told him a different story.

For a moment there, out on the prairie, he had been convinced that he and Dog were the ones being stalked.

And it wasn't a good feeling.

CHAPTER 6

The next two days were uneventful. No Indians, no mysterious creatures lurking in the night . . . in fact, Preacher and the other members of the freight caravan didn't see another creature except a few prairie dogs. The unvarying landscape was mind-numbing, but the wagons made good time.

Then it began to rain.

Preacher rode a few miles ahead of the caravan. He'd noticed the bank of blue-gray clouds building to the southwest early on the morning of the fifth day out from Independence. He pointed it out to Lorenzo, who was riding beside him.

"Yeah, I seen it," the elderly black man said. "Looks like we're gonna have a storm blowin' through."

"It might miss us," Preacher said. "Hard to tell just how far away anything is out here."

"That's the gospel truth! I never seen a flatter, emptier country than this here."

Preacher kept an eye on the clouds all morning. They loomed closer and closer, filling up half the sky until everyone in the wagon caravan, even the rankest greenhorn, couldn't help but notice them. Leeman Bartlett rode forward to talk to Preacher.

"Do you think we need to find shelter?" Bartlett asked as he cast nervous glances toward the billowing black clouds. Preacher knew that the sun shining on the clouds made them appear darker than they really were, but they were plenty dark enough to hold a lot of wind and rain, maybe even some hail.

In reply to Bartlett's question, Preacher swept a hand at the vast emptiness surrounding them and said, "That'd be a mighty fine idea . . . if there was any place to hole up. But you can see for yourself there ain't really any place like that out here."

"Then what should we do? Just keep going right into the teeth of that storm?"

Preacher shook his head. "No, I reckon it'd be best to stop. Maybe the worst of it will skirt past us." He didn't think that was likely, but stopping was just about the only thing they could do.

"Should we circle the wagons and unhitch the teams, like we do when we make camp?"

"No, leave 'em harnessed. We may have to move, if the water starts risin'."

Bartlett looked confused. "Are you talking about a flood? How would that be possible on flat ground like this?"

"You'd be surprised at the amount of rain that can fall in one of these cloudbursts."

Bartlett turned his horse and rode back to the wagons to pass along the order to stop.

There hadn't been much wind and soon it laid

down and was dead still. Lorenzo scratched his jaw and said, "I don't much like the way the air feels."

"Me, neither," Preacher said. Horse tossed his head, and beside them, Dog let out a little whine. "These two varmints agree, and I've learned over the years to always trust 'em." Preacher turned his mount. "Let's get back."

As they rode toward the wagons, which were coming to a stop about a quarter mile behind them, a hard gust of wind suddenly slapped them in the back. They grabbed their hats and kept riding.

Preacher had fought many battles in his life, sometimes against overwhelming odds. Some of the battles he'd had no business winning, but through guile, determination, and sometimes sheer luck and stubbornness, he had prevailed.

But against a fierce force of nature like the powerful storm rolling across the prairie toward them, there was no way to fight. All one could do was hunker down and hope.

Casey rode out to meet Preacher and Lorenzo, and as usual, Roland Bartlett was tagging along after her. The wind continued to rise. Casey had to shout to be heard above it.

"Preacher, what are we going to do?"

"Find a place to crawl into one of those wagons, otherwise you're gonna get wet," he told her as he reined in. He looked over his shoulder. He could see the rain, sweeping like a gray curtain toward them. They had a few minutes before the storm hit, but not much more than that.

"How bad is the storm going to be?" Roland called.

Preacher shook his head. "No way of tellin'." He

glanced again at the black-fanged clouds. "Bad enough, that's for dang sure!"

"Come on," Roland told Casey. "We'll find a spot for you in one of the wagons!"

They hurried off. Preacher and Lorenzo dismounted beside the lead wagon and tied their horses to one of the front wheels. The big gray stallion turned his rear end toward the storm and gave Preacher a baleful look, as if scolding him for bringing him out in weather like that in the first place.

Preacher told Dog to get under the wagon. The big cur obeyed, crawling underneath the vehicle, lying down, and resting his muzzle on his paws.

Leeman Bartlett hurried up. "Do we need to do anything else to prepare?"

"No, these wagons are loaded down with enough freight so they weigh plenty. They shouldn't go anywhere unless a damn cyclone comes along and picks them up."

Bartlett stared at Preacher. "Is such a thing even possible?"

"I've seen the destruction those twisters can leave behind," Preacher replied grimly. "It's possible, all right. But maybe we'll just get wet. Maybe the wind won't blow that hard."

As if to punctuate his words, thunder suddenly boomed as skeletal fingers of lightning clawed brilliantly across the sky. Under the wagon, Dog whimpered a little. He was a ferocious creature, but like all of his species, he didn't cotton to loud noises.

Preacher pulled back the canvas cover over the wagon bed. Inside, the vehicle was stacked with crates and barrels and burlap bags.

"Climb in," he told Lorenzo. "I'll give you a hand."

"How about you?" the old-timer asked.

"Don't worry about me. I'll find me a hidey-hole."

Preacher helped Lorenzo clamber into the wagon, then pulled the canvas tight so it would shut out as much rain as possible. The drops hadn't started to fall, but he knew it was only a matter of time—a minute, maybe two—before the deluge started.

Leeman Bartlett trotted up to him. "All the men are in the wagons," he said. "How long does a storm like this last?"

"Usually not very long. Fifteen minutes, maybe half an hour. I've seen downpours that lasted for days, but with them you don't get wind like this."

"We'd better get undercover," Bartlett said. "I think there's room for both of us in the third wagon."

Preacher followed Bartlett to that wagon. As Bartlett pulled back the canvas, Preacher saw Casey peering out at him through a narrow gap in the rear canvas flap on the second wagon. He smiled at her and tried to look reassuring.

He and Bartlett climbed into the third wagon. Preacher tied the canvas shut behind them. Thick black clouds covered the entire sky and didn't let much light through them, so it was almost pitch black inside the wagon. Preacher perched on a short keg of nails while Bartlett sat cross-legged on a wooden crate.

"Do you know what's in here?" Bartlett asked as he slapped a hand against the side of the crate.

"No idea," Preacher said.

"China. Fine china. Do you think they'll have a

use for it in Santa Fe, assuming we can get it there unbroken, that is?"

"I suspect they will. There are a lot of old, rich families in Santa Fe, and those grandees like to show off a mite for each other. They'll buy your china, and likely everything else you've got. Folks in *Nuevo Mexico* can get most things from Mexico City, but it's easier to bring freight in from the States. More caravans from St. Louis visit Santa Fe than ones from Mexico City."

"I hope you're right. I've sunk a great deal of money into this venture." Bartlett rubbed his face wearily. "It's not exaggerating to say that if it fails . . . I'll be ruined."

"We'll try to see to it that don't happen," Preacher said, but before he could go on, the rain hit. It slammed against the canvas with a loud sluicing sound. The wind howled louder.

Bartlett's eyes were big with awe at the sound of nature's fury. Preacher could see how wide they were, even in the dim interior of the wagon. With each gust of wind, the vehicle shook. The canvas cover billowed and popped against the steel hoops that gave it shape. If the storm lasted too long, it might rip the canvas right off the wagons. People and cargo would be in for a drenching if that happened.

"My word," Bartlett said quietly between booming peals of thunder. "I thought I had seen storms back in Pennsylvania. I'm not sure I've ever experienced anything to compare to this."

"These plains thunderstorms are the biggest I've ever seen." Water dripped through a tiny gap in the canvas and plunked down on Preacher's hat. "If it keeps up for very long, you're gonna be stuck here for the rest of today and probably most of to-morrow."

"Why can't we move on once the storm is over?"

"Because the trail will be too muddy," Preacher explained. "The wheels would bog down in a hurry. You'd have to use two or three teams on each wagon just to pull them loose, and even if you did that, you'd probably be stuck again before you went twenty yards. It'll be better just to wait and let the sun dry the ground some tomorrow before you try to move."

"I'll bow to your superior wisdom, sir. I'm not fond of the delay, but I suppose in a journey of this magnitude, a difference of a day or two doesn't have much significance."

"That's the truth," Preacher agreed. "The trip to Santa Fe is a long haul. You got to be patient."

The rain continued pounding down. The rumble of thunder was so loud the ground shook with each peal, and the lightning was so frequent that the flickering illumination cast by the bolts was almost as constant as firelight.

Preacher suddenly frowned as he heard a rum-bling noise that didn't seem to be caused by the thunder. He had heard something like it before and didn't like the sound. He leaned over to the canvas flaps at the front of the wagon and pulled them apart slightly, creating a narrow gap. He couldn't see anything except the wagon ahead of them in line, so he widened it a little more.

He put his eye to it and peered out.

What he saw brought a heartfelt exclamation from his lips. "Son of a *bitch!*"

"What is it?" Leeman Bartlett asked nervously.

For a moment, Preacher didn't answer. All he could do was stare at the broad funnel of madly whirling air that danced across the prairie toward the wagons. Ball lightning spiraled around it, marking its course over the plains. Preacher estimated that the giant tornado was at least a mile away, but it wouldn't take any time at all to cover that distance.

He found his voice again. "Cyclone," he told Bartlett. "A big one."

"My God. Is it headed toward us?"

"Appears to be. Hard to say, though, the way those things skip around."

"What can we do?" Bartlett asked, his voice cracking a little with barely suppressed fear.

"If you're a prayin' man, I'd get busy at it. If you ain't . . . this might be a good time to start."

Bartlett began muttering under his breath, but between the pounding rain, the howling wind, and the rumble of the approaching twister, Preacher couldn't tell if the man was praying or cursing. As for him, he sent up a brief plea to El Señor Dios, as the Mexicans called him.

Something else caught his eye, something that made him press his face closer to the gap in the canvas flaps. He saw a huge shape moving through the rain. It was nothing but a formless blob, but it was big. Something about the sight of it lumbering slowly along made a shiver go down Preacher's spine. Then the gray curtains of the downpour thickened, and whatever it was vanished from Preacher's sight.

He thought about Dog and Horse. He couldn't do anything about Horse, but there was room in the wagon for Dog and Preacher wanted his old friend with him. He told Bartlett, "Stay put."

The man clutched at his arm. "Good Lord! You're not going *out* in that, are you? What about the cyclone?"

"It'll get us or it won't," Preacher replied fatalistically. He pulled free from Bartlett's hand, pushed the canvas aside, and climbed out over the front of the wagon, dropping to the already muddy ground next to the stolid oxen.

Instantly, he was soaked to the skin. The rain lashed at him like something alive. He held on to his hat to keep it from blowing away. The storm was worse than he had thought. If he had known things were going to get that bad, he would have taken Dog into the wagon with him to start with.

"Dog!" he yelled over the racket. "Dog!"

He couldn't see much of anything. It was like he was in the middle of a waterfall. But after a moment he felt the big cur pressing against his leg. Preacher reached down and put his arms around Dog's thick, heavily muscled body. Lifting the animal wasn't easy, but he heaved Dog up until the big cur was able to scramble into the wagon. Preacher pulled himself in after him.

"That animal is soaked!" Bartlett protested.

"So am I," Preacher pointed out. The terrible, earth-shaking roar of the cyclone grew louder. "Get down and hang on!"

The wagon shook madly as Preacher pressed

himself to the floorboards, holding Dog tightly beside him with an arm around the animal. Dog whimpered and licked his face. Preacher expected that at any second the tornado was going to lift the wagon from the ground and suck it high into the air, spinning it madly at the same time.

He had looked death in the face many times, but he had probably never been closer to it until that very moment.

Although the wagon shook like it was about to fall apart, it remained on the ground. After a few seconds that seemed more like an hour, the shaking and the noise subsided slightly. Leeman Bartlett lifted his pale, fear-gaunted face and asked hollowly, "Is . . . is it over?"

"Maybe the worst of it," Preacher said. He let go of Dog and crawled over to the flaps at the rear of the wagon. When he pushed one of them back, rain slashed through the opening. He blinked water out of his eyes and looked for the tornado. A second later he spotted it, off the ground and pulling back up into the clouds. He thought it must have started lifting up just before it reached the caravan. If a monster like that had struck the wagons directly, it would have scattered them like a child's toys. They had definitely dodged one of nature's deadliest bullets.

But they weren't out of danger yet. As Preacher watched, a lightning bolt slammed into the prairie about a hundred yards away.

"The twister's gone!" he shouted over the roaring wind. "The storm's still a long way from played out, though. And there's nothin' sayin' another cyclone won't show up."

"Then we should all just stay put?" Bartlett asked.

"That's right. It'll blow itself out sooner or later."

And when it did, Preacher thought, there would be even more problems facing them.

Chapter 7

For more than an hour after the heavens opened up, the rain continued to pour down. At last the deluge began to slow, and when it did, it tapered off quickly and then came to an abrupt end. Mere minutes later, the sun started peeking through tiny rifts in the thick gray clouds.

That was the way of prairie thunderstorms, Preacher thought as he pulled the canvas back and got ready to climb out of the wagon. Once they were over, they were over.

But Lord, that one had left a mess behind.

The trail was a broad swath of thick muck and standing water. Preacher's boots splashed when they hit the ground. He sunk almost ankle-deep in the mud. When he turned back to the wagon to lift Dog down, the big cur looked at the mess and whined a little, as if to say he'd rather just stay right where he was, thank you very much.

Preacher grinned and said, "All right, if you want to be particular about it."

Bartlett looked down from the wagon as well. "Good Lord," he said. "It's a swamp out there."

"Yep," Preacher said. "Just like I told you. You couldn't go very far without boggin' down again. Better to wait until things dry out a mite."

The air was hot and steamy. Preacher took off his hat and sleeved sweat off his forehead as he slogged along the line of wagons, checking on the vehicles and telling the occupants that it was all right to come out again, if they wanted to.

Casey was a little flushed as she looked down from the wagon where she had taken shelter with Roland Bartlett. "What a terrible storm," she said. "I thought we were all about to blow away."

Preacher nodded. "We came mighty close. That cyclone almost got us."

"I hope I never have to go through anything like that again."

"It wasn't *that* bad," Roland put in. "At least we weren't alone."

Casey flushed a deeper shade of pink. Preacher managed not to chuckle. He figured there had been some clinging to each other going on in that wagon during the height of the storm.

He moved on and helped Lorenzo climb down from the lead wagon, then the two of them checked on the horses. The big gray stallion was wet and annoyed but seemed fine otherwise, as did the other horses. The same was true of the oxen hitched to the wagons. Considering the ferocity of the storm, they had all come through it pretty well.

They had been lucky, Preacher thought. Mighty lucky.

Lorenzo made a face as the mud tried to suck his

boots off with every step. "We ain't goin' anywhere any time soon, are we?" he asked.

"Not until tomorrow at the earliest," Preacher replied.

Word spread quickly among the bullwhackers that the wagons weren't budging. Several of the men who had been over the trail before came up to Preacher and told him they agreed with the decision.

"Gonna be a cold camp tonight," one of those veteran frontiersman said. "There's nothin' out here dry enough to burn right now."

Preacher knew that was true. Without a fire, they would have to make do with leftover biscuits for their supper, and no coffee. But that was still a lot better than going hungry, which he had done many times in the past.

Since the wagons weren't in their usual circle, Preacher rigged a makeshift corral with poles and a couple ropes. Then the bullwhackers unhitched the teams and drove them into the enclosure. The massive, stolid beasts of burden weren't easily spooked, so it was easy to keep them penned up. Preacher told a couple men to keep an eye on them, anyway.

The last of the clouds moved on, leaving the late afternoon sky clear and hot. It was sticky, miserable weather, and it wasn't long before everyone was on edge. Preacher was going to be glad when night fell. At least it would cool off a little then.

Remembering the thing he had caught a glimpse of during the storm, he told Lorenzo, "I'm gonna scout around a mite." The likelihood of finding tracks in the mud was slim, but it wouldn't hurt anything to take a look.

"You want me to come with you?" the old-timer asked.

"No, I'd rather you stay here and keep an eye on this bunch. Don't let them do anything stupid."

Lorenzo snorted. "You reckon they're gonna pay any attention to a black man?"

"Well, you try to talk sense to them, anyway," Preacher said.

He lifted Dog down from the wagon and swung up on Horse's back. Riding north, he kept an eye on the muddy ground as he searched for signs. Dog splashed along through the puddles.

Preacher cast back and forth for quite a while but didn't find anything, and Dog didn't react to any unusual scents. Just as Preacher had suspected, the downpour had washed away any tracks or smells. As the sun lowered toward the horizon, he called Dog to his side and said, "We might as well ride on back to the wagons."

He was about a mile from the caravan, he judged. As he headed south again, movement to the east caught his eye. He reined in and his eyes narrowed as he peered into the distance. After a moment, he was able to focus on the moving objects well enough to recognize them as several men on horseback.

The riders were headed west along the trail, toward the stalled wagons. Not knowing who they were but being naturally cautious, Preacher muttered, "We'd better get back there," and heeled Horse into a ground-eating lope.

As he rode up to the wagons, Lorenzo came out to meet him. "Find anything?" the black man asked.

Preacher hadn't explained what he was looking for, since to tell the truth, he didn't really know. He shook his head and said, "Nothin' unusual, except for some fellas comin' in from the east on horseback."

Lorenzo's hands tightened on the flintlock rifle he carried. Even though he lacked Preacher's experience on the frontier, he was smart enough to know that strangers could mean trouble.

"You know who they are?"

"Not a clue," Preacher said as he dismounted. He looped Horse's reins around one of the wagon wheels. "Where's Bartlett?"

"Last I seen of him, he was goin' through the wagons, checkin' to see if the rain damaged any of the freight."

Preacher walked along the line of wagons until he found Bartlett, who was climbing out of one of the vehicles. "Riders comin'," Preacher told him.

"Is that a problem?"

"Most likely not, but it could be, if they're lookin' for trouble. Get your men together."

Bartlett nodded and hurried off to do as Preacher said. The mountain man walked on past the wagons until he reached the end of the caravan. Then he waited for the riders to arrive. They were already in sight and coming steadily closer—close enough for Preacher to be able to count them.

Five men, and one of them was leading a pack horse. Not a real threat, considering that Bartlett had twenty bullwhackers working for him, but

Preacher was still wary. His instincts wouldn't allow him to be otherwise.

"Preacher?"

Casey's voice came from behind him. He looked over his shoulder and saw her plodding through the mud toward him with a worried expression on her face. Not surprisingly, Roland trailed after her. So did Lorenzo.

"Someone is following us?" Casey asked.

"Somebody's goin' the same direction we are," Preacher said. "It ain't necessarily the same thing."

"You don't think they could be some of Beaumont's men, do you?"

Back in St. Louis, Casey had worked for Shad Beaumont, a prominent criminal. Beaumont was dead, but ever since they had left St. Louis, Casey had worried that some of the surviving members of his organization might come after them and seek vengeance.

Preacher didn't think that was likely, but he couldn't rule out the possibility entirely, which was yet another reason to be cautious. He told Casey, "I'd be mighty surprised if those fellas had anything to do with Beaumont, but if they did and if they're lookin' for us . . . well, we'll deal with it, that's all."

"Who's Beaumont?" Roland asked.

Casey looked over at him and shook her head. "No one. He's dead. But some of the men who worked for him might have a grudge against Preacher and Lorenzo and me."

"Oh." Roland was clearly puzzled, but he didn't indulge his curiosity. Preacher figured Casey hadn't told him she used to work in a whorehouse, and she probably wouldn't tell him unless she was forced to for some reason. Her past didn't matter to Preacher and she knew that, but likely Roland would be a different story.

As the riders came closer, Preacher's keen eyes saw that they were all wearing buckskins. A couple sported coonskin caps, the others broad-brimmed felt hats like the one Preacher wore. He recognized them as fellow mountain men, even though he had never seen any of them before.

One of the men edged his horse in front of the others as the party closed to within thirty feet and reined in. The self-appointed spokesman was tall and rangy in the saddle, with a gray-shot brown beard that jutted from his angular jaw. He put a grin on his face and nodded to Preacher, who walked out from the wagons to meet him.

"Howdy."

"Afternoon," Preacher said as he returned the nod. He had his rifle cradled in his arms with his thumb looped over the hammer. The stranger couldn't fail to note that sign of being ready for trouble. As a matter of fact, the man's own rifle was resting across the saddle in front of him, also ready for quick use.

"Looks like you folks are a mite bogged down," the man commented. "We saw that storm blowin' through, but we were lucky and the worst of it missed us. Looked like it was a ring-tailed roarer, though."

"It sure was," Preacher agreed. "A big cyclone came down from the clouds, and for a minute I thought it was gonna carry us off."

The man shook his head. "I saw one of those

things down in Texas once. It'd be mighty fine with me if I never saw another one."

"Same here," Preacher said.

The man leaned over and spat. "Name's Garity." He waved a hand at his companions. "This here's Levi Jones, Walt Stubblefield, Micawja Horne, and Edgar Massey. We're headin' for New Mexico."

"They call me Preacher."

He saw the looks of recognition that appeared on the faces of all five men. They knew the name, all right. Most folks who roamed the wild places west of the Mississippi did.

"Preacher, eh?" Garity said. "Didn't know you'd started guidin' wagon trains to Santa Fe. I reckon that's where these wagons are goin'?"

"That's right. What do you plan to do in New Mexico?"

It was an unusually blunt question. Whenever folks met somebody for the first time, they normally waited for the other fella to offer whatever information he wanted to about where he came from and where he was going . . . and what he planned to do once he got there.

Garity frowned. "Figured we'd do some trappin'."

"Ever been to that part of the country before?"

"Nope. I'd wager you have, though, what with you bein' the famous Preacher and all."

Preacher stiffened at the edge of mockery in Garity's voice. The man obviously didn't think that based on looks alone, Preacher lived up to his reputation.

Preacher didn't give a damn about that, but he didn't like the predatory gleam he saw in Garity's eyes when the man looked at the wagons . . . and at Casey.

"Yeah, I've been there several times. Pretty country. The trappin's better farther north, though. That's where the real fur trade is."

"Yeah, but there's more competition up there," Garity pointed out. "We figure the field'll be clearer down south." He scratched at his beard. "How long do you folks figure on stayin' here?"

"Until the trail dries out enough that the wagons won't get stuck when they try to move," Preacher said. The answer was obvious, so he didn't see any harm in giving it.

"Muddy as it is, that may be a while. Anything we can do to give you a hand?"

Preacher shook his head. "Nope. I reckon we'll do just fine."

"All right, then. I reckon we'll mosey on." Garity lifted a finger to the brim of his hat. "You folks be careful, now."

He jerked his head at his companions. They moved their horses over to the side of the trail and rode around the wagons. Preacher saw that each of them eyed Casey as they moved past her. That wasn't surprising. A man could go a long time out there without seeing a woman, and an even longer time without seeing one as pretty as Casey.

She wasn't the only thing that interested the men, however. They looked long and hard at the wagons, too, as if they were weighing how much money the freight in the vehicles might bring in Santa Fe.

Preacher kept an eye on the men until they

vanished into the setting sun. Leeman Bartlett came up beside him and said, "That was a rather rough-looking bunch."

"Yeah," Preacher agreed. "I wouldn't trust any of 'em. Good thing is, there were only five of 'em. We outnumber 'em four to one, so there ain't much chance they'll try to bother us."

"But our guards should be especially alert tonight anyway, don't you think?"

Preacher grinned at the man. "You're learnin', Mr. Bartlett. You're learnin'."

CHAPTER 8

Preacher and Bartlett put on extra guard shifts for the night. The ground was too muddy to sleep on comfortably, so after their cold supper, the men who didn't have sentry duty climbed into the wagons and tried to find enough room to stretch out. That wasn't easy, especially for someone like Preacher with his long legs.

He managed to doze off on top of some crates, but his slumber was restless. After a while, he sat up, pulled on his boots, and climbed out of the wagon. The night was quiet and peaceful. The air had cooled off a little, and there was a breeze out of the north. It wasn't as sticky, which boded well for the ground drying out some the next day.

Something nuzzled his hand. He looked down and saw that Dog had crawled out from under the wagon. The big cur was covered with mud. He had romped in it for an hour around dusk, deciding it was all right after all.

"You're a mess, you know that?" Preacher said

with a grin as he gave Dog's ears an affectionate scratch. "You—"

He stopped short as Dog suddenly stiffened, growled, and pressed against his leg. The animal's ears pricked up, and he lifted his head as he pointed his muzzle toward the north.

"Whatever that damned thing is, it's out there again, ain't it?" Preacher asked softly.

As if in answer, Dog growled again.

"I've had enough of this," Preacher muttered to himself. Earlier, he had seen Leeman Bartlett climbing into one of the wagons to try to get some sleep. With Dog at his heels, he stalked over to that wagon and pulled the canvas back. "Bartlett!"

"What? Wh-what?" Sputtering a little, Bartlett raised up and stuck his head out through the opening. "What's wrong, Preacher?"

"You have any newspapers or anything like that?"

"Why, as a matter of fact, I brought along a stack of Philadelphia papers. I thought the American settlers in Santa Fe might like to see them."

"Gimme one of them," Preacher snapped.

Bartlett hesitated, and Preacher knew the man intended to sell the papers in Santa Fe, not share them for free. But after a couple of seconds, Bartlett said, "Very well. Just a moment."

After a minute of rustling around inside the wagon, Bartlett climbed out and handed Preacher a newspaper. He was wearing high-topped boots and a nightshirt, which gave him a rather ludicrous appearance. "What's going on?" he asked. "Is there a problem?"

"Somethin's been followin' us," Preacher replied,

"and I'm sick and tired of it. I'm gonna find out what it is."

He handed Bartlett his rifle, then took several sheets of the newspaper and twisted them into a makeshift torch. Getting out flint and steel, he struck sparks until he managed to catch the paper on fire.

Then he pulled one of the pistols from behind his belt, cocked it, and strode away from the wagons, thrusting the burning paper in front of him.

"Damn it, whoever you are, show yourself!" he bellowed.

Behind him, men began to crawl out of the wagons, awakened by the shout, and they called questions to each other as they wondered what was going on.

Preacher turned his head and barked a command. "Stay close to the wagons!"

He strode forward again, moving the burning paper from side to side. The torch wouldn't last long, only a few more seconds, before it burned down close enough to his fingers to make him drop it.

Suddenly he saw something glow up ahead of him. Two somethings, actually, like a pair of embers in the remains of a campfire. The way the two glows were set, he knew they were eyes.

What they belonged to was another question. As Preacher thrust his pistol out in front of him, the eyes abruptly rose higher and higher and then just as abruptly disappeared. At the same time, the flames singed Preacher's fingers and he had to drop the burning paper. It sizzled out instantly as it hit the mud.

Preacher wanted to pull the trigger, but he had never shot a gun without knowing what he was shooting at, and he didn't want to start. He held his fire with his finger still taut on the trigger, ready to squeeze it.

He heard a few small sucking sounds. The mud tugging at the feet of whatever was out there, he thought. The thing was leaving.

But it would be back, Preacher told himself. It had been dogging their trail for several days, and he didn't think it would stop just because he had yelled at it.

He didn't think their stalker was human. A man would have shown himself already. Judging by the glimpse Preacher had gotten of the thing during the storm, it was too big to be a man. That meant it had to be some sort of animal, but if that were true, it had a keener intelligence than most animals, or else it would have forgotten about the wagons and wandered off by now.

Preacher stayed where he was with the pistol pointing out into the darkness until his instincts told him the thing was gone. He didn't tuck the weapon away when he finally started back toward the wagons. In fact, he drew the other pistol and held it ready as well, just in case something came at him out of the shadows.

Nothing did. By the time he got back to the wagons, the entire camp was awake and waiting to find out what was going on. Casey, with a blanket wrapped around her shoulders, came up to him and asked, "What was out there, Preacher?"

The mountain man shook his head. "I don't know. Some sort of animal. I saw its eyes glowing in the light, but only for a second. Then it turned around and left."

Roland Bartlett was standing beside Casey. He said, "Well, then, if it was just an animal, we don't have to worry about it, do we?"

"I didn't say that," Preacher replied. "Whatever that thing is, it's pretty big, and it's smart, too. It'd be a good idea to keep our eyes open. But then, that's always a good idea out here."

The men began to head back to their wagons to get some more sleep. Casey came over to Preacher and laid a hand on his arm. "Do you really think we're in any danger from this thing?" she asked.

Preacher smiled, but the expression didn't hold any real humor. "We've been in danger from one thing or another ever since we left St. Louis," he told her. "And if you recollect, it was a mite perilous back there, too!"

By morning, the trail was still pretty muddy, but the big puddles of standing water were beginning to dry up. The sky was mostly clear, the cool breeze from the north was still blowing, and Preacher thought maybe the trail would be dry enough by midday for the wagons to pull out.

He told Leeman Bartlett they would remain where they were for the time being, then saddled Horse and rode out to the area where he had seen the glowing eyes the night before. Dog trotted alongside him. Since the rain had stopped before Preacher went out and challenged the thing, he thought he might be able to find its tracks.

Sure enough, the marks were on the ground,

leading off to the northwest. But the mud had been soft enough at the time the tracks were left that it had flowed back into them, blurring and obscuring any details. Even though Preacher dismounted and studied the tracks closely, he couldn't tell what sort of animal had made them.

He could follow them, though, and he did so, swinging back up in the saddle. Dog ranged ahead of him as he rode northwest.

The wagons fell out of sight behind him. Preacher was a little worried about Garity and the other hard-looking men who had ridden past, but he didn't expect them to double back and attack the wagons. They had struck him as men who wouldn't risk anything unless the odds were on their side.

Eventually, the tracks led to a rain-swollen creek and vanished into the fast-moving water. The creature must have plunged right in, demonstrating a complete lack of fear where the flooded creek was concerned. As Preacher reined in and sat on the bank, frowning at the rushing stream, he wondered what sort of varmint would do a thing like that.

He wasn't going to try to swim Horse across the creek. It would be too easy for both man and horse to be swept away. He turned the gray stallion and called, "Come on, Dog," to the big cur. They headed back toward the wagons, which were several miles away.

Preacher had covered about half that distance when a series of faint popping sounds came to his ears. He stiffened in the saddle for a second as he immediately recognized the sounds for what they were.

Gunfire.

"Son of a bitch," he muttered as he leaned forward

and dug his heels harder into Horse's flanks. The animal responded by leaping into a gallop.

Preacher couldn't hear the shots anymore over the pounding of Horse's hooves. Maybe the situation wasn't as bad as he thought it was, he told himself.

But he couldn't convince himself of that, and sure enough, when he came in sight of the wagons, he saw a number of men on horseback riding back and forth, firing rifles toward them. Since the wagons weren't pulled into a circle, the traditional defensive formation, the bullwhackers and the other men had been forced to take cover underneath the vehicles. As Preacher raced closer, he saw puffs of powdersmoke coming from under the wagons and knew Bartlett's men were putting up a fight.

Preacher figured Garity and the men who had ridden by the day before had joined up with some others and come back to attack the freight caravan.

He was coming at them from behind, so they didn't seem to know he was there. When he was within rifle range, he reined Horse to a halt and was out of the saddle even before the stallion stopped moving. He pulled the long-barreled flint-lock rifle from the fringed sheath strapped to the saddle and rested it across Horse's back.

Preacher eased the rifle's hammer back and lined the sights on one of the attackers. He would be shooting the man in the back, which he didn't like, but since the varmint was trying to kill folks Preacher had befriended, the mountain man figured he had it coming. Preacher took a deep breath and squeezed the trigger.

The black powder went off with a dull boom as

the rifle kicked back hard against Preacher's shoulder. The cloud of smoke that poured from the muzzle obscured his vision for a second, but as it cleared, he saw the man he had targeted was on the ground, kicking out his life spasmodically. The heavy lead ball had slammed into his back and driven him right out of the saddle.

Preacher didn't try to reload the rifle. The other attackers would have noticed that one of their number had been shot down from behind. As some of them wheeled their horses around to search for the source of the new threat, Preacher jammed the rifle back in its sheath and vaulted into the saddle. He sent the stallion lunging forward again and put the reins in his teeth, guiding Horse with his knees. Preacher pulled both pistols from behind his belt.

The guns were double-shotted and carried a larger than usual charge of powder, which made them mighty lethal, but he had to get closer to use them. He was relying on Horse's speed and elusiveness for that. As the attackers who had turned toward Preacher opened fire, the big animal swerved from side to side, responding swiftly and surely to the pressure of the mountain man's knees on his flanks.

Preacher felt as much as heard the hum of a rifle ball passing closely by his head. The sensation was nothing new to him, so he didn't let it spook him. Instead he kept riding, drawing ever nearer to the attackers. Soon he was close enough to recognize some of them, and just as he'd expected, the man called Garity was among them. Preacher saw clearly the man's beard and rawboned shape.

He was also close enough to use the pistols, and

as Garity tried to draw a bead on him with a rifle, Preacher whipped up his right-hand gun and fired.

The two balls spread out as they flew through the air. One of them missed Garity entirely, but the other tore through his left arm. The impact of the shot made him drop his rifle and slew around in the saddle. He had to grab his horse's mane to keep from falling.

Preacher heard Garity yell in a hoarse voice, "Let's get the hell out of here!"

The men turned their horses and jabbed in their boot heels. The animals took off at a run, headed west along the trail.

Preacher started to fire his second pistol after them, but he let go of the trigger before the weapon went off. The chances of him hitting any of them were slim, and he wanted to have a loaded gun handy if they happened to turn around and try another attack.

It didn't look like that was going to be the case. The raiders showed no signs of slowing down as they gave up their attack and galloped off along the Santa Fe Trail.

Preacher rode straight to the wagons. Bartlett, Roland, Casey, and Lorenzo crawled out from under a couple vehicles and hurried to meet him. Their clothes were smeared with mud, but he didn't see any bloodstains on them.

A wave of relief went through him as he realized the young woman and the elderly black man hadn't been hurt. In the time he had known them, he had grown quite fond of them both.

That was true the other way around, too. Casey asked anxiously, "Preacher, are you all right?"

"Yeah, I'm fine," he told her as he dismounted. "They threw a little lead at me, but none of it came close."

Bartlett said, "It was that man Garity and his friends, the ones who were here yesterday! I got a good look at the scoundrels."

"Yeah, it was them, all right," Preacher said, "and a dozen other polecats to boot. Garity's bunch must've been plannin' on meetin' up with those other fellas, and when they did, he told them about these freight wagons."

"Were they always planning to rob us?" Roland asked.

Preacher shrugged. "No tellin'. They may have been on their way to the mountains to do some trappin' just like Garity said, and decided to take advantage of the opportunity fate put in their way. Or they could've been highwaymen all along."

"Well, the important thing is that we defeated them and sent them packing," Bartlett said.

Preacher shook his head. "No, the important thing, the thing we got to remember, is that they're still out there. Only one man got hisself killed." Preacher jerked his head toward the corpse that lay on the ground about a hundred yards away. The man's horse had deserted him, following the other horses when the rest of the bunch galloped away. "And at least one of them is wounded," Preacher went on, "maybe more, but really, we didn't do all that much damage to them."

"Then you think they'll come back?" Roland asked with a frown.

"They don't have to," Preacher said. He pointed west along the trail. "They're between you and the place where you're headed. All they've got to do is wait for you to come to them."

CHAPTER 9

Bartlett sent a couple of the bullwhackers to fetch in the body of the dead man. The powerfully muscled freighters were able to carry the corpse without much trouble. They laid it out next to one of the wagons so Preacher could have a look at it.

The man was skinny and had a scraggly black beard. One corner of his mouth was twisted grotesquely because of a knife scar that ran raggedly up his cheek. It looked like somebody had shoved a blade in his mouth and cut his face half open.

Preacher had never seen him before.

"This ain't one of the fellas who was with Garity yesterday," he said as he hunkered on his heels next to the corpse. "I've seen his sort before, though."

"What sort is that?" Bartlett asked.

"The one that'll do some trappin' or some other kind of honest work if he absolutely has to, but he'd rather steal from other folks and enjoy the fruits of their labor."

"Then we shouldn't be mourning him too much, I suppose."

Preacher snorted as he straightened to his feet. Since Casey was out of earshot at the moment, he said, "Hell, when we pull out you can leave the bastard layin' here for the wolves, for all I care."

Bartlett shook his head. "No, he's still a human being. We'll give him a decent burial."

"Suit yourself. Don't expect me to pray over him."

"I can do that. I brought a Bible with me, of course."

Digging a grave in the mud proved to be a difficult chore, and the men given the task by Bartlett were muttering curses under their breath before they were finished. The hole kept filling up with water. Finally they got the grave deep enough, and Bartlett had the dead raider wrapped in a blanket. A couple of the bullwhackers lowered him into the soggy earth.

Bartlett got out his Bible, asked God to have mercy on the soul of the departed, whose identity was unknown, and then motioned for his men to fill in the grave. By the time that was done, it was early afternoon and the sun had passed its zenith.

Preacher walked out on the trail and tested its firmness with his boots. Hours of sun and wind had dried the ground somewhat. Bartlett followed the mountain man and asked, "Do you think we can leave now?"

"We'll give it a try," Preacher replied with a nod. "If it looks like the wagons are about to bog down, we can always stop again."

Bartlett called orders, and the bullwhackers hitched up their teams. Roland saddled Casey's horse and then his own. Preacher grinned as he heard Lorenzo grumbling about how nobody saddled his horse for him. He had to do it himself despite the fact that he was an old man.

"I reckon it's better to be a pretty girl than a old geezer," Lorenzo muttered.

"I don't know about that," Preacher said. "Casey's had a hard life at times."

"Yeah, well, so have I. It don't matter none. Nobody fusses over me."

Preacher suddenly lifted up Lorenzo's hat and planted a kiss on top of the old man's bald head. "There," he drawled. "That make you feel better?"

"Gimme that hat!" Lorenzo snatched it away from Preacher and started swatting at the mountain man with it. "Didn't nobody ever teach you about respectin' your elders?"

Despite the tomfoolery, several worries nagged at the back of Preacher's brain, and hoorawing Lorenzo wasn't going to make them go away.

When everything was ready, Bartlett rode along the line of wagons and waved his hat over his head. "Move out!" he shouted. "Wagons *ho!*"

The bullwhackers popped their whips and bellowed at their teams. The oxen leaned forward against their harnesses and lurched into motion. With loud sucking sounds, the wheels pulled free of the mud. The sounds continued as the wagons rolled along the trail.

Preacher watched the wheels. They left deep ruts behind them, but they kept turning. It was the best he could hope for. Progress would be slower than usual as the oxen trudged through the mud and fought its clinging grip on their hooves, but any progress was better than none.

Bartlett, Roland, and Casey were at the head of

the caravan. Preacher rode up alongside them and said, "Looks like there's a good chance the wagons won't get stuck."

"Splendid!" Bartlett said. "Finally we can put more ground behind us."

"Well . . . maybe not as much as you'd hope."

Bartlett looked over at Preacher with a frown. "What do you mean? The wagons are moving."

"This morning while I was out trying to track the critter that was lurkin' around camp last night, I came across a creek. Reckon in normal times it wouldn't be much more'n a trickle, maybe even a dry wash, but after that gullywasher yesterday, these ain't normal times. The stream was flooded."

"You mean we won't be able to ford it?" Roland asked.

Preacher nodded. "That's what I'm sayin'. I don't know for sure that it crosses the trail, but it was runnin' northeast to southwest, so there's a good chance it does. And if it does, we'll probably have to wait for the water to go down before we can get to the other side."

Bartlett said, "How long will that take?"

"Depends on how much water's runnin' in it. Might just be a few hours, in which case we might be able to ford today while it's still light. But it could be as long as another day."

"Another day lost!" Bartlett exclaimed. "My God, does everything out here in this wilderness conspire to cause trouble for a man and ruin his plans?"

"Sometimes it seems like it," Preacher admitted. "But your plans ain't ruined, just delayed a mite. We'll get across sooner or later. It's still possible we won't have to ford that creek at all."

That much luck was not with them, however. Less than an hour later, Preacher spotted the dark, muddy line of the flooded creek stretching across the trail in front of them. He reined in and pointed it out to Bartlett.

"Should we stop the wagons?"

Preacher shook his head. "No, there's no reason not to push on until we get to the creek. That way we'll be ready to ford it as soon as we're able to. I'll ride ahead and take a look."

He had barely pulled out ahead of the others with Horse moving at an easy lope when he heard hoofbeats right behind him. He glanced over his shoulder and saw Casey following him. She came up even with him.

"No need for you to come along," he told her. "You can go back with Roland and his pa if you want to."

"But I don't want to," Casey snapped. "I want to talk to you, Preacher."

He bit back an exasperated curse. If she wanted to have that conversation, then maybe it was time. They could clear the air instead of having the future hanging over them all the way to Santa Fe.

"All right," he said. "Go ahead and talk."

"You've made it clear over the past few days that you don't want to have anything to do with me."

"Now that just ain't true," he said. "I think you're a fine gal, and I like havin' you around."

"So if I come to your bedroll tonight, you won't turn me away?"

"I didn't say that. Just because I like you don't mean I think it's a good idea for the two of us to, well, you know . . ."

"Is it because I was a whore? Because you can't stop thinking about all the other men who have been with me?"

Preacher snorted. "Hell, no. You know better'n that, Casey. If there's one thing the frontier's taught me, it's that yesterday's dead and gone. What we did then don't matter anymore. Since nobody knows if he'll be around to see the sun come up the next mornin', tomorrow don't mean a whole hell of a lot, neither. What we do today, that's what counts the most."

"That's what I think, too," she said. "I just don't understand why you don't like me as much anymore."

They had reached the rain-swollen creek. As they sat on their horses beside it, Preacher said, "Likin' you don't have anything to do with it. I just figure you'd be better off with somebody besides a shiftless old goat like me."

"I keep telling you, you're not that old. Anyway, that's not your decision to make."

"I reckon I've got a say in it, though."

Casey laughed. "You know a lot about a lot of things, Preacher, but evidently not that much about women."

He frowned and said, "I don't mean to hurt you, Casey, and I reckon we'll be travelin' together until we get to Santa Fe, for sure, but after that I don't know yet where I'll be goin' or what I'll be doin'."

She looked out over the churning water. "You want to abandon me in Santa Fe, is that it?"

"I'd never abandon you," Preacher said.

"Well, that's what it sounds like to me."

With that, she wheeled her horse around and rode back toward the wagons. Preacher shook his head and muttered a curse. That hadn't gone the way he wanted it to, but that was pretty much the story of his life where gals were concerned. Casey was right about one thing. Despite his experience, women were mostly a mystery to him and probably always would be.

He forced his mind onto a more pressing problem, namely the flooded creek. The stream was wider there, so the water level wasn't as deep as it was farther upstream, but it was still deep enough and flowing fast enough that Preacher didn't think it would be a good idea to take the wagons into it just yet. He had a hunch that by morning, the creek would have gone down enough they could ford it without too much difficulty.

When the wagons arrived, he gave that bit of good news to Leeman Bartlett. The man nodded and said, "Thank goodness. We'll only lose a few hours that way."

"Yeah. We'll make camp right here and wait it out."

The wagons were arranged in a circle with the livestock in the middle, and the men searched the surrounding prairie for buffalo dung that was dry enough to burn. By the time dusk began to settle over the landscape they had gathered enough to make a decent fire. They could have hot food and coffee again, and that would make everybody feel better.

As they were tending to their horses, Lorenzo said quietly to Preacher, "I saw Casey cryin' a while back, after she talked to you. What'd you say to the gal, Preacher?"

"Dadgum it! I tried to get her to see that there ain't no real future for her and me. Sooner or later she's gonna want to settle down, and I ain't cut out for that."

"Has she said anything to you about settlin' down, Preacher?" Lorenzo asked.

Preacher frowned. "Well . . . no, now that you mention it, she ain't."

"Then maybe you done jumped the gun a mite. Maybe you should'a just let things stay like they were until we get to Santa Fe. You coulda worried about it then."

"Yeah, could be you're right," Preacher muttered. "Would've been simpler that way, that's for damn sure. I don't know how well it would've gone over with young Bartlett, though."

"Roland ain't a bad sort, but he ain't near man enough for a gal like Casey. He's got a heap of growin' up to do first."

"Maybe I'll go talk to her. Try to set things right for a while, anyway."

Lorenzo nodded. "Be a good idea, I'm thinkin'."

The sun had gone down, and the night shadows were gathering. Preacher walked toward the fire, looking for Casey as he approached it. He didn't see her, but Leeman Bartlett was there.

"Did you happen to notice where Casey got off to?" Preacher asked the older man.

"She was over by that wagon with Roland." Bartlett pointed to one of the big, canvas-covered vehicles. He frowned worriedly. "Preacher, what sort of woman is Miss Casey? I'm afraid that Roland has, ah, developed an affection for her."

"She's one of the finest gals I ever met," Preacher answered honestly.

"Are the two of you . . . I mean, I hope you'll bear no ill will toward Roland because of what I just said."

Preacher shook his head. "Don't worry about it, Mr. Bartlett. I ain't lookin' for trouble. Not woman trouble, nor any other kind."

Leaving Bartlett by the fire, he walked toward the wagon the man had pointed out. He didn't see Casey and Bartlett at first, but then he glanced underneath the vehicle and spotted their feet. They were on the far side of the wagon, inside the circle with the oxen and the horses.

Preacher was about to step over the wagon tongue when he heard sobbing. That made him move even quicker. He came around the wagon and saw Casey and Roland standing there. Roland had his arms around her, but he wasn't actually hugging her. His arms just sort of encircled her, and he patted her awkwardly on the back with one hand as he said, "Casey, don't cry. Please don't cry."

She had her hands to her face. She sagged a little against Roland.

"Casey," Preacher said. "There ain't no need to carry on so. I didn't mean—"

"You!" Roland said as he looked past Casey at Preacher. He put his hands on her shoulders and moved her gently aside. He came toward Preacher, saying, "Leave her alone. You're the reason she's crying, you—"

"Careful there, boy," Preacher warned in a low rumble. "I don't cotton to bein' called names."

"Oh? Well, let's see how you cotton to this!"

With that exclamation, Roland leaped at Preacher, swinging a fist straight at the mountain man's face.

CHAPTER 10

Preacher's instincts took over, as they always did when he was attacked. He pulled his head to the side to avoid the punch. Roland's fist sailed past, missing Preacher's ear by a couple inches. The miss threw Roland off balance and made him stumble forward.

Preacher's right fist came up hard, burying itself deep in the young man's belly. Roland bent over, gasping for breath.

Preacher gained control of himself and grabbed Roland's shoulders. He slung him to the side, sending him sprawling on the muddy ground.

"Stay down, boy," Preacher warned him. "Don't you come at me like that again."

"Preacher, no!" Casey cried. "Leave him alone."

"That's what I'm tryin' to do, damn it," Preacher snapped.

Panting, Roland lifted his mud-splattered face. "I won't let you . . . treat her that way," he said as he struggled back to his feet. As soon as he had them planted under him, he launched himself at Preacher again.

Preacher didn't want to hurt the young man, but it wasn't in him to let someone attack him without fighting back. When the Good Lord made him, He hadn't included the ability to run from trouble.

Nimbly, Preacher stepped aside from the charge and grabbed the front of Roland's shirt. He threw the young man to the ground again. Stubbornly, Roland struggled back to his feet.

Some of the bullwhackers had noticed what was going on and started yelling, "Fight! Fight!" The men began to converge, hustling around the wagons to watch. Preacher caught glimpses of Lorenzo and Bartlett among them.

For the most part, he ignored the spectators. Pointing a finger at Roland, he said, "Now that's enough. I don't want to fight you—"

"You're gonna have to," Roland interrupted. "I'm going to thrash you, Preacher."

"Not on your best day and my worst one, boy," Preacher said.

"You've got to pay for hurting Casey—"

She broke into his breathless declaration, saying, "Roland, no! You don't have to defend me." She came up beside him and clutched his arm. "I'm fine."

He looked over at her. "He made you cry."

"It doesn't matter. I was just being foolish."

Roland shook her off. "I don't care. I won't let him get away with it."

With clenched fists, he started toward Preacher again.

Preacher held up a hand, palm out. "Blast it, Roland, back off. I don't want to hurt you."

"You'll have to kill me to stop me," Roland said through gritted teeth.

"Roland!" Leeman Bartlett called out sharply. "Stop this foolishness right now. I won't have my son brawling in the mud over some woman. Stop it, I say!"

Roland ignored the orders his father barked at him, just as he ignored Casey's pleas to end the fight. His face was set in grim lines, as he continued his menacing advance toward Preacher.

The mountain man watched him closely, wondering if he would have to knock the boy out to get him to settle down. Preacher was ready to react if the youngster threw a punch.

Before that could happen, a shrill scream of terror suddenly split the night. It came from outside the circle of wagons. Everyone's head jerked in that direction. A shot boomed out, followed by another scream.

Preacher reacted instantly, jerking the pistols out of his belt and breaking into a run toward the sounds. As he pushed his way through the oxen, which slowed him down, he heard a man yell, "No, no!" then the plea abruptly choked off in a hideous gurgle.

Preacher broke free of the livestock and hurdled a wagon tongue. It was dark on that side. Only a faint flickering glow from the campfire reached the area, but it was enough to show Preacher a huge, swiftly moving shadow. He couldn't make out any details. The thing was just a deeper patch of darkness.

Both pistols roared and bucked in Preacher's hands as he fired. It was too dark for him to tell if he hit the thing, but he didn't see how he could have missed at that range. He jammed the empty guns behind his belt and yanked his heavy hunting knife from its sheath. He wasn't sure how much good the blade would do against a monster, but he would put up the best fight he could.

As he stood ready, the misshapen form wheeled around and lurched away, vanishing into the thick shadows of the night in a heartbeat.

It left behind something on the ground.

Preacher moved over to the dark, sprawled shape and dropped to a knee. He recognized the harsh, bubbling sound he heard as the sound of a man trying to draw breaths through a ravaged throat. He put out a hand, felt the hot wet stickiness of freshly spilled blood. Preacher rested his hand on the man's chest and found a faint heartbeat, but a second later it grew still. The tortured breathing stopped.

The man was dead.

There was nothing Preacher could do for him. There never had been. The mountain man turned his head and bawled, "Somebody bring a light!"

Men were making their way toward the spot. Some of them had grabbed rifles from the wagons. One of them turned back to fetch a lantern.

The bullwhackers babbled questions as they crowded around Preacher. He said, "Hold on, hold on. I know you all want to know what happened, and so do I. Let's wait for that light."

Lantern light bobbed with each step as the man carried it all the way around the circle instead of cutting through the center where the oxen were milling around. A faster and certainly easier route.

Preacher ordered, "Everybody step back and give him some room," as the man approached.

He held the light high above his head as he came up to the scene of the tragedy. Startled curses came from the men as the flickering glow washed over the bloody corpse lying on its back. Lifeless eyes stared up from the man's pale, bearded face.

Preacher recognized the man as one of the bull-whackers but didn't know his name. "Who is it?" he asked in the stunned silence that followed the curses.

"His name was Hammond," Leeman Bartlett replied in a stunned, hollow voice. "Ben Hammond. My God, what could have done that to him?"

The man's throat was nothing but a raw, gaping wound. Blood had poured from it, flooding down the front of his shirt. Preacher was surprised Hammond had lasted as long as he had.

That wasn't his only injury. Several deep gashes started on his forehead and angled across his face. One eye had been popped from its socket, and most of his nose was torn away. Similar gashes criss-crossed the luckless bullwhacker's chest. His bloody shirt was shredded.

Roland and Casey had joined the others gathered around Preacher and the dead man. Casey made a horrified sound and turned her face away from the gruesome sight. Roland slipped an arm around her shoulders and pulled her against him.

"Are those . . . claw marks?" the young man asked, sounding like he couldn't believe what he was saying.

Preacher had already figured that out. From the size of the shape he had glimpsed in the darkness and the way it had mauled Ben Hammond, there was only one thing the monster could be.

"Yeah, those are claw marks," he answered Roland's question. The fight between them seemed to have been forgotten. "The marks of a grizzly bear on a rampage."

"A grizzly bear," Bartlett repeated. "That hardly seems possible. They live in the mountains, don't they?"

"Most do," Preacher said, "but sometimes they start to roam, and you can find 'em just about anywhere west of the Mississippi."

"You reckon that's what's been followin' us?" Lorenzo asked.

Preacher nodded. "I know it is. Dog's not scared of much of anything in this world, but even he's liable to get spooked by a griz. Same goes for the horses. They catch even the faintest scent of a grizzly bear, they're gonna get nervous. A bear doesn't mind gettin' wet, so that's why it was out wanderin' around durin' that storm when I caught a glimpse of it." Preacher got to his feet and shook his head. "It all makes sense now, and the only reason I didn't think about a grizzly bear sooner is because like you said, Mr. Bartlett, you just don't think about runnin' into the critters out here on the prairie."

"But what can we do about it?" Bartlett wanted to know.

Preacher nodded toward the dead man. "You can bury this poor fella. The griz is gone. I saw it take off for the tall and uncut after I took those shots at it."

"Maybe you wounded it," one of the men suggested. "Maybe it went off to die."

Preacher shook his head. "Not likely. Even if I winged the thing, it'll take more'n that to put him down. You can't shoot a grizzly once or twice and kill it, not unless you're a good enough shot to put a ball right through one of his eyes into his brain. Even then, he's liable to stay on his feet for a little bit before he realizes he's dead. And it don't take long for one of those varmints to do a lot of damage. Looks like he swatted Hammond three or four times. Probably didn't take more than a few seconds."

"Everyone stay alert tonight," Bartlett ordered.

As if he had to tell them to do that, Preacher thought wryly. All the bullwhackers were so spooked and upset by Hammond's death they might not sleep at all.

"And stay together as much as you can," Preacher added. "I don't know what Hammond was doin' over here by himself, but the bear might not have come after him if he hadn't been alone and well away from the fire. He was just too temptin' for ol' Ephraim to resist."

"Old Ephraim," Roland repeated with a surprised look on his face. "The bear has a name? You . . . you know this bear?"

Preacher grinned humorlessly. "That's just somethin' mountain men sometimes call a grizzly. I ain't rightly sure how it got started, unless one time a fella saw a griz that reminded him of a friend of his called Ephraim, and the name stuck."

One of the bullwhackers stepped up and said,

"Ben was worried about one of the wheels on his wagon. He thought a hub nut was workin' loose. I reckon he came around here to check on it."

"A man's life is a mighty high price to pay for somethin' like that. Like I told you, stay together as much as you can. And keep your rifles handy."

The bullwhackers began to drift back toward the fire, muttering among themselves and looking around nervously as they did so. Preacher couldn't blame them. The night held more terror than it had before. They had seen for themselves how swiftly and brutally death could strike.

The man who had told Preacher about Hammond checking on the wheel lingered, as did the man who held the lantern. "Ben and me were good friends," the first man said. "I'll fetch a shovel and start diggin' a grave for him so he can be laid to rest proper-like."

Preacher nodded. "I reckon he'd appreciate that. I'll give you a hand. Lorenzo, how about you stay and stand guard while we're doin' that?"

"Sure, I can do that," the old-timer said. "I hope that grizzle-bear don't come back, though. I ain't never seen one of the critters, and it'll be just fine with me if I never do!"

Bartlett said, "Now that he's made his kill, what do you think the chances are that he'll leave us alone the rest of the journey, Preacher?"

"That's hard to say," Preacher replied. "He's been stalkin' us for several days. I don't see any reason for him to go off and leave us alone now. Besides, he didn't get a chance to drag Hammond off before I ran up and scared him away, so he didn't get what he really wanted."

"Do you mean . . . food?" Roland asked hollowly.

"He's probably been livin' on prairie dogs. That ain't enough to keep a big varmint like him goin'. He needs some bigger prey." Preacher peered off into the blackness, as if he could see the bear lurking in the darkness. "And I reckon we're it."

CHAPTER 11

Nothing more was said that night about the fight between Preacher and Roland Bartlett. Ben Hammond's sudden, unexpected, and bloody death had everyone too shaken up to worry about such things.

Preacher thought about it, though. Roland had made it pretty clear how he felt about Casey. The question was whether she would give up on her feelings for Preacher and turn to the younger man instead.

It would sure simplify things if that was what happened, Preacher told himself.

That wasn't the only thing on Preacher's mind. He pondered the advisibility of going out to track down and kill that rogue grizzly, perhaps taking Lorenzo with him. The old-timer didn't know all that much about the frontier yet, but he was smart and brave and would do what Preacher told him to do without arguing about it. Preacher was convinced they hadn't seen the last of the bear, so the question was whether he went after it or waited for it to come to them again.

On top of that were the other troubles that had plagued the caravan since its departure from Independence. The terrible storm and the cyclone it had spawned could have meant disaster for the wagon train. Likewise the raid by Garity and the rest of that outlaw bunch. In both cases, luck had been with Preacher and his friends, and they had dodged pure catastrophe by the narrowest of margins.

How long could their luck hold? Preacher asked himself that question, but he didn't have any answers.

He wasn't an overly superstitious man, but he couldn't help wonder if Hammond's death was an omen. Maybe fate had turned on them and was no longer on their side.

Those thoughts ran through Preacher's head while he helped dig Hammond's grave. Lorenzo stood nearby with his rifle ready, keeping a watchful eye on the darkness outside the circle of light cast by the lantern. Preacher and a couple bullwhackers got the grave dug fairly quickly. Hammond's body was wrapped in a blanket. The actual burial would wait until dawn.

With everything going on in his mind, Preacher's slumber was restless that night. He spent a lot of time prowling around the camp, rifle in hand and both loaded pistols in his belt, just waiting for trouble.

It didn't show up. The bear didn't pay a return visit to the camp, and neither did Garity and his men.

As the sun peeked over the horizon, the members of the party gathered by the grave. Once again, Leeman Bartlett brought out his Bible and said words over the deceased. Since Ben Hammond had been one of them and not an outlaw, the prayers were more extensive. Some of Hammond's friends spoke as well, testifying to what a good fella he had been and how he hadn't deserved to end up like that.

A lonely hole in the ground was how he would end up, Preacher mused. A forgotten grave, tended by no one, mourned by no one. Six months after he'd been laid to rest, no one would even be able to tell he was there. The earth would have reclaimed him. Preacher had long since resigned himself to that same fate. No man who lived a life such as he did was going to die in bed with a bunch of kids and grandkids and great grandkids around him.

At least he hoped not.

When the speechifying and praying was finally over, some of the men got to work filling in the grave while Preacher, Lorenzo, and Leeman Bartlett walked over to the creek bank to look at the stream. It had gone down quite a bit during the night, as Preacher had thought it probably would.

"What do you think, Preacher?" Bartlett asked. "Can we make it across?"

"I reckon so," Preacher replied. "The creek's still runnin' pretty fast, but it ain't near as deep now. You'll be all right."

"Good," Bartlett said fervently. "Being stuck here for two nights is more than enough." A smile creased his lined face. "I'm ready for some good luck for a change."

He just didn't know how lucky they really were, Preacher thought.

They'd had breakfast, so all that was left to do was hitch up the oxen and saddle the horses. As Preacher was putting his saddle on the big gray stallion, Lorenzo came up to him and asked, "Are you thinkin' about goin' after that bear, Preacher?"

The mountain man smiled. "You must've read my mind, Lorenzo. I pondered on it, sure enough. But I reckon it might be better if I stayed with the wagons. Ain't no tellin' when Garity and his bunch might make another try for 'em."

"Well, that's true. I figured I'd go with you if you went, and I got to tell you, I wasn't lookin' forward to it. I hope that bear just leaves us alone from here on out."

Preacher hoped so, too, but he was going to be surprised if things turned out that way.

The wagons crossed the creek without incident and rolled on west as the sun rose higher in the sky. Since the oxen had had a day to rest, they seemed stronger and pulled harder in response to the popping of the bullwhips and the raucous shouts of the freighters. The miles fell behind them.

Preacher rode in front with Bartlett and Lorenzo most of the time, galloping ahead every now and then to get the lay of the land. The terrain wasn't quite as flat. There were some rolling hills, and Preacher had reined in at the crest of one of those long, gentle slopes with Dog beside him when he spotted some movement in the distance. It was too far away for him to identify. Could have been some buffalo or antelope . . . or men on horseback. Preacher couldn't tell. But whatever it was, they were moving away from the trail.

Even though the distant movement wasn't an immediate threat, it was a good reminder that they weren't alone out there, Preacher told himself. The landscape might seem vast and empty, but it really wasn't.

When he returned to the caravan, he saw Casey and Roland riding together beside one of the wagons. The young woman hadn't spoken to him all day. That was all right with Preacher, but still he felt a little pang of loss. Casey was a fine gal. Although he had enjoyed the time they spent together he knew she would be better off with somebody other than him.

The jury was still out on whether that particular somebody was Roland Bartlett.

Other than the one glimpse Preacher had of movement in the distance, they didn't see anyone all that day or the next. In fact, a week went by without the wagon train encountering anything except wildlife. The days were long, hard, and tedious, but Preacher knew there wouldn't be many more of them before the caravan reached the Cimarron Cutoff.

Of course, once they got past that point, the trip would just get even harder.

Casey had been avoiding him for the most part, and when she did speak to him, she only said what she had to. Preacher wished there had been some way to handle the situation without offending her, but like everything else in life, it was what it was.

She came to him one night and said, "Preacher, I need to talk to you about something."

He frowned. "Sounds a mite ominous."

"No, we just need to get something settled."

He shrugged. For a second there, he had thought she was going to tell him that she was in the family way, since they had been together a number of times during the trip from St. Louis to Independence. Preacher knew it was possible there were some half-breed Indian kids with his features running around various villages where he had wintered, but he was reasonably sure he didn't have any children by white women. He wasn't certain what he would have done if Casey had told him she was expecting.

"I was about to take a walk around the camp," he told her. "Why don't you come with me? We can have a little privacy for our talk."

"That's a good idea."

He pulled one of the pistols from behind his belt and handed it to her. "Here, you hang on to that," he said. "Just in case we run into any trouble. I'll carry my rifle."

"Fine. You know I can handle a gun."

"Wouldn't have given you one if I didn't."

They left the campfire and the wagons, walking out about fifty yards, then turning to stroll around the circle. Preacher held his long legs to a gait that Casey could match.

He waited for Casey to start since she was the one who had asked for the conversation. The silence between them drew out until it started to get awkward.

Finally she said, "I'm sorry about what happened back up the trail. That business with Roland, I mean."

"Don't worry about it," Preacher told her. "It wasn't your fault, and anyway, no harm was done."

"It *was* my fault," she said. "I got angry and frustrated with you, and I turned to him for comfort. He took that to mean . . . more than it did."

Preacher frowned. "Roland's not a bad sort, for a greenhorn."

"I know that. But he can't compare to you, Preacher." She held up a hand to stop him when he started to speak. "Oh, I know it was never going to last between us. We were never going to get married and settle down and raise a passel of kids. In fact, I'm not even sure if I can have children. I had some problems a few years ago . . ."

"You don't need to talk about that," Preacher said gruffly.

Casey took a deep breath. "Anyway, I knew not to expect too much from you." He could hear the smile in her voice as she added, "You're already married to the wilderness."

"You'll find you a nice young fella one of these days. Maybe Roland, maybe somebody else, but I'm sure it'll be all right."

"I'm not," she said. "How could I ever marry a . . . a respectable man, after all the things I've done? It wouldn't be fair to him. I'd have to lie to him, because if I told him the truth, no decent man would ever want me."

"You might be wrong about that," Preacher said. "If a fella really loves you, he ain't gonna care all that much about what happened before. All that's really gonna matter to him is the here and now."

"Do you honestly believe that?"

"I do."

She slipped her arm through his. "I hope you're right, Preacher. I really do."

"So what are you gonna do about Roland?"

"I don't know. Wait until we get to Santa Fe and see what happens then, I suppose." She laughed. "He's madly in love with me."

"Well, of course he is. I reckon most of them bullwhackers are, too."

"No, they just want me to crawl into their bedrolls with them. Roland has all sorts of romantic notions, though."

"With a name like that, I reckon he'd have to."

"What do you mean?"

"Friend of mine from the mountains up north named Audie, he's a real educated fella and knows all sorts of things. I recollect listenin' to him recite this poem once about a French knight named Roland, and ever'body knows them French fellas are romantic."

"What happened to the Roland in the poem?"

Preacher didn't want to tell her that the knight wound up getting killed in battle. He scratched his beard and grinned. "Well, I don't rightly remember the end of the poem. You see, the rest of the fellas was passin' around a jug while Audie was recitin' . . ."

Casey laughed. "You don't have to explain. I understand."

They had walked a complete circuit of the camp while they were talking. Preacher glanced toward the wagons and said, "I expect we better get back 'fore folks start to worry about us."

"You mean Roland?"

"Well, if anybody tells him they saw the two of us goin' for a walk together, he's liable to get upset again."

"I appreciate you not hurting him before."

"Like I said, he ain't a bad sort, just young and inexperienced. He'll learn, if he lives long enough."

Casey stopped and turned so she was facing him. "I want a good-bye kiss," she said firmly.

"We ain't sayin' good-bye," Preacher objected. "It'll be another week or more before we make it to Santa Fe, and it ain't like you'll never see me again once we get there."

"Yes, but we're saying good-bye to what might have been between us. From here on out, we'll just be friends."

"Can you live with that?"

"I'll have to." She smiled up at him, close enough that he felt the warmth of her breath on his face. "But I want that kiss first."

"Well, hell," Preacher said. "I can do that."

He thumbed his hat back, slipped one arm around her, and bent his head to bring his mouth to hers. She wrapped her arms around his neck and pressed herself against him. He responded to the heat of her firm body and the sweet urgency of her lips and told himself he might kick himself in the future for practically pushing her into Roland Bartlett's arms. But some things were meant to be, and some weren't.

The kiss lasted for a long moment. Then he pulled back, smiled down at her, and said, "All right, we best get back now."

"Preacher . . ."

"Don't argue with me, now," he said.

"Preacher!"

The moon and stars were bright enough for him to see the shocked expression that suddenly appeared on her face. At the same time, he caught a whiff of a rank, musty odor. His blood turned cold in his veins.

"That damn bear's right behind me, ain't it?" he said.

CHAPTER 12

Casey nodded as she continued staring in horror over Preacher's shoulder. For a split-second, the mountain man felt like a damned fool. He had told everybody else to stay close to camp and always be in a group, and yet here he had wandered off. Even worse, he'd brought Casey with him.

He shoved those thoughts out of his head. He didn't have time for them.

Instead he said, "Gimme that pistol I gave you."

She swallowed hard, but she pressed the weapon into his hand. "Preacher, what are we going to do? You said you couldn't kill that creature with pistols."

"What's he doin'?"

"Just . . . just standing there. My God, he's huge!"

"Bears don't see too good," Preacher said. "They rely on their hearin' and their sense of smell. He knows we're here, and he's just tryin' to make up his mind what to do about us. How far away is he?"

"About . . . twenty feet, I guess."

A big grizzly could cover that distance in the space of a heartbeat.

"Start backin' away from me, slow and easy," Preacher said. "Be as quiet about it as you can. Since I'm in between you and him, he may not be able to tell you're movin' away from him."

"What about you?"

"I'm gonna stay right here and keep him occupied, if he gets feisty before you get back to the wagons."

"But he'll kill you," Casey whispered.

"Not without a fight," Preacher said. "When you get to the wagons, tell everybody what's goin' on. With one rifle, it takes a mighty lucky shot to put down a monster like this. But if twenty men are pourin' lead into him at the same time, even a big ol' griz can't stand up to that."

"Preacher . . ."

"Go," he said through clenched teeth. "Do it, Casey. Back away slow."

With a stricken expression on her face, she began to do as he told her. She took several shaky steps backward. When she was about ten feet away, Preacher said, "All right, turn around and walk toward the wagons. Don't run. That'll just draw the bear's attention. Move, Casey."

Again, she followed his orders. But as she walked, she kept glancing back over her shoulder at him.

Preacher wanted to look at the bear, but he continued to stand rock-still. After a moment, with his body concealing the movement, he lowered his rifle to the ground and slid his other pistol from behind his belt. He looped his thumbs over the hammers. Casey was only about ten yards from the wagons when Preacher eased back both hammers, with a metallic click.

He heard a sudden chuffing noise and recognized it as the sound a bear makes when it breaks into a charge toward an enemy. He twisted around and threw himself to the side as he brought the pistols up.

The bear was practically on top of him, moving with blinding speed. The pistols in Preacher's hands roared and spouted fire as he dived out of the way of the attack.

All four lead balls from the double-shotted pistols struck the bear, most likely failing to penetrate the thick layers of fat and muscle that coated the animal's enormous body and reach a vital organ. Chances were the wounds would sting like hell and irritate the varmint even more, but Preacher had to make the effort.

The bear let out an angry bellow as it swiped a huge paw studded with razor sharp claws at the mountain man. The bear was fast, but so was Preacher. His dive took him out of reach and the bear missed.

Preacher hit the ground on his shoulder and rolled over. He couldn't reach his rifle. The bear was between him and it. With the pistols empty, that left his knife as his only weapon. When he was younger he had fought a grizzly with a knife and killed it. That battle had left him severely injured. He was facing a much bigger bear than that one had been. It topped seven feet easily.

Preacher scrambled to his feet and darted to the side. The bear lunged after him. There was nowhere to get away from it, no tree to climb, and on open ground the bear could outrun him. Still, he could make the thing chase him and lead it away from the wagons.

"Come on, you hairy son of a bitch!" he yelled. "Come and get me!"

He whirled and sprinted away. Roaring, the bear lumbered after him. The creature didn't seem to be moving that fast, but it covered the ground and closed the gap in a matter of seconds.

Preacher was vaguely aware that Casey had started yelling and screaming for help as she reached the wagons. He expected the men to start shooting at the bear, even though he was sort of in the line of fire. He was surprised, when he heard hoofbeats pounding nearby.

"Preacher!" That was Lorenzo's voice. "Preacher, over here!"

Preacher jerked his head in the direction of the shout and saw the old-timer galloping toward him. Man and horse were silhouetted against the light from the campfire. A couple other riders followed closely behind Lorenzo.

Preacher darted toward them. Hope leaped in his chest. If he could avoid the bear's claws long enough to get on one of those horses, they could race back to the wagons before the massive creature could stop them.

The bear was fast, but its great weight gave it so much momentum it couldn't stop or turn quickly. Preacher zigzagged across the prairie, relying on his instincts to tell him when to change direction. The riders closed in on him. Lorenzo slowed his mount and extended an arm. Preacher reached up and grabbed it.

Lorenzo might be old, but his wiry body had a lot of strength in it. With the horse still moving, he hauled Preacher up and swung him onto the animal's back behind the saddle. Preacher grabbed hold with his legs and put an arm around Lorenzo's middle.

"Let's get the hell outta here!"

Lorenzo sent the horse running toward the wagons while the two men with him fired their rifles at the bear to distract it. Preacher recognized them as Leeman and Roland Bartlett. Their bravery and quick thinking in making the rescue attempt impressed him.

The bear bellowed as the shots struck it, but the wounds didn't slow it down. It swatted at the riders, and one of its paws clipped a horse's rump, making the horse scream in pain as the claws ripped gashes in its hide. The horse leaped high in the air, almost unseating its rider, Roland Bartlett. He had to hang on for dear life as the horse hit the ground again and dashed toward the wagons.

Preacher glanced over his shoulder. If Roland had fallen, it would have been all over for him.

The horse carrying Preacher and Lorenzo reached the circle of wagons and leaped over a wagon tongue. Bartlett and Roland followed closely. The bullwhackers who had crowded up behind the wagons with their rifles opened fire on the bear. Preacher slid down from the horse and ran back over to one of the gaps between wagons to watch the assault.

He had no way of knowing how many times the bear was hit. All he could tell for sure was that the bear swung around, bellowing in pain and rage, and disappeared into the night like a big, hairy, moving mountain. The shots trailed off. There was nothing left to shoot at.

Casey came running up to Preacher and threw her arms around him. "Are you all right?" she asked anxiously.

"Don't worry, he didn't lay a claw on me," Preacher told her. "I ain't quite sure how I managed to stay out of his reach, but I did."

"Thank God," she murmured as she hugged him and pressed her face against his chest.

"Whose idea was it to bring the horses out there and fetch me?" he asked.

She looked up at him. "That was Roland's idea."

Preacher saw that the young man had dismounted, along with his father. Roland held the horses, his expression stony, as his father went over to join Preacher and Casey.

"Good Lord, what a narrow escape!" Bartlett said. "Are you injured, Preacher?"

The mountain man shook his head. "Nope. Thanks to you and Roland and Lorenzo."

"That beast is a behemoth. Surely it must be the largest bear there ever was."

"I reckon there's probably been bigger. But it's plenty big enough, that's for sure."

"At least it shouldn't bother us anymore."

Preacher frowned and asked, "What makes you say that?"

Bartlett returned the frown. "Well, you shot it at close range with those pistols, and I'm certain my men hit it numerous times with their rifles. Surely after this encounter the beast will slink off somewhere and die of its wounds."

"I wouldn't be so sure of that," Preacher said. "Bears are mighty tough critters, and like I told you before, they're hard to kill." He shrugged. "But maybe you're right. I'll do some scoutin' when it gets light, see if I can find the body."

The camp was settling down now that the danger was over, at least for the time being. Preacher went over to Roland Bartlett, who had started unsaddling his horse.

"I'm obliged to you," Preacher said as he held out his hand. "Casey told me it was your idea to ride out there and get me."

Roland hesitated. He had seen Casey hugging him, Preacher knew, and was still jealous. He didn't know that the relationship between the two of them was definitely over, and Casey's hug had been because she was relieved Preacher was still alive.

After a moment, Roland shook hands with him. He didn't appear too friendly about it, but he gripped Preacher's hand firmly enough.

"It seemed to be the only way to save your life," he said. "I'm glad we were able to get to you in time. My father is counting on you to help us get to Santa Fe safely."

"I'll do my best," Preacher promised.

"I suppose Casey owes her life to you yet again," Roland went on. "If you had panicked when that bear showed up, it probably would have killed both of you."

"More'n likely," Preacher agreed. "Casey and I are square. She's helped me out plenty of times. That's what friends do for each other."

"Friends, eh?" Roland sounded like he didn't believe that.

Preacher nodded. "Yep. Ask her yourself."

"No offense, but what I ask Casey or don't ask her is none of your business, Preacher."

"That's exactly right," Preacher responded, hoping that Roland would understand what he was getting at. But if he didn't, it was the youngster's own fault for being so dense.

Everybody was on edge because of the bear, so it was no trouble getting extra volunteers to stand guard that night. The creature didn't make a return appearance, and no other problems cropped up.

Preacher saddled Horse the next morning after breakfast. Lorenzo came up to him and asked, "You goin' lookin' for that bear?"

"Thought I would. If it's dead, then these folks can relax. About that, anyway," Preacher added. "There are still plenty of other things out here that can kill 'em."

"That's the truth. You want me to come with you?"

Preacher shook his head. "No, you stay with the wagons. I won't be gone long."

Before he left, he found Leeman Bartlett and told the man, "You'll be seein' the Arkansas River off to your left today. The trail's gonna run beside it for a ways. I don't reckon you'll get that far before I get back, but just in case I get held up somehow, be on the lookout for a creek that'll run into the river from the north. That'll be Mullberry Creek. Right there's where you want to ford the Arkansas and angle off southwest. You'll be able to see the wagon tracks on the other side of the river."

"You mean that's the beginning of the Cimarron

Cutoff?" Bartlett said. "I have a map that I've studied quite a bit."

Preacher nodded. "That's it. When you get there, you'll be just past halfway from Independence to Santa Fe."

"Halfway?" Bartlett's eyes widened. "It seems like we've already been traveling forever."

"That's because all this country out here looks so much alike. It'll change some once you're on the Cutoff." Preacher chuckled. "Won't get any better, though. Just flatter and drier and hotter. And emptier."

"That seems hard to believe."

"You'll see it for yourself soon enough. When you do ford the Arkansas, whether it's today or tomorrow, be sure to stop and fill all the water barrels. You need to be careful with the water once you start across the desert. It'll take several days, maybe close to a week, to get to Cimarron Springs. That's the first dependable water you'll find."

"Why are you telling me all this?" Bartlett asked. "You'll be with us, won't you?"

"That's the plan," Preacher said with a note of grimness in his voice. "But anything can happen out here, like you saw last night with that blasted bear. It came damn close to rippin' me open with those claws. If anything happens to me, you need to know where you're goin' and how you're gonna get there. Listen to the men with you who have made the trip before. They'll know what they're talkin' about. You can count on Lorenzo to help out all he can, but he ain't never been this far west until now."

Bartlett nodded solemnly. "All right, Preacher. I understand. But I hope I won't have to worry about any of this. I'd like for you to be with us every step of the way to Santa Fe."

"That's the plan," Preacher said again as he clapped a hand on Bartlett's shoulder. "Now, I'm gonna go see if I can find me a bear."

CHAPTER 13

Blood was splattered on the short, coarse buffalo grass at the spot where Preacher had confronted the bear. That was proof the creature had been wounded, but it didn't tell Preacher how bad the bear's injuries were. He didn't find enough blood to convince him the bear was mortally wounded.

The rusty red droplets on the ground made the trail easy to follow. The bear had headed north. Dog bounded out ahead of Preacher and Horse, using his keen sense of smell to track the massive grizzly.

Preacher wondered if there had been something wrong with the bear to start with. While grizzlies could be found anywhere on the frontier, it was much more common for them to be in the mountains. Something had led the beast to wander out onto the plains.

Preacher followed the blood trail for several miles before it petered out. Dog still had the scent, and they continued their pursuit of the grizzly almost due north.

Preacher was convinced the bear wasn't seriously injured. It couldn't have gone that far if it was on the verge of bleeding to death. The wounds might fester and kill the beast eventually, but it would take time for that to happen.

He reined in and called, "Come on back, Dog!"

The big cur stopped and looked back at Preacher. He whined a little.

"I know, you got the scent and you don't want to give up the trail," Preacher said. "But I don't think we're gonna find that varmint any time soon and I don't want to be away from the wagons all day. That bastard Garity and his bunch could still be out here somewhere. Maybe the bear'll just keep goin' and not bother us no more."

Dog barked.

"Yeah, I ain't convinced of that, neither, but we can't rule it out. Now come on, you fleabitten old coot."

Dog rejoined him reluctantly, glaring so fiercely that Preacher had to chuckle.

"Yeah, I know, you could call me a fleabitten old coot, too, if you wanted to. I'm damn sure gettin' there."

They angled southwest, since the caravan would have put a few more miles behind it. Preacher hoped to intercept the wagons, but when he and his companions reached the Santa Fe Trail, the canvas-covered vehicles were nowhere in sight.

Preacher swung down from the saddle and knelt to study the ruts. The dust in them had been disturbed recently. He glanced at Dog and said, "Looks like they beat us here. They're makin' good time.

Probably be at Mullberry Creek crossin' before the day's over."

Confident that the wagons were in front of him, Preacher let Horse rest for a little while, then mounted up again and rode after the caravan. He could see the silvery ribbon of the Arkansas River off to his left as he followed the trail.

By early afternoon he spotted the wagons in front of him. Urging Horse to a slightly faster pace, he soon caught up. The bullwhackers paused in their incessant yelling and cursing to wave greetings to him as he rode past the wagons.

Lorenzo, Casey, Bartlett, and Roland were riding together in front of the wagons. They heard Preacher coming and reined in to wait for him to catch up. As the mountain man brought Horse to a stop, Bartlett asked, "Well, did you find the carcass of that bear?"

Preacher shook his head. "Nope. He was wounded, sure enough. I found blood to prove that. But he was still movin' just fine, headin' north. I followed the trail for several miles before I turned around and came back."

"You think he's going off to die?" Roland said.

"Don't know that," Preacher replied. "Fact is, I've got a hunch he wasn't hurt that bad. But I'm hopin' he's been stung enough by our guns to teach him he ought to leave us alone."

Bartlett frowned. "I wish he was dead. That way we'd know he couldn't threaten us anymore."

"Even if he was, there'd still be plenty of other things you got to look out for." Preacher nodded toward the edge of the trail. "Like that rattler over yonder."

The others looked where he indicated. Lorenzo said, "Lord have mercy. That there is the biggest snake I ever seen."

Coiled in the short grass at the edge of the trail was a thick-bodied rattlesnake. It was watching them intently with its inhuman eyes. Preacher moved Horse a little closer, and the rattles on the end of the snake's tail started making their eerie buzzing sound as they vibrated.

Horse shied a little. "Take it easy," Preacher told the stallion as he pulled his rifle from its sheath. "I know you don't want to get any closer to that varmint. I don't blame you."

He cocked the flintlock, drew a bead with it, and squeezed the trigger. As the rifle boomed, the snake's head, which had raised in a threatening posture, exploded in a spray of gore as the lead ball struck it. The thick, ropy body immediately uncoiled and began whipping about in death convulsions. Casey made a noise of disgust and looked away.

"See, that's just what I mean," Preacher said as he lowered the flintlock. "Out here, if it ain't one thing that'll kill you, it's somethin' else."

The wagons reached the Mullberry Creek crossing of the Arkansas River late that afternoon, late enough so that Preacher decided it would be better to wait until the next morning to ford the river.

Nobody had forgotten how close the grizzly had come to the camp, so even though Preacher didn't believe the bear was anywhere nearby, the guard was doubled again and those who slept did so lightly.

After a quiet night, the bullwhackers hitched the teams to the wagons and drove them into the broad, slow-moving river. The surface of the water sparkled in the early morning sun. The wagons crossed without incident and headed southwest with full water barrels, following the ruts of the Cimarron Cutoff that Preacher pointed out.

The landscape soon proved Preacher right again. It wasn't long before the terrain grew flatter, the air hotter and drier than it had been on the other side of the river. The grass was sparse, and there were long stretches of rocky, sandy ground that didn't look like it would ever be good for much of anything.

As Casey rode next to Preacher, she asked, "Nobody lives here in this wasteland, do they?"

"You'd be surprised," he told her. "There are a lot of Comanch' in these parts."

"Comanche Indians, you mean?"

"That's right."

"Like those Pawnees we saw not long after we left Independence?" Leeman Bartlett said.

Preacher had to smile at that. "The Pawnee are good fighters, and I wouldn't want 'em mad at me if I could avoid it, but to say that they're like the Comanch' . . ." He shook his head. "There ain't no other Injuns like the Comanch'. The Sioux are probably better when it comes to ridin', and the Blackfeet got ever'body beat when it comes to bein' plumb mean, and the Apaches can sneak around better'n any of the other tribes . . . but the Comanch' can do all of that, almost as well as them other tribes. Pound for pound, I reckon they're the most dangerous critters I ever seen, including that grizzly bear."

"Are we going to run into any of them?" Roland asked. He had started scanning the horizon nervously as Preacher spoke.

"It wouldn't surprise me a bit."

"Will they attack us?"

The mountain man shrugged. "That depends on how many of them there are . . . and what sort of mood they're in. All Injuns like to barter, and that includes the Comanches. There's a good chance they'll let us trade some bright-colored geegaws for safe passage through their land. Or they might decide to attack us and try to take the wagons and everything in 'em. We just won't know until the time comes."

From the worried looks on the faces of his companions, Preacher knew it would be all right with them if they didn't encounter any Comanches on the journey. He felt the same way . . . but he didn't expect it to happen.

When they made camp, Leeman Bartlett asked, "Should we forego having a fire tonight? It might be wise not to announce our presence to those savages."

Preacher shook his head. "Go ahead and build a fire. Build a big one. It won't make any difference. You can't take this many wagons through the desert without the Comanch' knowin' you're here. Two or three people might be able to dodge 'em by layin' low and makin' cold camps, but not a party this big. They'll know."

"Then we might as well make them think there are a great many of us," Bartlett said. "I'll tell the men to walk around a lot and make it look like there are more of them than there really are."

"Now that's not a bad idea," Preacher said.

That evening, Lorenzo asked Preacher, "What you said about two or three folks bein' able to slip through here by layin' low and not buildin' no fires . . . is that what you intended for us to do if it was just you and me and Casey?"

Preacher shook his head. Keeping his voice low, he said, "Hell, no. If it was just the three of us, I never would've brought us this way. We'd have taken the northern route, gone over to Bent's Fort, and then cut down to Santa Fe through Raton Pass. Wouldn't have been any trouble on horseback."

Lorenzo narrowed his eyes shrewdly. "Then the only reason we're goin' the way we are is so you can try to keep these pilgrims from gettin' theirselves killed."

"Since we've come as far with 'em as we have, it didn't seem right to just go off and let 'em shift for themselves. The northern route may not be quite as dangerous as the cutoff, but it ain't exactly what you'd call safe, neither, and it takes a week longer. That's more time for trouble to happen. I reckon it all sort of balances out in the end."

Lorenzo grunted. "If you say so, Preacher. You ain't steered us wrong yet. I sure hope we don't run into any of them heathen redskins, though."

Preacher lifted his coffee cup. "I'll drink to that."

A heavy guard was put on again. Preacher knew that contrary to what some folks thought, Indians would attack at night if it struck their fancy. In fact, down along the Colorado River in what was now the Republic of Texas, folks had recently started using the term "Comanche moon" to describe the sort of full moon the Comanch' liked to raid by.

He thought it was more likely, though, that the Indians would wait until they had gotten a better look at the wagon train before they struck. They would have to gauge whether they wanted to fight . . . or bargain.

Another day and more endless, desolate miles rolled past. Following Preacher's advice, Bartlett and his men were careful about how much water they drank. The oxen got a full ration from the barrels, because without those beasts of burden the wagons weren't going anywhere, but the men could make do with less.

Preacher figured they were halfway to the springs where the Cimarron River made its northernmost loop. He had stopped at that marshy pool a couple times before and hoped nothing had happened to it since the last time he was in those parts. If the spring had gone dry for some reason, it would be a long and mighty thirsty trip to the next water.

Roland and Casey were spending nearly all their time together, Preacher noted. With the threat of the Comanches hanging over them, it really didn't make much sense to worry about affairs of the heart, but Preacher couldn't help but be pleased anyway.

As they rode alongside the wagons, Lorenzo caught him smiling at the two youngsters during the third morning since hitting the cutoff. The old-timer said, "Mighty pleased with yourself, ain't you?"

"What are you talkin' about, old man?"

"You know dang good and well what I'm talkin' about," Lorenzo shot back. "You wanted that boy to court Casey, and he's sure doin' it. Best he can, anyway, out here in the middle of the most godforsaken country I ever seen. Any fella out here who wanted to bring a bouquet of flowers to his sweetheart would be purely out of luck."

Preacher shrugged. "I'm thinkin' she'll be better off with young Bartlett than she ever would be with me. I never intended on draggin' her all over the mountains with me. That's no fittin' life for a woman."

"What about for an old colored man?"

"That's up to you," Preacher said. "You're welcome to come along when I leave Santa Fe, assumin' we both get there alive. You might decide to stay there, though. Find you some Mexican *mamacita* to look after you in your old age."

Lorenzo snorted. "Slave or not, I been bossed around my whole life. I'd like to know what it's like to really be free for a spell."

Preacher was about to say something in response when he suddenly stiffened in the saddle. He stood up in his stirrups and peered off to the left of the trail.

"What is it?" Lorenzo asked sharply.

"Saw somethin' out yonder. It's so hot and hazy in these parts, it's easy to see things that ain't really there. Mirages, I think folks call 'em. But I'd swear I saw somebody movin' out there."

Lorenzo pointed in the other direction. "Like them over there?"

Preacher looked that way. Heat waves rippled up from the ground, distorting what he saw, but after a moment his vision focused well enough for him to make out a line of riders moving in a parallel course to the wagons. He looked back to the left and knew he hadn't been mistaken. There was a column of riders on that side of the caravan, too.

"Lordy, lordy," Lorenzo breathed. "Are those fellas who I think they are, Preacher?"

"That's right," the mountain man said. "The Comanch' have come callin'."

CHAPTER 14

Preacher and Lorenzo were riding a few yards ahead of Casey, Roland, and Bartlett. In a low voice, Preacher told the old-timer, "Drop back and let the others know what's goin' on, if they haven't spotted those Injuns themselves. Tell 'em to stay calm and not start raisin' a ruckus."

Lorenzo nodded. Rather than turning around, he slowed his horse and let the other three riders catch up with him.

Preacher glanced right and left. There were two outriders on each side of the caravan. They had to have seen the Comanches, but were riding along as if they hadn't, gradually working their way closer to the caravan. That was smart of them, Preacher thought. If they turned and made a run for the wagons, that would likely prod the warriors into chasing them.

Preacher noticed a couple rocky humps up ahead, the first real landmarks he had seen in quite a while. The trail ran between those shallow hills. It was the perfect place for an ambush, and he had no doubt Comanche warriors were waiting on both of the knobs. He held up his hand in a signal for the wagons to stop. If they got caught in that gap, they wouldn't have a chance.

Preacher wheeled Horse around and waved for the outriders to come in the rest of the way. Leeman Bartlett hurried up to him and asked, "Do we need to pull the wagons in a circle?"

"If you do that, they'll know you're gettin' ready to fight and they'll go ahead and jump us," Preacher said. "We might still be able to talk our way out of this. Let me give it a try. Spread the word, ever'body needs to have his rifle handy."

Bartlett nodded. "What are you going to do?"

"Let 'em know we want to parley." He urged Horse forward again.

"Preacher, be careful!" Casey called out behind him. Preacher acknowledged her concern with a slight wave.

Slowly, he rode out about fifty yards in front of the wagons and stopped. He sat in his saddle, waiting, apparently as calm as if nothing unusual or threatening was happening. The columns of Comanches flanking the caravan halted as well.

A few minutes dragged by, then a party of half a dozen warriors appeared in the gap between the knobs and rode toward him. They took their time about it. The Indians knew that waiting would stretch the nerves of their potential victims tighter and tighter.

The Comanches came to a stop about twenty feet in front of Preacher. He held up a hand, palm out, in the universal sign of peaceful greeting.

As had happened with the Pawnee, one of the warriors rode forward as a spokesman. When the Comanche brought his pony to a stop, Preacher said, "Greetings, brother."

He hoped his grasp of the Comanch' lingo wasn't rusty and he hadn't told the varmint to go do unspeakable things to himself. The warrior didn't look offended, so Preacher supposed he had made himself clear.

The man was short and stocky and looked tough as year-old jerky. He said harshly, "Who are you to call a warrior of the Comanche, brother?"

"I am known as Preacher."

If he had been hoping for a sign of recognition at the mention of his name, he was sorely disappointed. Clearly, it didn't mean anything to the Comanche.

"I am Lame Buffalo," the man said, "and I am brother to no white man."

"Then I would be a friend, if not a brother."

Lame Buffalo shook his head. "The white men are not friends. They are flies, buzzing around the heads of the Comanche and eating the droppings of our horses. They are to be tolerated, not befriended."

And you are one arrogant son of a bitch, Preacher thought. He almost muttered it aloud in English but bit back the words in time to prevent them from escaping. He had no way of knowing if Lame Buffalo spoke any of the white man's tongue. Just because he wasn't speaking it, didn't mean he couldn't savvy it.

Preacher turned slightly in the saddle and waved

his left hand toward the wagons behind him. "We wish to take our wagons through your land safely. We mean no harm to the Comanche people. We are peaceful traders."

"You take white man's goods to the land of the Mexicans?" Lame Buffalo asked.

He knew good and well that's what they were doing, Preacher thought. Lame Buffalo had probably seen dozens of freight caravans bound for Santa Fe. He might well have looted some of them.

But Preacher just said, "That's right. We carry only trade goods. No guns." The Comanches would be more likely to attack the caravan if they thought they might get their hands on some weapons. A few of the band carried flintlocks, but most were armed with bows and arrows or lances.

Preacher doubted Lame Buffalo would take his word, and sure enough, the leader said curtly, "Show me."

Preacher nodded. "Come with me."

Turning his back on the Comanches wasn't easy, but he did it and acted unconcerned as he rode toward the wagons with Lame Buffalo following him. Preacher saw the nervous faces watching them and made a motion with his hand, hoping they would understand he was telling them to stay calm. He smiled at Casey, Lorenzo, Bartlett, and Roland, who sat together on their horses next to the first wagon.

"This is Lame Buffalo," he told them in English. "He's gonna take a look at the goods we're carryin'."

"Are you going to offer to pay him to let us pass?" Bartlett asked.

"That's the idea. Be even better if he sees somethin' that strikes his fancy and suggests that we bargain with him."

Preacher glanced at the Comanche. Lame Buffalo's face was still stonily impassive. He gave no sign that he had understood any of the exchange between Preacher and Bartlett.

Preacher spoke to the bullwhacker in charge of the first wagon's team of oxen, a man named Fawcett. "Pull that canvas back, would you, Cliff?"

Fawcett went to the rear of the wagon and untied the canvas flaps. He threw them open so Lame Buffalo could look into the wagon. The Comanche leaned forward on his pony and frowned as he peered into the vehicle at the crates and barrels stacked in its bed.

"Hold on a minute," Preacher told him. He dismounted and climbed into the wagon. He pulled his knife from its sheath and used the blade to pry the top off a barrel of sugar. Scooping up a handful of the stuff, he held it out to Lame Buffalo. "Try this."

The Comanche frowned. His eyes narrowed in suspicion. But he couldn't resist the temption. He reached out and took a pinch of the sugar from Preacher's hand.

Preacher pinched some of it between the fingers of his other hand and lifted it to his mouth. He tasted the sugar and licked his lips to show Lame Buffalo how good it was. Still looking wary, Lame Buffalo tried it as well.

The warrior kept his face carefully impassive, but Preacher saw the pleasure that lit up Lame Buffalo's eyes for a second. He held out his hand for more of the sugar, and Preacher dumped the whole handful in his palm.

Lame Buffalo turned his pony and kicked it into a run toward the rest of the warriors who blocked the trail. He shared the sugar with them. Preacher heard them laughing.

"What're you doin', Preacher?" the bullwhacker asked.

"You've heard about catchin' flies with honey, Cliff?" When the man nodded, Preacher went on, "Well, I'm tryin' to catch some Comanch' with sugar."

Several of the warriors let out shrill yips and thrust their lances into the air. Lame Buffalo turned and rode back to join Preacher by the wagon. He pointed to the barrel and said, "We will take it all and not kill you."

Preacher shook his head. "One bag."

Lame Buffalo's face darkened with anger.

"And a bolt of cloth, your choice," Preacher added.

Lame Bear appeared to be considering the proposal. After a moment, he said, "Show me."

That was the beginning of a long, tense negotiation that lasted over an hour. The Indians had them outnumbered two to one, and everybody in the wagon train knew it. Impending violence was thick in the air.

Lame Buffalo had to look in every wagon and decide what he wanted. Every time he made a demand, Preacher made a counteroffer. Finally, they reached an accord. In return for the sugar, the cloth, some salt, a couple women's hats with bright-colored feathers, and a bag of nails—Preacher had no idea what the Comanches intended to do with those, but he had a brief moment of hesitation when he guessed it might have to do with torturing prisoners—the Comanches agreed not to kill them all and burn their wagons. It seemed like a fair enough deal to Preacher.

Lame Buffalo waved some of his men over to gather up the spoils. The warriors took the goods and galloped back to rejoin the others. Lame Buffalo said, "One more thing, and then you can pass."

"What's that?" Preacher asked. He suddenly had a very bad feeling.

Lame Buffalo nudged his horse over next to Casey's and reached out to grab her arm. "The yellow-haired woman goes with me, too!" he shouted.

Casey let out a frightened cry. Preacher knew Lame Buffalo didn't really mean it. The Comanche was just playing with them, in the sometimes cruel fashion of his people. Preacher opened his mouth to tell Lame Buffalo he couldn't have her, figuring the man would demand one more piece of tribute since he had been denied his latest demand. It was one more way of establishing his dominance.

But Roland Bartlett didn't know that, and Preacher didn't have time to tell him. The young man yelled, "Take your hands off her, you filthy savage!"

Roland jerked his pistol from his belt, and despite Preacher's warning shout, he whipped the gun up, cocking it as he did so, and pulled the trigger. Smoke plumed from the muzzle as the pistol boomed.

Lame Buffalo jerked to the side but managed to stay on his pony. Eyes wide with pain and shock, he looked down at his bare chest, where blood welled from the black-rimmed hole made by the pistol ball. He swayed for a second, then toppled from his mount.

The fragile truce that had existed a second earlier was blown to hell, just like Lame Buffalo.

CHAPTER 15

Preacher knew the rest of the Comanches would be startled by what had happened to Lame Buffalo, and it would be a second before they reacted. He used that second to cut down the odds a little more by yanking his rifle from its sheath and snapping it to his shoulder. He fired without aiming, letting instinct guide his shot, and one of the warriors in the trail let out a cry and pitched off his pony to fall in a limp heap.

"Everybody in the wagons!" Preacher bellowed. "In the wagons now!"

The sideboards of the vehicles would stop an arrow and would probably stop a bullet. The thick canvas covers over the wagon beds might stop one of the feathered missiles. They would be better off fighting from inside, rather than underneath.

Preacher slapped Horse on the rump. The stallion took off at a dead run, with Dog following him. Preacher knew he didn't have to worry about the Comanches catching his trail partners. They were faster than the Indian ponies and wouldn't let them get close enough to shoot them with arrows. They wouldn't return to the wagons until Preacher summoned them.

Preacher reloaded the flintlock as the Comanches *ki-yipped* and charged the caravan. All around him was chaos as frightened men scrambled into the wagons looking for cover. From the corner of his eye he saw Roland Bartlett grab Casey and practically throw her into the lead wagon. Preacher wanted to kick the addle-brained boy six ways from Sunday for what he'd done, but it was too late for that. Survival came first.

One of the warriors charged, his lance leveled to pin Preacher to the wagon behind him. He finished priming the rifle, lifted it to his shoulder, centered the sight on the Indian's chest, and pulled the trigger. The Comanche was only a few yards away, and he went flying backward off the pony as the ball from Preacher's rifle smashed into his chest like a giant sledgehammer. The lance slipped from the fingers of an outflung hand and skittered across the ground at Preacher's feet.

He snatched it up and thrust it into the side of another warrior who had gotten too close. The man screeched in pain as the lance's sharp tip pierced his vitals. Even as he was dying, he swung his bow toward Preacher and tried to loose an arrow, but the mountain man knocked the bow aside with the barrel of his rifle.

Preacher slid under the wagon as arrows thudded into the sideboards and bounced off the wheels. He rolled all the way to the other side and came out with pistols in both hands. The weapons roared and spat flame and smoke, and two more of the Comanches went down.

"Preacher!" Lorenzo yelled from the rear of the wagon. "Preacher, get in here, you crazy fool!"

Lorenzo had a point. With his guns empty, Preacher was in a bad spot. But he wasn't defenseless. As long as he drew breath, the man called Preacher wouldn't be defenseless.

He jammed the guns behind his belt, ripped his knife from its sheath, and dodged the thrust of a lance. Grabbing the shaft of the Comanche weapon, he dragged its owner off his pony. As the man fell, Preacher thrust up with the knife to meet him. The blade went deep in the warrior's body. Preacher pulled the knife loose and shoved the dying man away.

An arrow whipped past his ear. He turned and leaped for the wagon's tailgate. Lorenzo waited there to grab him and pull him in. The old-timer caught Preacher's wrist and hauled him through the opening.

Preacher sprawled on top of some crates. Lorenzo asked, "Are you all right?"

"Yeah!"

"We're in one hell of a mess, ain't we?"

"Reckon we'll just have to fight our way out of it," Preacher said.

Guns boomed all along the line of wagons. The defenders were outnumbered, but their firepower helped offset that disadvantage. Preacher reloaded his pistols, and winced as an arrowhead ripped through the canvas near his head. He saw several arrows sticking through the canvas whose shafts had not penetrated into the wagon.

Lorenzo took his rifle and clambered over the freight to the front of the wagon. His rifle blasted. "Got one of 'em," he shouted.

Preacher leaned out through the opening at the rear and blew away two more Comanches. One of them had an old blunderbuss in his hands. The ancient weapon discharged as he fell, blowing a hole through the wagon's canvas cover.

Preacher ducked back inside to reload again. "Did you see Roland throw Casey into the lead wagon?" he called over the roar of gunfire and the shrill cries of the Comanches.

"I ain't sure, but I think so," the old-timer replied. "That boy sure played hob, didn't he?"

"We'll talk about that later," Preacher said. *If we live through this*, he added silently.

Screeching unnervingly, the face of one of the Indians suddenly appeared in the gap at the back of the wagon. The warrior thrust the lance in his hand at Preacher, who twisted aside, reversed one of the pistols, and smashed the butt into the center of the warrior's face. Blood spurted and bone crunched under the impact. The Indian fell backward, either dead or out cold.

Coolly, Preacher went back to reloading. Just as he had the pistols ready to go again, Lorenzo let out an excited whoop.

"They're leavin'!" he shouted triumphantly. "They're givin' up, Preacher."

Preacher crowded up beside him to look out. The Comanches were galloping off, twisting around on their ponies to throw a few last arrows and derisive cries toward the wagons.

"Leavin', maybe," Preacher said with a grim note in his voice. "But givin' up . . . I don't think so."

The caravan's defenders had done quite a bit of damage to the Indians. A number of bodies were sprawled on the ground around the wagons. But even so, the Comanches still outnumbered their enemies. And they wouldn't likely abandon their efforts to avenge Lame Buffalo's death.

Preacher went to the back of the wagon, climbed over the tailgate, and dropped to the ground. He kept a close eye on the bodies as he hurried to the lead wagon. It was possible some of those warriors weren't dead. They might regain consciousness and try to carry on the fight. It was even possible some of them were shamming, in hopes of luring the white men into the open. If any of the varmints tried to rear up and shoot an arrow into him, Preacher was going to be ready.

When he reached the lead wagon, he called, "Casey! You all right in there?"

She stuck her head out through the rear opening in the canvas cover. "Preacher, thank God! Are you hurt?"

He shook his head. "Nary a scratch so far."

"I'm all right, too, and so is Roland."

Preacher hadn't asked about the youngster, but he supposed he was glad Roland wasn't hurt. If not for his impulsive action, though, they might have gotten through the confrontation without any violence.

Lorenzo came up beside Preacher. "What do you need me to do?"

"Go up and down the wagons and find out how everybody's doin'," Preacher told him. "See if we've got any dead or injured. Wounded men will need to be patched up while the Comanch' are off lickin' their own wounds and figurin' out what to do next."

Leeman Bartlett had emerged from the wagon where he had taken cover. He joined the small group beside the lead wagon and suggested, "Perhaps we should make a run for it."

"That might work if we were all on horseback," Preacher said. "With a bunch of oxen pullin' heavy wagons, there ain't no way in hell we're outrunnin' anybody, let alone those Injun ponies." Preacher looked around. "Let's see if we can get the wagons pulled over to the side of the trail and form 'em into a circle."

Roland jumped down from the lead wagon. "I'll spread the word," he volunteered.

Preacher nodded curtly. Roland had gotten them into that mess, so it was fitting he try to help get them out of it.

For a fleeting second, Preacher debated the wisdom of trying to call a parley with the Indians. If he offered to turn Roland over to them, they might agree to let the rest of the party go. He was the one who had killed Lame Buffalo and started the fight, after all.

But as quickly as the idea came into Preacher's head, he discarded it. He couldn't do that, and he knew it. For one thing, Casey would likely never forgive him for it, and for another, Lame Buffalo was partially responsible for what had happened, too. If he hadn't been such an arrogant horse's rear end and grabbed Casey like he did, Roland wouldn't have had any reason to shoot him.

Still carrying his pistols, Preacher walked from

body to body, checking to make sure they were dead. Eight of the Comanches were lying on the ground, including Lame Buffalo, and all of them had crossed the divide.

Whips popped and bullwhackers shouted curses as they got their teams moving again. The wagons lurched forward. Preacher kept an eye on the area where the Indians had disappeared, and tried to look in every direction at once. He didn't think the respite would last very long.

Bartlett came up to Preacher. "Our horses are gone!"

"I ain't surprised," the mountain man said with a nod. "The Comanch' grabbed 'em."

"How do we get them back?"

"More than likely, you don't. You'll have to walk or ride the wagons. Maybe a few of 'em followed my stallion. I ran him off when the attack started. He'll be back, and with some luck, he might have a couple of your saddle mounts with him."

"This is terrible," Bartlett complained. "Just terrible."

"Talk to your son," Preacher said. "He's the one who got trigger-happy."

Bartlett frowned. "But that savage grabbed Casey. He was going to drag her off with him."

"No, he wasn't," Preacher said. "He just wanted to show what a big man he was. We would have offered him something else in trade instead of Casey, and that would have been the end of it."

"You sound awfully certain of that."

"I am. Seen it happen before. I would've handled it without anybody gettin' hurt, but Roland didn't give me a chance."

"We don't all know as much about life on the frontier as you do, Preacher."

"That's why you asked me to come along," Preacher snapped. "Let's get those wagons pulled in a circle."

He retrieved his rifle and reloaded it while keeping watch all around them. He didn't expect the Comanches to allow them to circle the wagons in a defensive arrangement without attacking again, but to his surprise, that was what happened. The Indians were probably doing some considerable wrangling among themselves about what to do next. Either that, or one of their medicine men was trying to whip up some powerful medicine to protect them when they attacked.

As soon as the wagons were in position, the men began unhitching the teams and leading them into the center of the circle. While that was going on, Lorenzo came up to Preacher and reported, "Ain't nobody on our side dead, but we got half a dozen wounded men."

"Any of 'em hurt too bad to fight?" Preacher asked.

"Only one. Some of his friends loaded him in one of the wagons."

Preacher nodded. "We'll see if Casey can look after him. Tell Roland to stay with her."

"That boy ain't going very far away from her," Lorenzo said with a snort.

"That's good. I'm countin' on him to keep her safe when those Comanch' hit us again."

"When's that gonna be, you think?"

"Soon," Preacher said grimly. "Any time now."

As the minutes dragged past he came to the conclusion the Comanches were deliberately stringing it out. They wanted the men with the wagons to get nervous. When Preacher looked at the bullwhackers and listened to their worried, low-voiced conversations, he knew the tactic was working. Their nerves were quickly stretching to the breaking point.

Since the lull in the fighting continued, Preacher walked out several yards from the wagons and gave a piercing whistle. He repeated it a couple times before he saw Horse and Dog trotting toward him over the prairie. Two more of the saddle mounts trailed the stallion and the big cur. Preacher held his rifle ready for instant use as he watched the animals come in.

When he got them safely inside the circle of wagons, he found Leeman Bartlett and told him about the extra horses that had avoided capture.

"That's one bit of good luck, anyway," the man said. "Lord knows we can use all of it we can get."

"I want half the men to rest while the other half stand guard," Preacher said. "Those Injuns could come from any direction, so we got to look ever' which way we can."

Bartlett nodded. "I understand. I'll give the orders." He hesitated. "Preacher, I know you're right about what Roland did. I'm sorry."

"We'll worry about that later. Right now let's just try to get through this alive."

He went to the wagon where the seriously wounded man had been placed and found Casey wrapping strips of cloth around the man's midsection to serve as makeshift bandages. He appeared to be unconscious.

"An arrow went all the way through his side," Casey said. "He lost a lot of blood, but I cleaned the wounds. I'll bind them up and maybe he'll have a chance."

Preacher nodded. "The fella's better off that the arrow came out the other side. Gettin' one of the blamed things out usually tears a fella up worse'n it did goin' in."

Roland was hovering over Casey as she worked. He clutched a rifle in his hands and had a pistol behind his belt. He glared at Preacher and said, "My father tells me you think *I'm* to blame for this attack."

"I won't lie to you, boy," Preacher said. "You caused it, all right. You lost your head and shot Lame Buffalo when there wasn't any need."

"No need? My God, man, that savage was trying to kidnap Casey!"

Preacher was getting tired of explaining what had really been going on. He said, "It was just part of the game. We would've bartered for her, and she wouldn't have gone anywhere."

"How in blazes was I supposed to know that?"

"Maybe if you'd waited a minute instead of pullin' that trigger—"

The wounded man let out a groan.

"That's enough," Casey said sharply. "Arguing about it now isn't going to change things. Roland, you don't have to stay here with me."

"Yes, he does," Preacher said. "I want him to watch out for you when the Comanch' jump us again."

"I thought they ran away," Roland said.

Preacher made a disgusted sound. "We're damn lucky they ain't back already."

Casey said, "No one has to watch out for me. Give me a pistol and some powder and shot, and I'll handle my share of the fighting."

As Preacher looked at her determined face, he knew she meant it. He said, "That ain't a bad idea. Roland, you've got extra pistols in the freight these wagons are carryin'. Go rustle up one for her. I'll stay here for the time bein'."

Roland looked like he wanted to argue, but after a second he nodded. "I'll be right back," he told Casey. He climbed out of the wagon.

"Don't you think you were too hard on him?" Casey asked when Roland was gone.

"I didn't say anything that wasn't the truth."

"Maybe not, but he's just learning his way around out here, like I am."

"He won't live long enough to learn much of anything if he don't start payin' more attention to the folks who know better."

"Maybe you're right. But I was scared that Indian was really going to take me with him, and I was glad when Roland stopped him."

Preacher shook his head. "I never would've let that happen. I'd have shot the varmint myself before I let him carry you off."

Casey's voice softened a little as she said, "I know that. I just didn't stop to think about it at the time."

Preacher didn't have anything to say to that. He hunkered on his heels in silence as Casey sat beside the wounded man.

He didn't stay that way for very long. A shout went up somewhere outside, and a second later Preacher heard running footsteps approaching the wagon. He straightened as much as he could in the cramped confines of the wagon and shoved the canvas flaps aside to see Lorenzo hurrying toward the wagon.

"Preacher!" the old-timer called. "It's them Injuns. They're attackin' again!"

CHAPTER 16

Preacher bit back a curse. Roland hadn't come back yet with that pistol for Casey. He pulled one of his own pistols from behind his belt and pressed it into her hand.

"Did this fella you patched up have a powder-horn and shot pouch?" he asked.

She shook her head. "I didn't see them if he did."

"All right. You got one shot here. If you need it, make it count. I'll send Roland back here if I see him."

"Don't worry about me, Preacher. I'll be fine." Her face was pale with fear, making the scar on her cheek stand out more than usual. He squeezed her shoulder reassuringly and climbed quickly out of the wagon.

He saw dust boiling up from the hooves of the Indian ponies as the Comanches charged toward the circled wagons. They must have been making medicine to have taken this long to attack again, he thought. He shouted to the men crouched behind the wagons, "Hold your fire until they're closer!"

He added the same advice he had given Casey. "Make your shots count, boys!"

They had plenty of powder and ammunition. What they wouldn't have was a lot of time to reload. If they didn't break the back of the charge with their first volley, some of the warriors were going to make it into the circle.

Preacher took up a position at the back of the wagon where Casey and the wounded man were. Lorenzo stood at the front of the next wagon in line. Leeman Bartlett was a couple wagons away. Preacher didn't see Roland.

"Where's Roland?" he called to Lorenzo. "Have you seen him? He was gonna fetch a pistol for Casey."

The old-timer shook his head. "Don't know. Ain't seen hide nor hair of him this last little while."

Preacher didn't have time to worry about Roland. He brought his long-barreled flintlock to his shoulder and aimed toward the charging riders.

"Roland!" Leeman Bartlett suddenly screamed. "My God! Roland, come back!"

Preacher lowered his rifle and looked around to see Bartlett clambering over a wagon tongue, leaving the circle. Preacher ran after him. He hurdled the wagon tongue and grabbed Bartlett's arm. The Comanches were only about five hundred yards away.

"What the hell's wrong with you, Bartlett?" he demanded. "You gone loco?"

Bartlett pointed a shaking finger. "Look!"

Preacher's face grew grim as he spotted the mounted figure riding toward the onrushing warriors. Roland had gotten hold of one of the extra horses and was meeting the Comanche charge by himself. It was the most foolhardy thing Preacher had ever seen.

Despite that, he felt a surge of admiration for the youngster. It was a crazy, futile gesture on Roland's part . . . but there was no doubt it took courage to do what he was doing.

Preacher shoved Bartlett toward the wagons. "Get back in the circle!" he ordered.

"But my son—"

"There's nothin' you can do for him."

Nothing any of them could do, Preacher thought.

Except maybe him.

"Go on," he told Bartlett. "I'll see if·I can get him."

Bartlett stumbled over the wagon tongue as he climbed back into the circle. Preacher whistled for Horse and Dog. The stallion and the big cur responded instantly. As Preacher swung up into the saddle, he called, "Lorenzo!"

The old-timer stuck his head around the back of a wagon. "Preacher, what in hell's name are you doin'?"

"Goin' after that fool kid. Count ten and then have everybody fire."

"Preacher—"

"Just do it!"

Preacher leaned forward in the saddle as he urged Horse into a run. The stallion galloped at a breakneck pace after Roland, eating up the ground.

Preacher counted off the seconds in his head as he rode. When he reached seven, he hauled back hard on the reins. The Comanches were less than two hundred yards away, and Roland was about halfway between him and them. At the count of eight, Preacher dropped out of the saddle. His feet hit the ground and dug in, and as he counted nine in his head, he pulled Horse's head down hard. The stallion knew what he wanted and fell to the ground beside Preacher.

"Dog! Down!" the mountain man yelled.

Dog hit the dirt, too, and as he did, the ten-count ended in Preacher's head. From the wagons, shots roared in a concentrated volley. Like the humming of a flight of giant insects, the heavy lead balls buzzed through the air above Preacher, Horse, and Dog and smashed into the Indians and their ponies.

Roland's horse was hit, too. It went down hard, sending Roland flying through the air. Preacher didn't know if any of the shots had struck the youngster. That had been a calculated risk in his hastily-formed plan.

One thing was certain: if Preacher hadn't done *something*, Roland would have been slaughtered by those Comanch' in a matter of seconds. The desperate gambit had nothing to lose.

Clouds of dust rolled through the air as a dozen or more of the Indian ponies spilled, going down in a welter of thrashing limbs. Preacher was up again instantly, vaulting into Horse's saddle. He raced toward the spot where Roland's motionless body sprawled on the ground.

The fierce volley from the wagons blunted the Comanche charge as Preacher hoped. The warriors who were still mounted reorganized a short distance away. Recognizing Preacher and Roland as targets too tempting to pass up, arrows began to fly through the air as Preacher galloped toward Roland, who was apparently unconscious and defenseless.

Preacher reached his side in a matter of heartbeats and was out of the saddle, lifting him and throwing him over Horse's back. The stallion jumped as an arrow grazed his rump.

Preacher leaped into the saddle and grabbed the reins. He wheeled Horse and sent the stallion racing toward the wagons again. With his other hand, he held Roland's limp form in place in front of the saddle. Dog ran ahead of them. Arrows whipped through the air around them.

Preacher soon outdistanced the Comanche bows, and the few warriors who had flintlocks weren't good shots with them. Even so, he didn't slow down until he had leaped Horse over a wagon tongue and was back in the circle.

Bartlett and some of the other men rushed to gather around him. "My God!" Bartlett cried. "Is he dead?"

"I don't think so," Preacher said as hands reached up to take hold of Roland and lift him down from the stallion's back.

"Whoo-eee!" Lorenzo said. "I never seen nothin' like that before, Preacher! You coulda got yourself blowed all to hell tryin' somethin' like that."

"Yeah, but I didn't." Preacher dismounted and waved a hand at some of the men. "Get back to the wagons and watch out for those Comanch'! Reload those rifles, if you ain't already done it."

The men had placed Roland on the ground. Bartlett knelt beside his son and felt for a heartbeat.

"He's alive!" Bartlett announced a second later. "I don't see any blood on him."

"I think it just knocked him out when he got throwed off his horse," Preacher said.

Casey came pushing through the crowd. "Roland! Is he all right?"

Bartlett looked up at her. "He's alive, my dear. I think he's going to be fine."

"What in the world was he trying to do?" Casey demanded of Preacher.

The mountain man shrugged. "Looked to me like he was tryin' to fight off those Injuns all by his lonesome."

"Because you told him it was his fault they attacked us!"

"I told him the truth," Preacher said bluntly. "What he did with it was his own lookout."

Casey glared at him for a second, then dropped to her knees beside Roland. She took hold of his shoulder, lifted him, and pulled his head into her lap. His eyelids began to flutter. After a moment, his eyes opened and he looked up into Casey's worried face.

"I . . . I'm alive?" he asked hoarsely.

"You are," she told him. "But that was a foolish thing to do, Roland."

"I thought . . . it might help," he said. He looked over at Preacher. "I thought it might . . . make amends."

"Throwin' your life away hardly ever does anybody any good," Preacher said.

Roland wasn't listening to him. He was looking at Casey again.

Preacher left them there like that and went

back to one of the wagons, peering past it at the Comanches. They had withdrawn again but hadn't gone out of sight. They sat out there, about two dozen of them, watching the wagons. The odds were no longer overwhelmingly on their side.

"What do you think they're gonna do?" Lorenzo asked as he stood beside Preacher.

"They've hit us twice, and we've hurt 'em bad twice," Preacher said. "Some of 'em will be thinkin' by now that it's time to cut their losses and go home."

"But not all of 'em."

Preacher shook his head. "No, not all of 'em. The hotheads are still gonna want blood. It's just a matter of how many are left on each side, and if they can convince the others to go along with 'em."

Bartlett came up to them and said, "Preacher, I . . . I don't know how to thank you for saving my son's life. Roland would be dead now if you hadn't gone out there and brought him back. I've never seen such a thing."

"And you ain't likely to see it ever again," Preacher said, "because most fellas'd have more sense than to try a damn fool stunt like that. But he's back and he ain't dead, and there ain't no need to say anything else."

"All right," Bartlett said. "But I won't forget, Preacher. Not ever."

"Preacher." Lorenzo pointed toward the Indians. "Looks like the hotheads won the argument."

The Comanches were charging again. Preacher called out to the other defenders, "Get ready! Here they come!"

When the warriors were just outside easy rifle

range, they swung to the side and began riding in a circle around the wagons. They yipped and shouted and waved their bows and lances in the air.

"What are they doing?" Bartlett asked.

"Showin' off," Preacher said. "They ain't attackin' after all. They're just tellin' us how fierce they are before they leave."

"You mean they've given up?"

"That's what it looks like to me. For now, anyway. There's no guarantee they won't try to rustle up some more warriors and come after us again later. But for now . . . I'd say it's over."

"Thank God," Bartlett said fervently.

The Indians made several circuits around the wagons, yelling ferociously and gesturing threateningly with their weapons. Then they turned and rode up the trail to the site of the first battle to retrieve the bodies of their comrades who had fallen there.

"I'll bet I could tag one of the red bastards from here," one of the bullwhackers said as he sighted over the barrel of his rifle.

"Leave 'em alone," Preacher said sharply. "They're lettin' us get out of here with our hair. It'd be plumb stupid to antagonize 'em. Anyway, they're gatherin' up their dead. Show some respect."

"Respect?" the man repeated. "For those red heathens?"

"They're honorable enemies, and they were here before we were. Sure, they came along and pushed somebody else out, but they were still here before we were."

The man shrugged powerful shoulders. "Whatever you say, Preacher."

"It won't hurt to keep an eye on 'em. If they try to jump us again, then you can shoot as many of 'em as you want to."

Within fifteen minutes, the Comanches were gone from sight. Preacher knew they might come back, but his instincts told him the trouble was over.

"We got some daylight left," he told Bartlett. "Best hitch up the teams and get movin' again."

While that was going on, Roland sought out Preacher and said, "Casey tells me you saved my life. Thank you."

"You're welcome."

"I'm sorry I acted rashly in shooting that Indian. I really thought he was going to take Casey with him."

"Well . . . I reckon it ain't your fault you didn't know no better."

"I'll do anything and everything in my power to protect her."

"That's good to know. Just be sure you know what you're doin' when you do it."

Roland nodded. Preacher had the feeling the young man still didn't like him very much, but at least Roland had had the gumption to speak plainly.

A few minutes later, the oxen were hitched up and the wagons were rolling again. Since there was only one extra horse, the men who had been working as outriders took the places of the wounded bullwhackers. Casey rode in one of the wagons with Roland. He had volunteered to take over for one of the wounded men, but Casey insisted he rest after being knocked out, and Bartlett agreed with her.

Preacher picked Lorenzo to ride the extra saddle mount starting out. "We're gonna have to take the place of all those other outriders," he told the old-timer. "That means scoutin' the flanks and our back trail as well as keepin' an eye on what's up ahead."

Lorenzo nodded in understanding. "You go ahead," he told Preacher. "I don't mind bringin' up the rear for a while."

Preacher lifted a hand in farewell as Lorenzo wheeled his horse and rode toward the rear of the caravan. Preacher moved out ahead, wondering how they could get their hands on some more horses, knowing that wasn't likely to happen short of Santa Fe.

For the rest of the day, Preacher and Lorenzo circulated around the wagons as the heavy vehicles made their slow, steady way southwestward. They checked in every direction for any sign of the Comanches or other trouble approaching the caravan. Nothing threatening appeared. Hot, tedious hours crept by, and finally the sun lowered toward the horizon and Preacher began looking for a good place to make camp.

He found it near a cluster of rocks and motioned for the bullwhackers to pull the wagons into a circle again. It was a good thing they would reach the springs tomorrow, he thought. The water in the barrels was starting to run a little low.

After the strain of the day everyone was exhausted, but the possibility the Comanches might return had the men so on edge that sleep was difficult. Preacher had no trouble getting volunteers to stand guard.

When he checked on the wounded man, Casey reported, "He seems to be sleeping peacefully and doesn't have any fever. I think there's a good chance he'll be all right."

"It's thanks to you taking care of him if he is," Roland said.

"How're you doin', boy?" Preacher asked. "You must've hit your head pretty hard to get knocked out cold like that."

Roland shrugged. "I've got a headache, but that's all."

"Seein' straight?"

"As far as I can tell."

"All right." Preacher turned back to Casey. "If you need me, give a holler."

She nodded. "I will."

Despite the tension in the camp, the night passed quietly. The wagons rolled out the next morning without incident, and the day passed, with long hours of slow, hot travel toward Santa Fe.

Late that afternoon, Preacher spotted a patch of green ahead and felt his spirits surge. Vegetation meant the springs were still flowing. He rode ahead to make sure, then returned to the wagons to give the others the good news.

"Looks like the spring is in good shape," he told an exhausted-looking Leeman Bartlett. "I'm thinkin' after such a long haul and the trouble we've had, it might be a good idea to stay here a few days and let everybody rest up, includin' the oxen."

"That sounds like an excellent idea," Bartlett responded. "I couldn't agree more."

"Thing is, we'll still have to keep our guard up. Injuns have been using this spring for a whole lot longer than wagons have been goin' to Santa Fe.

Wouldn't surprise me none if they knew about the spring before there ever *was* a Santa Fe."

The spring emerged from the ground and formed a pool surrounded by a marshy area covered with reeds and grass. The Cimarron River itself was nearby, its banks lined with scrubby trees, but its water supply was actually less dependable than that of the spring. It had been Preacher's experience that the spring water tasted better than the river water, which was brackish at times.

The caravan pushed on. The worn-out bullwhackers had more life in their steps, as did the oxen. The big brutes smelled the water and were anxious to reach it.

"Be careful not to let 'em drink too much when we get there," Preacher warned the men as he rode alongside the wagons. "We don't need 'em boggin' down." He paused and then added, "The same thing goes for you men. You been on short water rations for a few days now. Fill your bellies too full and it's gonna make you sick."

By nightfall, the wagons were circled, camp was established, and morale was better than it had been for days. It was hard to believe that only one day earlier they had been battling for their lives against the Comanches. Fresh water and green vegetation did a lot to lift a man's spirits.

The man who'd had the arrow go through his body was awake and feeling better, thanks to Casey's nursing. The other men who had been wounded during the fight were recovering as well.

For the next two days, the men rested, filled the water barrels, and did routine repair work on the wagons. The arrows that had pierced the canvas had been removed, and the holes sewn up. Several of the burly bullwhackers proved to be surprisingly deft at the mending.

On their third night in camp, Preacher sought out Leeman Bartlett and said, "I reckon we'd better get back on the trail tomorrow, if that's all right with you. Once we leave the springs, another week should see us in Santa Fe." Maybe the last leg of the trip would prove to be the easiest, he thought.

The man nodded. "Whatever you think is best, Preacher. Although I must say, I'll miss this place. Compared to what we've seen so far of the Cimarron Cutoff, this is a veritable Eden." Bartlett paused. "I've started to think about what we'll do after we reach Santa Fe. I wish you'd come back to St. Louis with us and guide us west again on our next journey."

Preacher didn't even think about it. He shook his head and said, "Sorry, Mr. Bartlett. I ain't sure yet where I'll be goin' when I leave Santa Fe, but it ain't gonna be back to St. Louis. I've had my fill of that town for a good long while."

"Well, perhaps you'll reconsider. I'd pay you good wages."

Preacher smiled. "One thing a man like me ain't ever considered all that much is good wages."

He said good night to Bartlett and went to find Lorenzo. The old-timer was playing cards with some of the bullwhackers. "You up to standin' guard tonight?" Preacher asked him.

Lorenzo glanced up from his cards. "I reckon."

Preacher nodded. "Good." He looked out at the blackness surrounding the camp. "I got a feelin' . . ."

"A bad feelin'?" Lorenzo asked shrewdly.

"Just a feelin', that's all."

One of the bullwhackers said, "I hope them damn Comanches don't come after us again." The other men muttered agreement.

"Or those fellas who tried to rob us," another man put in.

Preacher hadn't forgotten about Garity, although it seemed likely to him the would-be thieves had already pushed on to Santa Fe. He left Lorenzo and the other men to their game and walked on around the circle of wagons. He found Casey and Roland sitting on a couple of crates Roland had taken out of one of the wagons.

The young man came to his feet as Preacher approached. "Is something wrong?" he asked.

Preacher had left the two young people alone while the caravan was camped at the Cimarron springs. He thought the bond between them had grown stronger, and that was a good thing. His hope was that when the wagons started back to St. Louis from Santa Fe, Casey would go with them. He wouldn't be surprised if she wound up marrying Roland Bartlett.

"No, nothin's wrong," Preacher told them. "Just thought I'd see how you two were doin' and let you know we're leavin' here in the mornin'."

Casey smiled up at him. "After everything we've gone through, it's been like paradise here, Preacher."

"Yeah. Roland's pa compared it to Eden. I reckon he wasn't far wrong."

"How long will it take us to finish the trip from here?" Roland asked.

"Another week, I'm thinkin'. If nothin' else happens along the way." He hadn't shaken the slight feeling of uneasiness that had cropped up in him earlier.

"I'm looking forward to seeing Santa Fe," Casey said.

"It's a right pretty town in its way," Preacher said. "And the mountains around it are even—"

The sentiment he was expressing was interrupted by a terrifed shout that suddenly ripped through the night, followed by the boom of a gunshot.

CHAPTER 17

Preacher wheeled around and broke into a run toward the source of the commotion. He heard growling and snarling and recognized the sounds of Dog fighting with something or someone. A man screamed, making Preacher think the big cur had gotten hold of someone.

He realized a second later the cries were coming from the wagon where he had been talking to Leeman Bartlett a few minutes earlier. Since he couldn't think of any reason why Dog would attack Bartlett, he decided something else must be going on.

Horror washed through him a moment later when he rounded the back of the wagon and saw a towering figure. The grizzly bear was back, and it had Bartlett.

The man shrieked in agony as claws and teeth tore into him. Dog was trying to help Bartlett by darting around and snapping at the bear, but the grizzly ignored him. The creature seemed intent on mauling Bartlett to the exclusion of everything else.

Preacher jerked his rifle to his shoulder. Bartlett was in the line of fire, but it didn't matter. He was doomed unless somebody did something fast. It might already be too late.

The light from the campfire that penetrated between the wagons was uncertain, but Preacher lined his sights on the bear's head and pulled the trigger.

The grizzly roared as its head jerked back, so Preacher knew his shot had found its mark. The brute didn't fall, but continued to savage Leeman Bartlett. Preacher suspected the ball from his rifle had struck the bear a glancing blow and bounced off the thick skull under the fur.

More men ran up in response to the screams and growls and gunshots. Roland shouted, "Pa!" and tried to rush past Preacher.

Preacher grabbed the young man's arm and dragged him back. "You'll just get yourself killed!" he said as he shoved Roland into the arms of several of the bullwhackers. "Hold onto him!"

Preacher dropped his empty rifle and pulled his pistols. He was going to have to get closer to the bear so he could fire a shot directly into one of the beast's eyes, to reach its brain and stop it.

He feared it was too late to help Leeman Bartlett. Bartlett's head lolled loosely on his neck, and his clothes, shredded by the grizzly's teeth and claws, were soaked with blood.

Holding the pistols ready, Preacher moved closer to the bear. Suddenly, the grizzly threw Bartlett's limp body aside like a child discarding a rag doll, its beady eyes focused on Preacher instead. With a thunderous roar, the monster charged.

"Everybody scatter!" Preacher shouted as he flung himself out of the way of the charging bear. The creature barreled past him with Dog still nipping at its heels. Yelling frightened curses, the other members of the party scrambled to get away from the grizzly.

The bear slapped at one of the bullwhackers who was too slow getting out of the way. The big paw smashed into the man's back and lifted him off his feet. The bullwhacker yelled in pain and flew through the air for a short distance before crashing to the ground. Stripes of blood angled across the back of his shirt where the bear's claws had ripped his flesh.

Preacher leaped to his feet and ran after the bear, yelling, "Hey! Hey, you big hairy bastard!" Reaching high, he reversed one of the pistols and slammed the butt into the back of the bear's head, then dropped into a crouch as the grizzly wheeled around and swung a vicious blow at his head. He straightened, so close he could smell the bear's fetid breath in his face.

Before Preacher could jam his pistol into the bear's throat, the bear caught him with a backhanded swing that landed on the side of the mountain man's head. The blow was a glancing one, strong enough to send Preacher flying off his feet, but not powerful enough to break his neck. He managed to hang on to the pistols as he rolled over a couple times on the ground.

The camp was full of yelling and cursing, and gunshots added to the chaos as the bullwhackers who had managed to reach cover opened fire on the bear.

The grizzly lunged back and forth, roaring out its defiance and anger. Suddenly it turned and ran straight at one of the wagons, crashing into the vehicle, causing it to shudder. Ripping off the canvas cover, the bear reached for the man inside and jerked him out of the wagon bed.

That grizzly was a damn smart critter, Preacher thought. Either that or guided by blind luck and instinct. The bullwhackers had to stop shooting for fear they would hit the man grabbed by the bear.

The bear lurched away from the wagon and threw the man among the livestock. The oxen were milling around in instinctive terror because of the grizzly's presence and would trample the bullwhacker if someone didn't reach him quickly.

Preacher darted into the press of oxen and reached the man's side. He bent down to grab his arm and pulled him to his feet. The man was only semiconscious.

Preacher hauled him out of danger and looked around for the bear. Not seeing the grizzly, he shouted, "Where'd the varmint go?"

Several men leaped down from the wagons where they had taken shelter and ran toward Preacher. "It got out of the circle and ran off!" one of them said. "We tried to kill it, but it seemed like it didn't even feel the shots!"

"Build the fire up bigger," Preacher snapped. "Get one started on the other side of the circle. I don't want that damn thing gettin' close to the wagons again without somebody seein' it!"

The bullwhackers hurried to carry out those orders. While they were doing that, Preacher went over to the last place he had seen Leeman Bartlett.

He found Roland sitting on the ground, cradling his father's bloody, ravaged body, rocking back and forth in shock and grief. Tears rolled down the young man's face. Casey knelt beside Roland with a comforting hand on his shoulder, but he didn't seem to know she was there.

Preacher looked at Casey with a question plain on his face. She shook her head. Bartlett was gone, which came as no surprise considering the amount of terrible damage done to him by the bear's claws and teeth.

"Why?" Roland moaned. "Why did that monster do such a thing? My father never hurt it! My father never hurt anybody!"

Preacher hunkered on his heels on Roland's other side. "I'm sorry," he said. "That varmint's crazy. Loco even for a bear. Somethin' drove it out here on the prairie in the first place, and the way it followed us all those miles just ain't normal. A bear's brain ain't very big, but this one's big enough to hold a powerful lot of hate."

"I can't believe he's gone," Roland choked out. "I just can't believe it."

"I reckon you don't want to be thinkin' about this right now, Roland, but you're the boss of this wagon train now."

Roland's head came up as he glared at Preacher. "You think I *care* about something like that now?"

"I know you don't," Preacher said. "But you got responsibilities."

"No. You're in charge." Roland's voice held a bitter edge. "My father listened to you and took your advice on everything. Every time there was trouble, you gave the orders. You're in charge, Preacher."

Preacher wasn't going to waste time arguing. Roland was too grief-stricken to be giving orders, anyway. Later on, he would be able to see the situation more clearly.

Preacher squeezed Roland's shoulder and repeated, "I'm sorry about your pa." Then he straightened and looked around. He saw the bullwhackers had followed his orders. The campfire was blazing brighter, and a fire burned on the other side of the circle, too. The light from the flames extended out from the wagons.

"I want a man on guard at every wagon," Preacher said. "How bad are those other two fellas hurt?"

"Charley's back is ripped up pretty bad," one of the men replied. "We'll clean it up. I think he'll be all right. Pettigrew's just shaken up from bein' tossed around by that bear."

Preacher nodded. He was glad to hear the other injuries weren't too serious. Leeman Bartlett's brutal death was plenty bad enough by itself.

When Preacher was satisfied the camp was well-guarded, he motioned for Lorenzo to follow him and returned to the place where Roland still sat, holding his father's body.

"Casey, why don't you take Roland into one of the wagons?" Preacher suggested. "Lorenzo and me will take care of his pa."

Roland looked up at him. "What are you going to do? There's nothing anyone can do for him now!"

"That ain't true. We'll clean him up, get him ready to be laid to rest proper-like in the mornin'."

Casey said, "Preacher's right, Roland. Come with me."

For a moment, Roland looked like he was going to argue. But then he sighed and eased his pa's body to the ground. He stood up shakily and allowed Casey to take his arm and lead him toward one of the wagons.

Preacher waited until the two of them had climbed into the vehicle, then said to Lorenzo, "Can you rustle up a blanket?"

"To wrap Mr. Bartlett in? Sure."

"I know which wagon his gear is in. I'll see if I can find him some clothes that ain't all tore up and bloody."

By the time half an hour had passed, they had Bartlett's body cleaned up, dressed in fresh clothes, and wrapped in a blanket as it was laid out under one of the wagons. First thing in the morning, they would dig a grave and give him a proper burial.

"I never did expect to see that damned ol' bear again," Lorenzo said as he and Preacher looked out at the night where the fearsome creature had vanished. "Why do you reckon it's followed us all this way?"

Preacher shook his head. "I don't know. Somethin' wrong in its head, more than likely. Just plumb loco, like I said earlier. But I do know one thing."

"What's that?"

"It's time for that varmint to die," Preacher said. "After we get Bartlett buried tomorrow, you and me are gonna do us some bear huntin', Lorenzo."

* * *

Bartlett was the one who had read from the Good Book at the previous burials. With him gone, that job fell to his son. Roland, who was still grief-stricken but more in control of himself the next morning, took on the task. His voice broke a few times as he read the Twenty-third Psalm and led a prayer, but he made it through the solemn ceremony.

When it was over, Preacher led Roland away from the grave while some of the bullwhackers filled it in. With Casey and Lorenzo accompanying them, they went to the other side of the camp.

"I've been thinking about what you said last night, Preacher," Roland mused. "About me being in charge. I'm not sure I'm up to the job."

"There's only one way to find out," Preacher said. "But I'll do whatever I can to help you out."

"What do you think we should do next? Move on to Santa Fe like we planned to do?"

"I don't think it would hurt anything to stay here one more day. That'll give Lorenzo and me time to do a little job."

Roland frowned. "What sort of job?"

"We're goin' after that griz."

Roland stared at him. "That won't bring my father back," he finally said, his voice grim.

"No, but maybe it'll keep the varmint from killin' anybody else. It's got a taste for blood, that's for dang sure."

"You went after it before, remember?"

Preacher nodded. "I remember. And I wish we'd caught up to it then. This time we won't come back until we do."

"You think we should wait here for you?"

"You've got plenty of supplies," Preacher pointed

out, "and the best water supply in this part of the country. I'm hopin' it won't take us long to find the bear. We might be back later today. But if it takes a few days, you'll be all right here. Just keep a full shift of guards on all the time."

"In case the Indians come back."

Preacher shrugged. "It could happen." He rubbed his bearded jaw. "And it'd be better if I was here to help you fight 'em off."

"I don't think there's any doubt of that." Roland frowned. "Why don't we compromise? You and Lorenzo see if you can trail the bear. But if you don't find it, come back tonight and we'll move out for Santa Fe tomorrow morning." He took a deep breath. "I hate the idea of letting that creature get away with killing my father, but as you pointed out, Preacher, I have other responsibilities now, like all the men who work for him. Who work for me."

Roland might still have a ways to go, but he was starting to grow up, Preacher thought. He said, "All right. We'll ride out now and be back tonight, one way or the other."

Roland nodded. "Thanks, Preacher. I feel like I ought to come with you, instead of asking you to avenge my father."

"Nope, be better for you to stay here," Preacher said with a shake of his head. "Somebody's got to be in charge, and I reckon that's you."

Roland drew in a deep breath. "That still sounds wrong to me, but I'll do what I can."

Preacher clapped a hand on his shoulder. "Just keep your guard up, son. That's the most important thing you can do right now."

Motioning for Lorenzo to follow him, Preacher

started toward the horses. He put his saddle on the big gray stallion while Lorenzo got the other horse ready to ride.

In a low, worried voice, the old-timer said, "You know, Preacher, I'm startin' to think that bear can't be killed. We done shot it and shot it, over and over, and the damn thing keeps on a-comin' back."

"Ain't nothin' ever lived that can't be killed," Preacher said.

"What if it ain't . . . a real bear? What if it's some kind of spirit?"

"A ghost bear?" Preacher shook his head. "It's real, all right. My jaw still aches from the wallop it gave me last night. It's real, and with enough powder and shot, it'll die."

Or else I'll die tryin' to kill it, he thought.

CHAPTER 18

Accompanied by Dog, they rode out of camp heading north, the same direction the bear had gone. The trail was harder to follow since the ground was hard and didn't take tracks well. Dog also seemed to have trouble picking up the scent.

Preacher's keen, experienced eyes were able to spot the little signs of the grizzly's passage: the rocks that had been overturned recently, the marks in the dirt left by a dragging claw, the occasional drops of blood that testified to the fact the bear was wounded again.

If Preacher had been the superstitious sort, he might have wondered about the bear, just like Lorenzo. There was no telling how many times the big varmint had been wounded, and yet it was still alive, still vicious, still determined to wreak havoc on the wagon train. Preacher had no explanation for how it had survived or why it was so hell-bent on delivering death and destruction to the caravan, but he had seen men who were hard to kill, as well as men whose violent actions made no sense. If a human could go crazy, he supposed a bear could, too.

After a while, Lorenzo said, "I hope you know where you're goin'. I don't see no trail."

Preacher pointed out the sign he was following. "If you're gonna live out here on the frontier," he said, "it's time you started learnin' some of the things that'll help keep you alive."

"I'm all for stayin' alive," Lorenzo said.

The bear's trail led due north, through some bleak, rugged country. "Looks like he's headed for Canada," Preacher commented after a while.

"How far's that?"

"Too far for us to follow him all the way there," Preacher replied with a smile. "Maybe we'll catch up to him."

Lorenzo was silent for a few moments, then asked, "What do you think about that young fella Roland? Is he gonna be able to take over and run things like his pa?"

"Maybe," Preacher said. "Bartlett didn't really know what he was doin', either. He just bought some wagons and freight and started out to Santa Fe, trustin' to luck."

"What was lucky was him runnin' into you. That whole bunch'd likely be dead now without the help you give 'em."

"Well, they gave us a hand back yonder in Independence, remember? Seems fittin' we'd do what we can to help them, too."

"Speakin' of Independence . . . Casey seems taken with the boy now. You finally got her to give up on you?"

"So it appears," Preacher said dryly.

"And that don't bother you none?"

"That was what I wanted. What I'm worried about now is what will Casey do when Roland starts back to St. Louis."

"Go with him?" Lorenzo suggested.

"I thought about that. What if some of your old boss's friends recognize her?"

The old-timer snorted in contempt. "I ain't sure Shad Beaumont ever *had* any friends. Just folks who worked for him and folks who was scared of him . . . or both, like me." Lorenzo shook his head. "But I been around them crooked folks enough to know they don't care about much of anything except money. They won't have no reason to bother Casey, even if somebody does recognize her."

"Roland might find out about her past if that happens," Preacher pointed out.

"That's likely to happen anyway, sooner or later." Lorenzo shrugged. "Roland'll just have to get over it, if it bothers him. Maybe it won't."

"Maybe not," Preacher said.

While they were talking, he'd kept his eyes on the ground ahead of them, intently picking out the little indications that the grizzly had passed that way. He hadn't seen any blood for quite a while, telling him the bear's wounds were superficial and had stopped bleeding.

Dog ranged back and forth in front of them, sometimes with the scent, sometimes not. Preacher lost the trail a time or two himself but was able to find it again.

Around midday, they came to a dry wash, about a dozen feet deep and steep-walled. The bear's tracks led right up to the edge. Preacher frowned as he swung down from the saddle and studied the ground. It looked like the bear had walked straight up to the wash and fallen into it. Preacher saw where the dust had been disturbed on the floor of the arroyo by the creature's landing.

More tracks led off to the west. Preacher pointed them out and said, "Looks like he got up and kept movin'."

"How come he fell off of there?" Lorenzo asked. "I know you said bears don't see too good, but there ain't no way he missed somethin' as big as this wash."

"Maybe he just didn't care," Preacher said. "Maybe he's dyin' at last, and he knows it."

"We gonna follow him?"

Preacher looked up, studying the sun's position in the sky. "Yeah," he said after a moment. "I think we can stay on his trail for a couple more hours if we need to, and still get back to the wagons before dark if we push the horses a little."

"You're the boss." Lorenzo looked and sounded a little nervous.

"You're not still worried about the bear bein' supernatural somehow, are you?" Preacher asked. "I tell you, the blamed thing's real, and it can be killed."

"Oh, I believe you," Lorenzo said. "But he's been mighty hard to kill so far, and I'm just wonderin' how much more damage he can do 'fore we finish him off."

"Not much, I'm hopin'," Preacher said.

They rode along the edge of the wash, following it as it twisted and turned in a generally westward direction. Preacher was able to see the tracks from up there. As far as he could tell, the bear wasn't making any effort to climb out of the wash.

After about a mile, he began seeing blood on the ground along with the tracks. One of the bear's wounds must have broken open, he thought. His anticipation increased. Mortality might finally be catching up to the giant creature.

He spotted something up ahead. A dark hole in the side of the wash marked the mouth of a cave. As Preacher and Lorenzo approached it, Preacher saw the tracks and the blood leading into the opening. Instinct had drawn the grizzly to a place where it could den up.

The two men reined to a halt. Lorenzo frowned at the cave mouth and said, "What do we do now? That damn thing found itself a hole to crawl into!"

"To crawl into and die, more'n likely," Preacher said. "But I ain't turnin' back until I know for sure."

Lorenzo looked over at him, frowning in surprise. "You don't mean to tell me you figure on goin' *in* that cave?"

"Chances are it ain't even a real cave, just a hollowed-out place," Preacher said. "Probably not more'n eight or ten feet deep. If I can get down there, I ought to be able to see into it enough to tell if the bear's dead."

"What if it *ain't* dead?"

Preacher thought about it for a minute. "Tell you what. We'll tie a rope around me and fasten the other end to Horse, so if I need to get out of there in a hurry, he can pull me out."

Lorenzo didn't look convinced, but he said, "All right. It's your skin. Just don't be expectin' me to climb down in there after you if you get in trouble."

"I don't," Preacher assured him. "Just keep your rifle handy."

He dismounted and took the coiled rope off Horse's saddle. He made a loop in one end and slipped it over his head and shoulders, tightening it under his arms and around his chest. The other end he tied to the saddle.

"Toss my rifle to me once I'm down there," he told Lorenzo. He led Horse away from the edge until he judged the stallion was far enough away to keep the rope taut. Then he backed to the edge. The rope stretched out tight between him and Horse.

"All right, old fella," Preacher called to the stallion. "Come toward me, nice and slow."

Horse started walking forward. As he did, Preacher leaned back against the rope and reached over the edge with a booted foot. He found a good place to brace it and then stepped back with the other foot. As Horse came toward him, Preacher was able to walk backward down the sheer wall of the arroyo. The sandstone face was rough enough to provide several good footholds along the way.

It didn't take long at all for Preacher to descend into the wash. "Keep comin', Horse," he called up to the stallion so he would have plenty of slack in the rope as he approached the cave. Now that he was closer, he could see that the bear's tracks definitely led into the dark opening.

Lorenzo threw the rifle down to Preacher. The mountain man held the weapon ready for instant use as he started toward the cave mouth. The opening was about five feet tall and four feet wide. Preacher crouched to look into it.

The bear exploded out of the cave with a swiftness and ferocity that surprised even Preacher. He pulled the rifle's trigger, making flame and smoke spew from the muzzle, but didn't know if he hit the grizzly or not. He had to move so fast to avoid the lethal swipe of a huge paw that he lost his footing and sprawled backward on the ground.

"Back, Horse, back!" he yelled. Instantly, the rope around him went taut.

As he slid backward over the dusty floor of the wash, being dragged by Horse, Preacher scrambled to get his feet under him. The bear charged after him. Preacher thrust the rifle out to block another blow from one of those paws. The impact knocked the weapon out of his hands and sent it spinning away, but at least it kept the claws from raking across his face.

Preacher tried to get turned around so he could walk back up the wall, but he didn't make it in time. His shoulder rammed against the sandstone so hard the impact took his breath away and stunned him. He felt his feet come off the ground, as the rope around his torso began to lift him.

The bear came at him again, reaching for him. Preacher had the presence of mind to draw his legs up and then lash out with them, kicking the bear in the chest. He wasn't strong enough to knock down such a behemoth, but the grizzly was staggered for a second. It threw back its head and let out an angry, frustrated roar.

It lunged forward again, enveloping Preacher in its powerful arms. As the creature pulled him against it, he reached for his pistols, hoping to blast both double-shotted loads into the bear's face at close range. As the bear's grip tightened Preacher's arms were pinned against his sides. Even though his hands were wrapped around the butts of the pistols, he couldn't pull them from behind his belt.

He jerked his head aside as the bear bit at him. The animal's hot breath washed across his face and was so foul it made him gag. Something was wrong with the bear, Preacher thought. Its insides were festering.

Knowing that wasn't going to do him any good. The grizzly was about to crush the life out of him.

Dog leaped from the bank and landed on top of the bear's head, snarling and snapping. The big cur hadn't been able to stand at the edge of the wash and watch his old friend battling for his life without jumping right into the middle of the fracas. Dog's sharp teeth tore into one of the bear's ears and started ripping at it. The bear roared in pain and let go of Preacher to reach up and remove the annoyance from the back of its neck.

With a pained yelp, Dog went flying away. The grizzly wheeled around and went after him.

Preacher started rising again as Horse lifted him. His wits returned to him, and he yelled, "No, Horse! Down!"

"Preacher, what the hell you doin'?" Lorenzo shouted in alarm. "Get outta there!"

"I ain't leavin' Dog down here!"

Preacher's feet hit the ground again. He grabbed the rope, pulled it loose, threw it off.

Without the rope, he was free to charge after the bear. As he looked past the varmint's considerable bulk, he saw Dog lying on the ground, apparently stunned if not worse. As he ran, Preacher pulled the guns from behind his belt and cocked them.

"Damn you, bear!" he bellowed. "I'm gettin' tired of fightin' you!"

The bear swung around again, distracted by the shout as Preacher had hoped. Dog was safe for the moment.

But only for the moment. If the bear killed Preacher, the big cur would be next.

Lorenzo's rifle boomed from the top of the bank. The bear stumbled a little as the ball smashed into its chest. "Die, you son of a bitch!" Lorenzo yelled. "Why won't you die?"

Preacher dodged aside as the grizzly swiped at him with both paws. He avoided the first blow, but the second one clipped him on the left shoulder and sent him rolling again. Fiery pain rippled down Preacher's arm from the gashes torn by the creature's claws.

Summoning up all the strength he could, Preacher surged back to his feet. He wouldn't have time to reload once he pulled the triggers. He had to save his shots until he was sure they would do the most good.

The bear charged him. Preacher spun away from the attack. As the bear lumbered past him, Preacher took a chance.

He jumped on the bear's back.

He looped his left arm around the bear's neck and tried to get his legs around the creature's thick body. As he burrowed against the thick, rank-smelling fur, he struggled to get the barrel of the pistol in his right hand against the creature's ear—another way to its crazed brain. The bear flailed around so much the gun muzzle kept slipping away from where Preacher wanted it before the mountain man could pull the trigger.

A claw hooked in his buckskin shirt without puncturing his flesh, but it was enough of a grip for the bear to tear him loose and fling him away. Preacher went rolling helter-skelter across the ground just as Dog had a few moments earlier. When he came to a stop, he tried to force his muscles to work, but his brain was too stunned. He rose slightly but slipped down again.

The bear lumbered toward him like a furry avalanche, it's angry roar reminding Preacher of the *rumble* of an avalanche.

A shaggy gray shape darted between Preacher and the grizzly. Dog was back on his paws, and he planted himself firmly in the bear's path, snarling and growling his defiance as he got ready to protect his friend to his last breath and last drop of blood.

The bear stopped a few feet away and roared again. Preacher saw shadows moving and looked up to see Lorenzo standing at the edge of the wash, lining up a shot with his rifle.

"Don't!" Preacher croaked. "Hold your fire, Lorenzo!"

The old-timer didn't lower his rifle, but he didn't press the trigger, either. He looked at Preacher and said, "What do you mean, don't shoot?"

"You ain't gonna kill him. You're just gonna make him mad."

"Looks to me like he's already mad."

As if to prove it, the bear bellowed again.

Breathing hard, Preacher said, "Look at him.

He's tired and hurt bad. He don't want this fight any more than we do."

It was true. The bear was swaying more than normal when standing on its hind legs. The beady little eyes were dim with pain and confusion. Since it hadn't attacked again, Preacher wondered if he could wait it out. Maybe the bear was finally about to collapse and die.

Instead, the great beast abruptly wheeled around and started to move away. It dropped to all fours and picked up speed as it swung along the bottom of the arroyo.

"Preacher?" Lorenzo shouted. "What do I do now?"

"Let him go," Preacher muttered. "Just let him go." To the big cur, who was straining to bound after the grizzly, he added, "Dog, stay."

As Preacher pushed himself into a sitting position, the bear disappeared around a bend in the wash. Preacher struggled to his feet, retrieved his rifle, and managed to get hold of the rope, which still dangled into the wash from Horse's saddle.

"I'm gonna tie this around Dog," he said. "Horse can lift him outta this hole and then pull me out the same way."

"But the bear—"

"The bear's done for," Preacher said. "You reckon he'd do that if he didn't know it was over?"

Lorenzo scratched his jaw. "Well, I dunno. Maybe not. What're we gonna do?"

"We're gonna go back to the wagons, and tomorrow we're headin' to Santa Fe."

Preacher might not be a superstitious man, and he knew it was going to bother him to let the bear go after making that promise to Roland Bartlett, but he was beginning to think of the grizzly as a force of nature, just like the tornado that had almost wrecked the caravan earlier in the journey. Some things it was a waste of time to fight. A smart man picked his battles.

And God help him, Preacher was done with that one.

CHAPTER 19

Dog didn't care much for having the rope tied around him like a sling and being lifted out of the wash by Horse. He whined as he began to rise into the air.

"Up you go," Preacher told the big cur. Lorenzo waited atop the bank for him.

Preacher had checked Dog for injuries and found some deep scratches where the bear had grabbed him and flung him away. The mountain man had some medicine made from roots and herbs in his saddlebags that would help the injuries. He intended to rub a healthy dollop of the stuff on his left shoulder and arm where the bear had clawed him. That arm was already getting a little stiff.

Lorenzo pulled Dog in, got the rope off him, and tossed it back down to Preacher. "There you go," he called. "Now get outta that hole in the ground. I don't like this place. That bear might come back."

Preacher thought that was unlikely, but he didn't waste any time getting the rope fastened around him, tucking his rifle under his arm. Horse backed up, taking most of Preacher's weight as he climbed out of the wash.

"Looks like that varmint got you pretty good," Lorenzo said as he gestured toward Preacher's wounded shoulder. "Get that shirt off and we'll clean it up."

Using water from their canteens, Lorenzo got the blood washed away. Preacher saw that the scratches were deep enough to be gory and painful. He took the medicinal ointment from his saddle-bags and rubbed a handful of the black, foul-smelling stuff on the wounds, then gave Dog the same treatment.

"That'll help heal up them scratches?" Lorenzo asked.

Preacher nodded. "Injuns been usin' things like this for hundreds of years. They generally know what they're doin'."

"Didn't you tell me that some of 'em will chant songs and dance around and then claim it gave 'em some sort of magic that'll stop a rifle ball?"

"Well . . . I never said they got *ever'thing* right," Preacher drawled.

He pulled his ripped and bloodstained shirt back on and they mounted up. After taking a good look at the sky and judging how much daylight was left, Preacher said, "Let's ride along this wash a little farther. I want to see if that bear collapsed and died."

"You sure we got time?"

"I'm gonna take the time. I made a promise to Roland, and I intend to keep it if I can. I'd like to be able to tell him I saw that beast's carcass with my own eyes."

A short distance farther on, the arroyo branched out into a maze of gullies and little canyons. The tracks had petered out as the floor of the wash became rockier, so they couldn't be sure which way the bear had gone.

Preacher reined in and sighed. "Might as well head back to the springs," he told Lorenzo. "We don't have the time to waste lookin' for that ornery critter. It'd take a couple hours to search all them gullies and canyons."

"You figure he's dead or soon will be, anyway, don't you?" the old-timer asked.

Preacher nodded. "As many times as he's been shot, as much damage as we've done to him, I don't see how he could survive for much longer. He smelled like he was rottin' away from the inside out."

"Maybe that's why he's so damn ornery."

"Could be," Preacher agreed. He swung Horse's head around. "Let's go."

He wished he was as confident as he had sounded when he answered Lorenzo's question. The grizzly had to be dying. It simply *had* to be.

But Preacher sure wished he could have seen the thing's carcass.

The sun had set but the western sky was still awash with gold and orange light as the two riders approached the springs near the bend of the Cimarron. Preacher had been expecting to spot the wagons up ahead, but so far he hadn't seen them.

A vague uneasiness began to stir inside him. It was possible Roland had ordered the men to move the wagons to another location, but Preacher had told the young man to stay put at the springs. He couldn't think of any reason why Roland would have gone against that suggestion . . . unless they were trying to get away from trouble of some sort.

As they drew closer to the springs, Preacher could tell the wagons definitely weren't there. Lorenzo saw that as well and asked, "Where the hell did they go?"

"I don't know," Preacher said, "but I don't like it. Come on!"

He heeled Horse into a run. The big gray stallion responded instantly, pulling ahead of the mount carrying Lorenzo. Preacher pulled his rifle from its sheath as he galloped toward the springs.

A shot rang out from the scrubby trees along the river. The ball kicked up dust a considerable distance in front of Horse. Preacher was about to veer the stallion in that direction and return the fire when he heard a man's voice shouting, "Don't shoot! Don't shoot! It's Preacher!"

That was Roland Bartlett, Preacher realized. He headed for the trees, convinced something had gone wrong while he was gone.

By the time he reached the trees with Lorenzo trailing about fifty yards behind him, several men had emerged from their cover and were waiting for him. Preacher recognized them as some of the bullwhackers. They were grim-faced and carried their rifles. One of them had a bloody bandage tied around his arm, and another man sported a similar binding on his thigh. They had been in a fight, no doubt about that.

Roland limped out to meet Preacher as the mountain man swung down from Horse's back. He had a bandage tied around his right calf. His face was pale with pain.

"What happened here?" Preacher asked. "Where are the wagons?"

"Gone," Roland replied in a choked voice.

"I can see that, damn it. Who took 'em?" Preacher knew it probably hadn't been the Comanches. Indians didn't have any use for wagons or slow-moving oxen.

"It was that man Garity and the other thieves with him. They must have been following us, just waiting for a good chance to jump us again."

"Garity," Preacher said. The name left a bad taste in his mouth. "I knew him and his bunch might still be around here, but I figured it was more likely they'd gone on to Santa Fe or wherever the hell else it was they were headed."

Roland shook his head. "I got a good look at him. It was definitely Garity and his men. We tried to fight them off, but they hit us without any warning and killed several of the men before we knew what was going on. The rest of us were cut off from the wagons and had to retreat into these trees. Some of them kept us pinned down while the others hitched up the teams and got the wagons moving."

A chill went down Preacher's back as a thought occurred to him. "What about Casey?" he asked. "Was she hurt in the fightin'?"

"I don't know," Roland replied, his voice more

tortured than ever. "She was with the wagons. Garity . . . Garity took her with them."

Preacher went cold all over when he heard those words. Anger boiled up inside him. "What the hell were you doin'?" he demanded. "You were supposed to have guards posted, and you should've been with the wagons, not down here by the river!"

"I know," Roland said, sounding miserable. "But some of the men decided they wanted to wash off, and I thought it would be better if they did that in the river instead of the pool at the springs, and . . . and—"

Preacher stopped him with a sharp slashing motion of his hand. "That's enough," he said coldly. "It was a damn fool thing to do, and just the sort of chance Garity had been waitin' for, I reckon."

"I know." Roland's voice sounded dull and defeated as he nodded. "It's my fault." His head came up. "That's why I'm going after them. I'm going to get Casey and the wagons back. I want Lorenzo's horse."

"And leave me stuck out here?" Lorenzo asked. He snorted. "Not likely."

"Hold on," Preacher said. "These horses been travelin' all day already. They're in no shape to be rode all night. Anyway, there ain't much light left. How good are you at trackin' in the dark?"

Roland grimaced. "I'm not a tracker at all. You know that, Preacher."

"So you figured I'd go with you, right?"

"I supposed you'd want to help Casey as much as I do." Anger flared in the young man's voice as he went on, "Or do you not give a damn about her now that she's with me?"

"She ain't with you," Preacher pointed out. "She's with Garity. And you're damn right I want to help her. We can't do that by rushin' off, just the two of us."

Roland glared at him for a moment, then sighed. "You're right, of course. Garity has at least a dozen men. But what are we going to do?"

Preacher looked at the sky, where the last light of day was fading. "We'll stay here tonight and pick up their trail in the mornin'," he said. "Did you at least see which way they were headed when they left?"

"They were following the trail southwest."

Preacher nodded. "They're headin' for Santa Fe. Nobody there will know the wagons and the freight don't belong to them. They can sell 'em all off and make a killin', then take the money and light a shuck out of there before anybody figures out the deal was crooked." Preacher tugged on his earlobe. "Maybe we can go after the varmints tonight after all. When did the raid happen?"

"Around the middle of the day."

"So they've had half a day to get a lead on us," Preacher mused. "But even on foot, men can move faster than those oxen pullin' those heavy wagons. We can catch up to 'em before the night's over."

Roland shook his head. "Some of the men are hurt too bad to march like that."

"Then they'll stay here with a couple men to watch over 'em while the rest of us go after Garity."

"We'll be outnumbered."

"Not for long," Preacher said.

* * *

Lorenzo didn't like it, but Preacher asked him to stay behind to help guard the wounded men. The old-timer had been in the saddle practically all day and was worn out.

"The same thing is true of you," Lorenzo pointed out, "and you got clawed by that damn bear, to boot."

"Yeah, but I'm a heap younger than you," Preacher responded with a grin.

"You just want me to give up my horse so that young whippersnapper can use it."

"Roland's spoilin' for a fight. We'll see to it that he gets one."

Reluctantly, Lorenzo agreed. "Don't push that horse too hard. It's already been a long way today."

Preacher nodded. "We'll take it as easy as we can. Most of the time we won't be movin' any faster than those men can walk."

In addition to Preacher and Roland, eight men were in the party going after Garity and the rest of the outlaws. Each man was armed with a rifle and a knife, and a couple had pistols as well. It wasn't much of an army, Preacher thought, but it would have to do.

Starting out, Roland was the only one who rode, since he had an injured leg. Preacher walked alongside him, leading Horse. The other eight men followed behind them. The stars were out and provided enough light for Preacher to follow the well-defined wagon trail.

"What about the bear?" Roland asked after a few

minutes. "I saw that you were hurt. You must have found it."

"We did," Preacher said. "Dog and me both tangled with the varmint close up, and Lorenzo shot the blasted thing again."

"So you killed it?"

"Well . . . it was alive the last time we saw it, but as bad hurt as it was, it's bound to be dead by now."

"But you're not sure?" Roland persisted.

Preacher shrugged. "I wish I was."

He knew logically that the bear couldn't have survived for much longer after their encounter earlier that day . . . but he had thought that on other occasions, too, he reminded himself.

Ghost bear. Spirit bear. The words forced themselves into his brain. He shoved them right back out. The bear was flesh and blood. He had felt it, smelled it, wrestled with it. Like everything else flesh and blood, it could be killed.

But he had to admit, that particular bear had been damned stubborn about dying.

"I hope Casey's all right," Roland said. "I . . . I hate to think about what might be happening—"

"Then don't," Preacher said. "Think about what we're gonna do when we catch up to that bunch."

"What *are* we going to do? We can't just burst into their camp and start shooting. Casey might get hurt, and besides, they outnumber us, like I said before."

"I plan to do somethin' about that."

"What can one man do?"

Preacher smiled in the darkness. "I've slipped into and back out of more than one Injun camp, and take my word for it, the Blackfeet and the

Sioux and the Comanch' are a hell of a lot harder to sneak around than those outlaws will be. I plan to find out just where Casey is—maybe even get her out of there before the shootin' starts."

"That would be wonderful," Roland said. "She's already been through enough in her life."

"Told you about her life, did she?"

"She told me enough," Roland snapped. "I don't care about her past, if that's what you're talking about, Preacher. It's a closed book as far as I'm concerned."

"That's a good idea," Preacher said with a curt nod. "I'd keep it that way, if I was you."

They dropped the subject of Casey, which was just fine with Preacher. He didn't know how much of the truth she had told Roland about her past, and he didn't care. That was between the two of them.

Preacher called a halt as the moon rose to let the men and horses rest for a few minutes. Later, around midnight, he estimated, they stopped again. The moon and stars wheeled through their courses in the sky as the party trudged on. Preacher could sense the exhaustion in the men.

Finally, he held up a hand and called softly, "Hold on. We'll wait here a bit."

"Don't we need to keep going?" Roland asked. "Casey's still up there somewhere. They can't be too far ahead of us now."

Preacher nodded. "That's what I want to find out. You fellas stay here. I'm goin' ahead to take a look around." He added, "Don't budge from this spot until I get back."

"We won't," Roland snapped defensively. He

knew their failure to do that at the springs had contributed heavily to the disaster that had befallen them.

Taking Dog with him but leaving the stallion behind, Preacher disappeared into the night.

Chapter 20

Time and experience and some good teachers among the Crow and other friendly tribes had given Preacher the ability to move with almost complete silence when he wanted to. He used that ability in the wee hours of the morning since midnight was long past. It was the best time to slip into an enemy camp, when sleep lay heavily on most of them.

Garity and his men were confident of their ability to protect themselves, so they had built a good-sized campfire when they stopped for the night. Preacher spotted the glowing embers of it when he was still several hundred yards away. When his keen eyes saw the orange coals, he stopped to size up the situation.

Now that he knew where to look, he could see the light-colored canvas covers of the wagons. The vehicles had been pulled off the trail a short distance and arranged in a circle. Garity knew enough to do that, anyway.

Preacher moved closer. When he was within a

hundred yards of the wagons, he dropped to a knee and put an arm around Dog's shaggy neck.

"Stay," he whispered in the big cur's ear.

Dog whined. He wanted to go with Preacher. The mountain man repeated, "Stay."

Dog wouldn't like it, but he would wait there until Preacher either returned or summoned him.

His boot moccasins made no sound on the hard ground as Preacher catfooted toward the wagons. He had left the long-barreled flintlock behind with Dog. It was too awkward to carry around while he was trying to be stealthy. He had his pistols, but if all went as he hoped, he wouldn't need them.

More important, he had his knife. It was the blade that was going to come in for some work tonight.

Already in a low crouch, he dropped to his knees and then stretched out on his belly to cover the last fifty yards in a crawl. Garity surely had sense enough to have posted some sentries. As he came closer, Preacher caught a whiff of pipe smoke, confirming his hunch. He followed his nose until he spotted a dark shape leaning against one of the wagon wheels.

Grinning to himself in the darkness, Preacher began crawling in a wide circle that would allow him to come up behind the guard. He didn't get in any hurry. Rushing things in a job like that could get a man killed. Minutes stretched by with Preacher moving only a few inches at a time.

Eventually, he was where he wanted to be: close enough to reach out and touch the guard as he silently rose to his feet. The man was still puffing on his pipe, blissfully unaware that he had only seconds to live. He had no idea what was about to happen until Preacher's left arm came around him and clamped down on his throat like an iron bar, stifling any sound and making the guard spit out his pipe.

By the time it hit the ground, the cold steel of Preacher's knife was buried in the man's back, the tip sliding between the ribs and delving deep to find the heart. The guard jerked a little but didn't struggle as he died.

Preacher pulled the knife out, lowered the corpse to the ground, and wiped the blood off the blade onto the man's shirt. He took the pistol he found behind the guard's belt, tucking it behind his own belt, but left the rifle.

Soundlessly, the mountain man moved around the outside of the circled wagons until he found another guard. That man died without any commotion as well, and Preacher commandeered another pistol. When it came time for a battle, his forces would be at least a little better armed than when they had started out.

Some of the thieves were sleeping under the wagons. Preacher found a vehicle where the ground underneath it was empty and crawled through the space into the circle. He lifted his head and studied the wagons as best he could. The moon was lower and the light wasn't as good. After a moment, he spotted a man standing guard *inside* the circle, next to the tailgate of one of the wagons.

Preacher was willing to bet Casey was inside that wagon and the sentry was there to prevent her from getting away.

He could do something about that, Preacher thought, and was about to crawl over to the wagon and get started on it, when some instinct warned him. A second later, he heard a swift padding of feet, followed by a shrill cry and the explosion of a gun.

Preacher jerked to his feet as shadows leaped through the night, hurdling wagon tongues and charging into the circle as they yipped. His brain worked swiftly and he realized the wagons were under attack by Indians. He suspected they were Comanches, and the possibility suggested itself they might be the remnants of Lame Buffalo's party, reinforced by more warriors from the same band!

Preacher didn't really care who the Indians were. They would kill him just like they would kill every other white man with the wagons if they could.

And Casey, too, he thought as he sprinted toward the wagon where he thought she was. He had to take advantage of the distraction to get her out of there. He couldn't afford to wait any longer.

The man guarding the wagon threw his rifle to his shoulder as a pair of the attacking Indians charged at him. The weapon boomed and sent one of the warriors flying backward, but the other one lunged forward and drove his lance into the guard's body. The guard screamed as the sharp-tipped weapon tore all the way through him and emerged from his back to hit one of the sideboards of the wagon behind him. For a second the dying man was pinned there until the warrior yanked the lance free with a whoop.

He was turning away from the crumpling guard when Preacher reached him. The mountain man's hands locked on the bloody shaft of the lance and wrenched it out of the warrior's hands. Preacher brought it up in a flash and thrust the tip into the

Indian's throat. He felt it grate against the upper end of the man's spine as blood gushed from the ripped-open throat.

Preacher shoved the dying warrior aside. "Casey!" he called as he leaped to the back of the wagon. "Casey, you in there?"

He heard a shocked gasp. Then a familiar voice cried, "Preacher! Preacher, is that you?"

He used his left hand to rip aside one of the canvas flaps while his right pulled a pistol from behind his belt. Gunshots were blasting all over the camp. He didn't have to worry about being silent anymore.

An arrow whistled past his head. He turned to see where it had come from and spotted one of the warriors trying to fit another arrow onto his bowstring. Leveling the pistol, Preacher pulled the trigger and sent a ball slamming into the man's body. The impact of the shot made the warrior drop his bow and arrow and spun him off his feet.

"Casey, come on!" Preacher said. "We gotta get out of here!"

"I can't!" she said despairingly. "I'm tied up."

Muttering a curse under his breath, Preacher clambered into the wagon. It was black as pitch in there, so he had to fumble around to find her, following her voice as she said, "Here! I'm here!"

He reached down, touched the fabric of her dress, and pulled his knife. Finding her ankles first and working carefully by feel so he wouldn't cut her, he worked the blade under the ropes binding her and severed them with a hard tug on the razor-sharp blade.

Whether her hands were tied in front of her or

behind her, he could deal with later, he decided. He sheathed the knife and put his arms around her, lifting her to her feet. Her wrists were bound in front of her, he discovered as she sagged against him.

"You all right?" he asked.

She nodded. He felt the movement of her head against his chest. "Yes, they didn't hurt me . . . too bad."

He wasn't sure what she meant by that, but again, it could wait until later when they were safely away from the battle raging outside the wagon. Shots continued to fill the night, along with shouted curses and the shrill cries of the attacking Indians.

He led her to the back of the wagon. "I'm gonna put you on the ground," he told her. "Get to the trail and run as hard as you can back the way we came from. Roland and some of the men are waitin' back there a ways."

Preacher heard the genuine concern in her voice as she asked, "Is he all right?"

"He caught a bullet in his leg, but he'll be all right. I reckon he'll be a lot better once he sees you again. Now go!"

He put his hands under her arms and swung her out of the wagon. She stumbled a little as her feet hit the ground.

"I'll be right behind you!" he said, then leaped out of the vehicle.

Something crashed into him just as he landed. The collision was enough to knock him off his feet. A weight came down on top of him, and foul breath gusted in his face. He was reminded of wrestling with the bear, but it was no giant grizzly trying to kill him. His hands grabbed bare flesh slick with sweat and grease, and he knew he was fighting with one of the warriors.

Preacher's eyes caught a glimpse of starlight winking on steel. He jerked his head aside. The knife skimmed past his cheek, leaving a scratch behind as it buried itself in the ground. Preacher brought an elbow up under the man's chin, catching him hard in the throat. At the same time, Preacher rolled to the side and threw the warrior off him.

His hand snatched up the knife the man had dropped and brought it around in a looping blow that plunged the blade into the man's chest. The warrior spasmed, his back arching up off the ground as he pawed at the knife's handle for a second. Then he sagged back in death.

Preacher scrambled up and looked around for Casey. He didn't see her, but he hadn't heard her cry out while he was struggling with the Indian, so he hoped she had gotten away and was running back up the Santa Fe Trail toward Roland and the other men. He headed in that direction, but his way was suddenly blocked by a pair of warriors.

One of them thrust a lance at him. He dived under it, rolled again, and lifted his leg to smash his heel into the man's groin in a savage kick. The Indian howled in pain as Preacher's foot crushed his privates and sent him staggering backward as he doubled over in agony.

Preacher flung himself aside as the second man jabbed at him. He caught hold of the lance and used it to brace himself as he pulled himself upright. He and the warrior panted in each other's faces as they struggled over the weapon.

Preacher's left shoulder and arm hurt like blazes.

The pain stole some of Preacher's usual strength in that arm, and he felt his grip on the lance start to slip.

Knowing he couldn't afford to weaken any more, Preacher used his legs to shove his opponent backward, then let go of the lance. The move gave him just enough time to pull one of the loaded pistols at his belt and cock it before the Indian caught his balance and lunged forward again with the lance. The tip landed in the space between Preacher's arm and his side. He fired the pistol at point-blank range as he thrust the muzzle at the warrior's chest. The shot blasted the Indian off his feet and left him lying on the ground, gasping out his life through the big, blood-bubbling hole in his chest.

A hand grasped Preacher's arm. He started to turn, intending to club the man who'd grabbed him with the empty pistol in his hand, but before he could launch the blow, the man said, "Good job! You blew the hell out of that redskin! We got the bastards on the run!"

Preacher recognized the voice. It was Garity himself, the leader of the outlaws, who had grabbed him, thinking Preacher was one of them.

At the same time Garity realized his mistake. He yelled a curse and swung a punch at Preacher's head. Preacher jerked free from Garity's grip and ducked under the outlaw's fist.

"Help!" Garity shouted. "Over here! Over here!"

Preacher hooked a hard left into Garity's belly and the man doubled over. Knowing the pistol in his hand was empty Garity straightened and slashed at Preacher's head with the barrel. The gun raked across Preacher's forehead, opening up a cut that leaked blood into the mountain man's eyes.

Garity had been right about the Indians: the ones who were left alive were retreating, and the sound of gunfire was dying out around the camp. Garity's men were able to hear his shouts. As they neared, Garity bellowed, "It's Preacher! Get him!"

Preacher had one loaded pistol left. He jerked it out. As he pointed it at Garity and pressed the trigger, someone tackled him from behind around the knees. His legs collapsed underneath him and the shot went wild. Someone else hit him and knocked him the rest of the way to the ground.

Fists and feet hammered into him. He reached up and grabbed the leg of a man trying to kick him. With a heave, Preacher sent the man flying into a couple of the others. All of them went down in a tangle.

At least half a dozen more of Garity's men surrounded him. They were liable to stomp him to death if he didn't get away. Hooking a foot behind a man's knee and sweeping his legs out from under him, Preacher tried to bolt up through the momentary gap in the circle of would-be killers surrounding him.

The opening was too small. One of the men got an arm around Preacher's neck and held on for dear life, squeezing tighter and tighter. Two men began pounding Preacher's ribs. Pain shot through him with each blow. Red rockets went off behind his eyes as the lack of air began to make everything spin crazily around him. The world seemed to be receding.

But he heard Garity say, "Don't kill him! Damn it, I don't want that bastard dead yet!"

That was the last thing Preacher knew except pain. A crazy blood-red whirling filled his head, then utter blackness.

CHAPTER 21

The first thing Preacher was aware of was light, bright and searing against his eyelids. Then pain came flooding in along with the radiance.

But he was alive, and while that surprised him at first, a moment later he began to remember how Garity had said he wanted Preacher kept alive.

That beat the alternative, Preacher supposed, but under the circumstances he wasn't sure how long it was going to last. He hurt like hell, from head to toe, and the heat that enveloped him felt like it was about to cook him. He was frying in his own juices.

He tried to force his eyes open but couldn't do it. The light was just too bright. Preacher knew it had to be the sun beating down on him. No campfire had ever been painfully brilliant.

Gradually he became aware that he was lying on his back with his arms stretched out on either side of him. His legs were painfully extended, too, and couldn't move. Once he had realized that, it wasn't much of a stretch to figure out he had been staked out on the ground.

He turned his head a little, though he hadn't really been aware of doing it. Something moved between him and the sun, blocking the bright light and searing heat.

"You're awake, are you, Preacher?" a mocking voice asked.

Garity. Preacher recognized the man's tone. Since Garity knew he had regained consciousness, there was no point in trying to conceal the fact.

Preacher managed to open his eyes and found himself staring up at Garity, although he couldn't see the man as anything except a black silhouette with the sun behind his head, radiating redly around it.

"I was beginnin' to think the boys were too rough on you, even though I told 'em to take it easy," Garity went on. "I'm glad to see you're still alive. I want your dyin' to take a long time."

Preacher didn't say anything. His lips were blistered, and his mouth felt like it had a wool sock in it. After a moment, he realized that sock was his tongue.

Garity turned his head and said to someone else, "Bring her over here."

Preacher's heart sank. The only "her" he knew of out there was Casey. He had hoped she had gotten away. Evidently that wasn't the case.

It was confirmed a few seconds later when she said, "Oh, my God, Preacher, I'm sorry. When I saw you weren't behind me, I . . . I turned back to see what had happened. I should have kept going."

He managed to husk, "Y-yeah . . . I reckon . . . you should have . . ."

"It wouldn't have mattered," Garity said. "As soon as I realized you were gone, I would've come after you and found you, darlin'. You're gonna be with me all the way to Santa Fe." He paused. "I know a fella who owns a whorehouse there. He'll pay me a tidy sum for a pretty little yeller-haired gal like you."

"Go to hell," Casey spat at him. "You'll have to kill me first."

"That's mighty big talk for a gal who can't do a damned thing to back it up." Garity laughed. "You might as well face it. From here on out, you do what I say." He shifted so the fierce sunlight slammed into Preacher's eyes again. "And right now I say you're gonna stand there and watch while Preacher dies, no matter how long it takes. And it's gonna take a *long* time."

"You bastard!" Casey's hands were still tied in front of her, but her feet were loose. She lunged at Garity and raised her hands as she tried to claw at his face. Preacher couldn't see it, but he could hear enough to guess what was going on.

Garity shoved her away with a laugh. "Hang on to her, boys," he ordered. "Make sure she keeps her eyes open."

"Let me go!" Casey cried. "Let me go, damn you!"

The men ignored her. She started to sob.

Preacher wanted to tell her it was all right, but he couldn't find the strength to form the words.

Despite the ordeal he was being forced to endure, his brain was still working, and one thought was crystal clear: Garity hadn't said anything about

Roland Bartlett and the other men from the wagon train.

That could mean Garity didn't know about them. If he wasn't aware Roland and the others were nearby, there might still be a chance to turn the tables on him.

That meant waiting for Roland to do something. Obviously hours had passed since the battle at the camp. Daylight had come again. From the angle of the sun shining down into his face Preacher guessed that the morning was fairly well advanced. Roland and the other men were close enough to have heard the shooting going on the night before. Yet they hadn't come to find out what was going on.

Preacher's already cracked and bleeding lips cracked a little more as he smiled faintly. He had told Roland to stay put. By God, it looked like the boy was going to do as he was told!

"Preacher . . ." Casey said tentatively. "Preacher, what are you smiling about?"

"Nothin'," he told her. Roland was their only hope. If that wasn't enough to make a man smile, he didn't know what was.

After a few minutes, he asked, "Casey, where are we?"

"Shut up," one of the men left to guard her said. "Garity didn't say nothin' about lettin' the two of you talk."

"He didn't say we couldn't, either," Casey argued. "Preacher's dying anyway. What difference does it make if he knows where he is?"

The men didn't answer for a moment, then one of them said, "I don't reckon it makes a damn bit of difference. Go ahead, tell him."

"We're the same place we were last night," Casey said. "Garity decided not to move the wagons just yet. He said he could afford to wait"—she choked up for a second—"to wait until you were dead."

"What about . . . them Injuns?"

"They're all dead except for a few who got away."

"I wonder . . . if it was that same bunch . . . of Comanch'."

"It must have been," she said. "They could have been following us, waiting for a chance to settle the score for what happened before. They might not have known that Garity stole the wagons. They must have thought Mr. Bartlett was still in charge."

Casey's statement agreed with the vague theory that had formed in Preacher's mind. The caravan had been jinxed from the start. Trailed by the Indians, trailed by Garity's outlaws, trailed by that damned bear . . .

Maybe he was the one who was jinxed, he thought. He had always had a way of attracting trouble, ever since he had left the family farm as a youngster and headed west. Maybe it hadn't been so lucky for the Bartletts and the others that he and Lorenzo and Casey had thrown in with them after all.

Leeman Bartlett hadn't been lucky, that was for sure. He had met a gruesome death, and several of the other men from the caravan had crossed the divide as well.

"Hoodoo," Preacher murmured. "I'm a hoodoo . . ."

"What are you saying, Preacher?" Casey asked. "I couldn't understand you."

"Nothin'," he breathed as he kept his eyes

screwed tightly shut against the sunlight. "Nothin' at all . . ."

The minutes were like hours, the hours like years. To Preacher it felt like he had been baking out there for all eternity. Given the sort of life he had led, all the men he had killed, he figured there was a good chance he would wind up shaking hands with the Devil when he died, but that day felt like he was getting a head start on Hell.

To make matters worse, ants found those blood-crusted wounds on his shoulder and arm and started chewing on them. Preacher felt the cords standing out in his neck as he strained and struggled to keep the cries of pain bottled up inside him. He didn't want to give Garity that much satisfaction.

At one point, Casey burst out, "For God's sake, can't you see how bad he's suffering? At least let me brush those ants off him."

"Garity wants him to suffer," one of the guards replied. "As a matter of fact, Dumars, why don't you fetch him? I got a hunch he'd like to see this."

"Can you watch the woman on your own?" the man called Dumars asked.

The other guard chuckled. "I hope to smile I can. I can watch her just fine. A little scar never bothered me none."

Preacher heard the footsteps as Dumars walked off. He came back a few minutes later with Garity, who let out a booming laugh when he saw the ants swarming on Preacher's shoulder and arm.

"Just when you figure things can't get any better," Garity said. "We got us a pretty little honey to keep us company on the way to Santa Fe, we're gonna be rich men when we get there and sell those wagons and all that freight, and we got Preacher dyin' to entertain us in the meantime." He leaned over the mountain man, blocking the sun from Preacher's face again. "How do you like those little critters, Preacher? Makes dyin' a mite more interestin', don't it?"

Preacher's eyelids flickered open. He whispered, "Why don't you go to—"

Before he could finish the curse, one of the other men broke in to say, "Somebody's comin', Garity!"

"Who the hell's that?" Garity muttered.

"Don't reckon we have to worry about him. It's only one man."

"Yeah, but he looks familiar," Garity said. "I think it's one of those fellas we took these wagons away from."

Preacher couldn't figure out why one man would be approaching the outlaw camp. Maybe one of the bullwhackers who were with Roland had slipped away from the others and planned on trying to join up with Garity's bunch.

Garity strode past Preacher. The shadow he cast was a blessed relief from the searing sun, but it lasted only a heartbeat and then was gone.

"He's stoppin', whoever he is," one of the other men said.

Garity raised his voice in a shout. "What do you want, mister?"

"I want to make a trade," came the reply, in a voice Preacher recognized.

Roland.

Casey had recognized the young man, too. "Oh,

my God," she said softly. "Doesn't he know that he's going to get himself killed?"

"What sort of trade?" Garity yelled.

"I want Preacher and the girl!"

That brought a laugh from Garity. "What in hell makes you think you can have 'em?" he asked.

"Like I said, I'll trade."

"You got nothin' left to trade for 'em," Garity replied scornfully. "We already took all your wagons and freight."

"But you don't have this money belt," Roland called back. "Two thousand dollars, Garity! It's yours if you send Casey and Preacher out to me! It's the last of my father's life savings, but I don't care."

Preacher wondered if Roland was telling the truth. He hadn't heard anything about a money belt with two thousand dollars in it, but on the other hand, neither Roland nor Leeman Bartlett had had any reason to tell him about it. Roland's offer to buy his and Casey's freedom might be genuine.

On the other hand, Roland could be running a bluff and trying to pull a trick of some kind. It probably didn't matter much either way, Preacher thought. Garity wasn't going to turn them loose. He was having too much fun tormenting Preacher, and he had plans for Casey. He might pretend to agree, in hopes of luring Roland closer just in case the young man really did have the money.

"Bring that belt on over here," Garity called. "I got to see the money before I make a deal."

"No!" Roland shouted back instantly. "Send Preacher and Casey to me. Don't come after them. I'll leave the money where you can find it."

Garity laughed again. "You damn fool! You expect me to trust you? You're one man, and you're on foot. You ain't got a chance." He turned his head and snapped orders. "Go get him and bring him to me. Get the horses and run him down, but don't kill him!"

"Roland, get out of here!" Casey screamed. "Go!"

"Too late, girl!" Garity said. "He ain't gettin' away!"

Casey ignored him and screamed again, "Roland, run!"

Several men on horseback pounded past the spot where Preacher was staked out. He wished he could see what was going on. He tried to lift his head but was too weak.

Casey stumbled forward and dropped to her knees sobbing, putting her in Preacher's line of sight. "What's . . . happenin'?" he asked her painfully.

"Roland's trying to . . . to run away," she sobbed. "But he's not going to make it."

Preacher heard excited whooping from the men who were chasing Roland on horseback. They regarded it as a game.

The next moment a sudden flurry of gunshots erupted. For a second he thought the men were shooting at Roland, despite Garity's orders not to kill the young man, but then Preacher realized the shots were coming from a different direction.

"What the hell!" Garity yelled.

Casey twisted around to look. "Wh-what is it?" Preacher asked her.

A look of hope appeared on Casey's face. "It's

the bullwhackers from the wagons," she told Preacher. "They're attacking Garity and his men!"

Preacher realized that Roland's offer to buy his and Casey's freedom had indeed been a trick. Roland had distracted Garity and his men and caused Garity to split his forces. The bullwhackers must have crawled around to the other side of the outlaw camp to launch their attack. It would have taken hours for them to get into position, but the plan stood at least a slim chance of working.

"Get back here!" Garity bellowed at the men who had gone after Roland. He started to run past Preacher, then stopped abruptly and pulled a pistol from his belt and pointed it at the mountain man. "This ends here and now, damn you."

He wasn't paying any attention to Casey. Still on her knees, she twisted and threw herself at Garity's legs. The unexpected impact jostled him just enough that when the pistol in his hand exploded, the ball slammed into the ground beside Preacher's ear, throwing dirt in his face rather than splattering his brains across the sand.

Casey dropped her shoulder and lunged at Garity's knees.

"You bitch!" he yelled as he went over backward. He slashed at Casey's head with the empty gun but missed.

Preacher blinked the grit out of his eyes and turned his head enough to see the deadly struggle going on. Casey scrambled to Garity's body and plucked the knife from his belt. She lifted it and tried to plunge the blade into his chest, but he rolled aside. The knife buried itself in the ground instead. Garity brought an elbow around and caught Casey in the jaw with it. The blow sent her sprawling.

The roar of gunfire continued. Preacher groaned in frustration. Every instinct shouted for him to get in the middle of the fight, but sturdy rawhide thongs bound him to the stakes driven into the ground. He couldn't move, no matter how hard he strained against them.

Only a few feet away, Garity heaved up onto his knees. He threw himself on Casey and groped at her neck, obviously intending to strangle the life out of her. Garity's face was red with rage. At that moment, he didn't care how much he could make by selling her to a whorehouse in Santa Fe. He wanted to kill her.

Preacher saw Garity's fingers lock around Casey's throat and knew she had only seconds to live. Every bit of resolve, every ounce of strength he could possibly summon up, he channeled into his left leg. The life he had lived had hardened Preacher's body, but more important than that, it had given him an iron will. He used that iron will as he heaved against the stake holding his leg.

And it moved.

Only slightly at first, but Preacher felt it shift. With a loud groan, he heaved again, and this time, the stake pulled free.

Preacher forced his muscles to work as he drew up his leg and then lashed out with it, slamming a kick with his bare foot into the middle of Garity's back. It broke his chokehold on Casey's throat and knocked him forward over her. Gasping for air, she had the presence of mind to snatch the pistol Garity had dropped on the ground. It was empty, but she grasped the barrel with both hands and swung the pistol like a club, slamming it into the side of Garity's head above the ear. Garity collapsed, half on top of her.

She shoved him aside and struggled out from under him. She looked like she wanted to keep hitting Garity with the pistol until his head was smashed to bits, but she dropped the gun and grabbed the knife. She swung around and started sawing at Preacher's bonds.

His hands came free, then his other leg. His hands were numb from being tied so tightly. He flexed his fingers as Casey helped him sit up.

"We've got to get out of here," she said. "Can you stand up?"

Preacher could see the battle continued around the wagons. Clouds of powdersmoke rolled thickly. The roar of shots mingled with shouted curses.

With Casey's help, he struggled to get to his feet. His legs wouldn't support him. She cried out as she strained to keep him upright. "Roland!" she called. "Roland, help!"

So Roland was still alive. Preacher was glad to hear that. The men Garity had sent after him must have turned back to the wagons when the shooting started.

The young man ran up to them and took hold of Preacher's other arm. "I've got him!" he said. "Casey, are you all right?"

"I'm fine, but we have to get away," she told him.

Concentrating on helping Preacher, they didn't

see Garity getting to his feet, but the mountain man did. He rasped, "Look out . . . Garity . . ."

Roland let go of Preacher's arm, reaching for the pistol behind his belt as he turned toward Garity. He was too late. In Garity's hand was a flintlock derringer he'd taken from inside his buckskins. He thrust it out in front of him and pulled the trigger as Casey cried, "No!"

Smoke and flame erupted from the derringer's muzzle. Preacher heard the ball thud into flesh, saw Roland stagger and fall. Casey let go of Preacher and launched herself at Garity again.

He met her with a vicious backhand that cracked across her face and sent her spinning off her feet.

Preacher fought to stay upright. He was weak and didn't have a weapon, but he would fight Garity with his bare hands if that was all he could do. He would fight to the last breath, too, and it looked like it might come to that. The shooting around the wagons was beginning to die down. Preacher knew from the grin that stretched across Garity's face that the bullwhackers hadn't won.

"You've caused me a hell of a lot of trouble, Preacher," Garity said. The insane rage that had filled the man earlier had faded. His eyes were filled with a colder, even more diabolical fury. "But you'll pay for it," Garity went on. "Damned if you won't."

Preacher took an unsteady step toward the man and clenched his fists. "Go ahead and . . . get it over with," he rasped.

"Not yet," Garity said. He looked past Preacher and nodded.

It was an old trick . . . but it wasn't always a trick. Preacher heard a heavy step behind him and tried to turn, but before he could move something crashed into the back of his head. For the second time in less than twelve hours, he was sent plunging into a black oblivion.

CHAPTER 22

It was a damn good thing he had a thick skull, Preacher thought as consciousness seeped back into his head. If he didn't, his brains would be scrambled good and proper by now.

Maybe they are and you just don't know it, he told himself.

He saw light and felt heat, but it wasn't the same as before. The glow that penetrated his closed eyelids danced and flickered, and the heat wasn't steady.

He was close to a fire.

And he was bound again, but not staked out on the ground. He was upright. When he shifted as much as the ropes around his arms would allow, he felt a rough surface scrape his back. After a moment he figured out that his wrists were tied together behind his back, and another rope wound around his torso binding him to what felt like a wagon wheel.

It was a wagon wheel, he saw when he forced his eyes open. He was tied to the front wheel, and

Casey was bound similarly to the rear wheel on the same side of the vehicle. Preacher looked past her and saw Roland Bartlett tied to another wagon. The left shoulder of his shirt was stained with blood where Garity had shot him with the derringer, and his head sagged forward. He was unconscious, but his chest rose and fell, so he was still alive.

They were on the inside of the circle. Preacher could see several other men were tied to wagon wheels, too. He recognized them as some of the bullwhackers he had left with Roland. They were the survivors from the bunch that had launched the attack on the outlaw camp while Roland provided a distraction.

Preacher wondered where Dog and Horse were. Probably within earshot, knowing his old friends. He figured they would come if he whistled to summon them, but that would expose them to danger at the hands of the outlaws.

Night had fallen. Preacher realized he had lost most of an entire day. The oxen were crowded over to one side of the area inside the circle of wagons, and a big fire had been built on the side closest to the wagons where the prisoners were bound. The outlaws were gathered around it.

One of the men had noticed Preacher lift his head. The man nudged Garity and jerked his chin toward the wagons. Garity looked around, saw that Preacher was awake, and grinned. He ambled over, carrying a jug. Preacher could smell the rotgut whiskey on Garity's breath, even from several feet away.

"Damn, you got a hard head!" Garity said, unknowingly echoing the same thought that had gone through Preacher's brain a few moments earlier. "I thought sure you was dead this time."

"Not even close," Preacher rasped, which was sort of a lie. He felt at least half dead.

But that meant he was still half alive, too, and that half was a hell of a lot stubborner than the dead part.

"I'll bet you're wonderin' why I didn't just go ahead and kill you."

"I don't waste my time wondering about what loco snakes like you do or don't do," Preacher said.

Garity went on as if Preacher hadn't said anything. "I'm tired of havin' to worry about you people poppin' up to cause trouble for me. Now that I've got you all here, I'm gonna finish you off once and for all."

Garity didn't know it, but he was wrong. Lorenzo and the bullwhackers who had been wounded too badly to come along on the rescue mission were still back at the springs. But it didn't really matter, Preacher knew. Those men wouldn't be able to help him and the other prisoners.

Garity waved a hand. "We got you all lined up here like targets, so that's what we're gonna do. We're gonna have some target practice." Garity stepped closer and poked a hard, bony finger against Preacher's bare chest. "Startin' with you, you son of a bitch. We're gonna shoot away little pieces of you and see how long we can keep you alive."

"What about the girl?" Preacher asked.

Before Garity could answer, Casey said hotly, "You might as well go ahead and kill me, too. I won't cooperate with you."

Garity leered at her. "You go ahead and fight all you want to, darlin'. Just makes it that much sweeter for me, and I'll bet most of the boys here feel the same way. The ones in Santa Fe will, too."

"I'll kill you," Casey said in a low, threatening voice. "You'll never be able to turn your back on me, Garity. You'll never be able to close your eyes. Because I'll find a way to kill you."

"I'd like to see you try, honey."

"But you don't have to worry about that," Casey went on. "I'll make a deal with you."

Garity shook his head. "You got nothin' to bargain with."

"You don't think so? Leave Preacher, Roland, and the other men alive. Tomorrow morning you can leave them tied up so it'll take them all day to get loose. By then you'll be far enough down the trail that they'll never catch up to you. If you do that"—Casey swallowed hard—"I'll make it worth your while. I give you my word on that."

"What can you do that'd make it worth my while?"

"I worked in a whorehouse from the time I was sixteen," Casey said with a defiant jut of her chin. "I promise you, Garity, I know some tricks that'll surprise even a man like you."

Garity looked at her and chortled. "You think so? You make it mighty temptin'."

Roland's head had started to lift during the last exchange. He heard enough of it, and understood enough, to prompt him to call out shakily, "N-no, Casey! Don't!"

"Shut up, mister," Garity snapped. "This is between me and this little trollop." He looked at Casey again and went on, "I'll admit you got me curious, but it ain't enough. I don't want no more trouble, so we're gonna just go ahead and shoot these other fellas. If I have to knock you out to get what I want from you, that's all right."

The oxen began to shift around nervously. Preacher noticed that and frowned. Something was bothering them, and it took a lot to spook those massive, stolid beasts. He peered through the gaps between the wagons, searching the night, but it was hard to see anything in the thick darkness, especially since his sight had been compromised by the bright flames of the campfire. He drew in a deep breath, thinking he might catch a whiff of a particular scent, but the smell of the woodsmoke covered up everything except the whiskey fumes Garity was breathing toward him from only a few feet away.

In fact, Garity lifted the jug just then and asked, "You want a drink, Preacher? One last drink before we start shootin' you to pieces?"

"I wouldn't drink after you if that was the last jug of corn squeezin's on earth," Preacher answered with a glare.

"I got news for you." Garity laughed. "As far as you're concerned, this *is* the last jug of corn squeezin's on earth! Because you're gonna be dead in a little while."

Preacher looked at the way the oxen had started tossing their heads around a little. Even though the possibility that had occurred to him was so far-fetched it was hard to believe, he took the chance anyway.

What did he have to lose?

"You'd better not shoot me," he said. "You'll be mighty sorry if you do."

"I don't think so," Garity responded. "Why in the hell would you say that?"

"Because if you kill me," Preacher said, "the spirit of my brother the bear is gonna come after you and tear you apart."

Garity and the outlaws stared at him. "Your brother the bear?" Garity repeated. "What in blazes are you talkin' about?"

"It's true," Preacher insisted. "Me and the grizzly bear are brothers. He's my totem animal, as the Injuns would say. He follows me around and protects me."

"And you had the gall to call me loco! That's the craziest thing I ever heard."

"If you don't believe me, go ahead and shoot me," Preacher said calmly. "The spirit bear won't just get you, though." He raised his voice as he looked around at the other outlaws and went on, "He'll come in here and kill all the rest of your men, too. Rip 'em into little pieces, that's what he'll do. If you don't believe me, ask them." He jerked his head toward Casey and Roland and the other prisoners. "They've all seen it with their own eyes."

"It's true," Casey said quickly. "The biggest bear I've ever seen in my life. It's terribly ferocious, and . . . and it follows Preacher around!"

She wasn't stretching the truth by much, Preacher thought. The bear had certainly seemed to be following him for hundreds of miles.

"I saw it," Roland put in. "The thing is a monster, and you can't kill it. Before we knew about its connection to Preacher, we shot it again and again, and it just kept coming. It . . . it killed my father."

Roland's voice broke, and there was no doubting his sincerity. He and Casey had caught on so quickly to what Preacher was doing. Several of the bull-whackers chimed in as well, telling Garity how fierce and massive the beast was.

They probably thought Preacher was stalling for time, clinging to life any way he could for as long as he could, just as he had done all those years ago when the Blackfeet took him prisoner and planned to burn him at the stake.

But there was a big difference. Preacher was stalling, sure, but he was also waiting to see if his crazy hunch might be true. No reason why it shouldn't be, he told himself. The oxen were nervous . . . and Garity's men were starting to get that way, too. He saw the furtive, worried looks they exchanged with each other.

"There's only one way you can kill me and keep the spirit bear from seekin' revenge," Preacher said.

"Yeah? How's that?" Garity asked with a sneer.

"In a fair fight. Turn me loose and you and me can settle this man to man, Garity. If I die fightin', it'll be an honorable death and the ghost bear won't have to avenge me."

Garity shook his head. "That ain't gonna happen."

One of his men spoke up. "Why not, Garity? You said yourself that Preacher's half dead. Hell, you can finish him off easy."

The other men nodded in agreement.

"Damn it, have you forgot who's givin' the orders here?" Garity snapped at them.

"Their lives are ridin' on it, too," Preacher said. "The ghost bear will kill 'em all."

"Shut the hell up about some stupid ghost bear!" Garity roared. "There ain't no such thing!"

"Then go ahead and shoot me," Preacher challenged. "See what happens."

Garity glowered at him for a long moment, then muttered, "Son of a bitch." He drew the knife at his belt and used it to point at two of his men. "Point your rifles at him while I'm cuttin' him loose. If he tries anything funny, go ahead and kill him."

"You're gonna fight him, Garity?" one of the outlaws asked.

"No, I'm gonna cut him loose and then kill him," Garity said. "It ain't gonna last long enough to call a real fight."

They would see about that, Preacher thought.

Garity moved closer to him and started sawing on the ropes that held him to the wagon wheel. After a moment, the ropes parted. Without them to hold him up, Preacher's strength deserted him momentarily and he fell to his knees.

Garity laughed. "See what I mean?" he told his men. "What's about to happen ain't a fight at all. It's gonna be pure slaughter."

With his hands tied behind his back, Preacher struggled to his feet. He dragged a couple deep breaths into his lungs, turned sideways, and held his bound hands away from him.

"Finish it, Garity," he said.

"Oh, I'll finish it, all right," Garity said meaningfully. He moved behind Preacher and roughly sliced the bonds around the mountain man's wrists, leaving a stinging cut on Preacher's arm in the process. Preacher pulled his hands in front of him. They were like chunks of dead meat. He shook them and flexed them. A million tiny knives pricked him as the blood began to flow again, but it was welcome torture. It meant that he would be able to use his hands again.

"All right," Garity said. He held out a hand to one of his men. "Gimme your knife." The man did so, and Garity threw the knife into the ground at Preacher's feet. The handle quivered a little as the weapon stood upright. "Whenever you're ready, Preacher," Garity said. "Just don't take all night about it. I'm gettin' a mite anxious to carve you into little pieces."

Preacher looked down at the knife, then up at Garity. "I don't think I can do it," he said. "I'm too beat up. I can't take you on."

"I knew it," Garity sneered. "What a damn coward."

"But I got a substitute," Preacher went on. "Somebody you can fight instead of me."

"Oh? Who's that?" Mockingly, Garity waved a hand at Casey. "The whore? Or that boy?" He pointed at Roland.

"Nope," said Preacher. "Him."

He nodded toward the far side of the circle, where the grizzly that had just climbed over a wagon tongue reared up to its full height and let out a soul-shattering roar.

CHAPTER 23

The oxen began to scatter, moving as fast as the massive brutes could move, as the bear charged through them and headed across the circle toward the fire and the humans gathered around it. The outlaws yelled in fear as they swung around and started firing toward it. Their pistols and rifles boomed, adding to the terrible racket as the bear continued to bellow out its rage and hate.

Preacher had no doubt it was the same bear, and he was more than halfway convinced the damn thing *was* some sort of avenging spirit. But it was flesh and blood, too, and as it reached the nearest man, it slapped him aside before he could get out of the way. The man flew through the air and came crashing down on the ground with his head twisted on his neck at an impossible angle.

As Garity watched the bear, Preacher leaped forward and snatched the knife from the ground, intending to plunge the blade into Garity's back. Sensing the movement Garity twisted aside and slashed at Preacher with the knife he still held.

Preacher jerked back. The tip of Garity's blade raked across his bare chest, leaving behind a fiery line that oozed blood into the thick dark hair on the mountain man's chest. Garity was off balance for a second because of the near miss, and Preacher's knife sliced across his forearm, but not deeply enough to make Garity drop his knife.

Garity howled in pain. "You bastard!" He came at Preacher, slashing wildly back and forth. In the face of the furious assault, Preacher had to give ground.

He was light-headed from exhaustion, hunger—it had been well over twenty-four hours since he'd had anything to eat—and the effects of being knocked out twice in that same period of time. He needed a few thick steaks, a jug of whiskey, and some real sleep.

Instead he had a vicious madman coming at him with a knife. Preacher's back bumped against the wagon wheel where he had been tied. He couldn't retreat any further. Garity thrust his knife at Preacher, who twisted aside and barely avoided the blade. Garity's arm went through the gap between two of the wheel's spokes. Preacher reached behind the wheel, grabbed Garity's wrist, and yanked it down as hard as he could. Trapped, the bones in Garity's forearm snapped with a crack like a tree branch breaking. He screamed and slammed a punch to Preacher's head with his left fist.

The blow knocked Preacher away from the wagon wheel. He watched as the bear lunged back and forth among Garity's men, mauling them. The claws dug so deep into one man's neck that his head was torn right off his shoulders. His body stumbled around for a second with blood spouting from the ragged stump of a neck before it collapsed. The head rolled into the fire and started to burn.

Cradling his maimed arm against his body, Garity dropped to his knees and fumbled behind the wheel for the knife he had dropped when Preacher broke his arm. He came up with the blade and leaped at Preacher again.

Jerking aside to keep from being gutted, Preacher kicked Garity in the chest and knocked the outlaw underneath the wagon. He would have dragged him out and finished him off, but at that moment, Casey screamed, "Preacher, look out! The bear!"

Preacher wheeled around and saw the bear charging toward him, leaving the bodies of Garity's men in a scattered shambles behind it. Blood welled from a dozen wounds in the grizzly's body, but it seemed as fierce and unstoppable as ever.

Far from being a totem animal that wanted to protect Preacher, like in the wild yarn he had spun to stall Garity, the bear was obviously out for Preacher's blood. The only reason it had torn into the outlaws was because they were between it and the mountain man.

"What the hell did I ever do to you, you son of a bitch?" Preacher yelled.

The bear's only answer was another ear-splitting roar. Preacher dived under a sweeping blow from one of the massive, claw-studded paws. The claws were stained red from all the blood they had shed.

Preacher darted in close to the bear. The knife in his hand flickered in and out. Bear blood dripped crimsonly from the blade. The grizzly lurched after Preacher.

They were well-matched, he thought. Both of

them more dead than alive. The bear had to be on its last legs, fueled only by its unshakeable, unfathomable rage.

Preacher wasn't just fighting for himself. He knew if the bear killed him, it would likely turn on Casey, Roland, and the other prisoners next. Tied to the wagon wheels like they were, they wouldn't be able to avoid the slashing claws and teeth. The bear would rip them to shreds.

So it had to end at long last. The bear wasn't going to get away from him. Or, in another way of looking at it, he thought, *he* wasn't going to get away from the bear. Whatever grudge the varmint had against him, it was time to settle it.

He wasn't quick enough to avoid everything the bear threw at him. A glancing blow knocked him off his feet and left a set of claw marks on his side. Preacher rolled as the bear reached for him. Overbalanced for a second, it fell to all fours.

Preacher seized the opportunity. He leaped onto the bear's back and locked his left arm around its neck. The grizzly reared up again, trying to throw him off, but Preacher hung on desperately.

He had been in that position before, when he was fighting the bear in the dry wash far to the northeast, but he'd had a pistol instead of a knife in his hand. He slammed the blade into the bear's body again and again and again, trying to drive it as deeply as he could. The bear clawed at the arm around its neck and roared. Preacher roared, too, an inarticulate cry of rage that was as animalistic as any sound the grizzly made. Blood flew in the air, some of it Preacher's, some of it the bear's.

Preacher pulled himself higher on the bear's

back and plunged the knife into the side of the creature's neck. He ripped it free, drove it home again. Blood spurted in a hot flood over his arm. Preacher struck again and again as the bear began to stagger back and forth.

Even in his berserk fury, a small part of Preacher's brain was rational enough to realize he would be crushed if the bear fell on him when it collapsed. He reached around as far as he could, slammed the knife into the front of the bear's throat, and then let go, leaving the weapon where it was. He dropped to the ground but lost his footing as he slipped in a puddle of blood. He fell as the bear turned toward him.

The grizzly let out one more roar, but the sound was a lot weaker. Preacher scrambled backward as the bear took a tentative step after him. It pawed futilely at the air as if striking at something only it could see.

Then, like a huge tree that's rotted at the base, it began to topple forward.

Preacher got out of the way just in time. The bear crashed to earth right beside him, and Preacher would have sworn he felt the ground shake under him. He pushed himself along the ground until he reached one of the wagon wheels. Reaching up, he grasped a spoke and tried to pull himself upright.

Iron will could push a human body only so far, and Preacher's body, slick with blood and leaking more of the precious stuff with every passing second, had reached its limit. He slid to the ground and fell onto his side. That left him looking directly into the face of the dead bear a few feet away. As he stared at the lifeless eyes, he felt a strange kinship, almost a sadness that the grizzly had reached the end of its trail at last, as someday he inevitably would, too.

"You and me, old son," Preacher whispered. "We're . . . a lot alike . . . ain't neither of us . . . fit for anywhere except . . . the wild places . . ."

The world went away again, and Preacher was sure it was never coming back.

A gentle swaying was the first thing he was aware of. He was rocking back and forth a little as he lay on something soft. A pile of blankets, maybe.

Then he took the time to be surprised that he was still alive.

His eyes opened. He saw something white arching over him. The great vault of heaven? Maybe he wasn't alive after all. Was he lying on clouds instead of blankets?

No, that wasn't possible, Preacher decided. A rapscallion like him wasn't going to wind up in heaven, and even if he did, he wasn't convinced it would be like the psalm-singers said, floating in the clouds with a bunch of angels in robes who flew around playing harps. Not hardly! For a man like him, heaven would be a beautiful morning in the high country, with a good rifle, a good horse, a good dog . . .

That white thing above him was the canvas cover stretched over the hoops of a big freight wagon, he realized as he forced the crazy thoughts out of his head. He was alive, and he was in the back of a wagon.

Lorenzo leaned over him and said, "I knowed you was too damn stubborn to die. I just knowed it."

"You . . . old coot," Preacher whispered. "Where . . ."

"You're in one of the wagons," Lorenzo answered, telling Preacher what he had already figured out. "We're on our way to Santa Fe."

"How . . . long . . ."

"Were you out? More'n two days. It was three nights ago you killed that ol' bear. Of course, you ain't been out cold the whole time. You'd come to ever' now and then and start to ravin' about this and that, but this is the first time you've made any sense. You was just so beat up and lost so much blood, it took you a while to rest up and start to recuperate. You're still a long way from bein' able to get up and dance a jig," Lorenzo added.

"How did you . . . find us?"

"Well, we sat around them springs for a couple o' days. The fellas decided you wasn't comin' back for us, so we set off on foot along the trail. The gent who was wounded the worst had passed away by then, so we buried him and the rest didn't want to stay there no more. The hurt ones claimed they was healed up enough to walk, so they did."

."And you found . . . the wagons?"

"Hard to miss 'em, there was so many damn buzzards circlin' overhead. Dead bodies ever'where, and folks tied to wagon wheels about to die o' thirst and hunger and exposure. We got ever'body loose, doctored up them what needed it, and started tryin' to figure out what to do next. We didn't have enough bullwhackers to handle all the teams, so we doubled up on some of 'em. Hitched two wagons together and used two teams to pull 'em, so it'd only take one man. That was Roland's idea, and so far it's been working."

"Roland . . . he's all right?"

"I'll go fetch him," Lorenzo said. "He'll want to know you're awake."

Preacher started to tell the old-timer to wait. He wanted to find out about Casey, and Horse and Dog, too. But Lorenzo had already swung a leg over the tailgate. He dropped out of the wagon and disappeared.

Preacher lay there and waited. There was nothing else he could do. He felt as weak as a day-old kitten. His head was fairly clear, though, and he was grateful for that. With all the punishment he had absorbed, he could have wound up a drooling idiot.

Of course, some might say he wasn't far from that at his best, he thought wryly.

A few minutes later, Roland climbed into the wagon, followed by Lorenzo. The young man had his left arm in a sling, and Preacher could tell by the bulkiness under his shirt that bandages were wrapped around Roland's wounded shoulder. He knelt beside Preacher and smiled.

"I'm glad to see you've come back to us, Preacher. I was worried that bear had done too much damage to you, on top of everything else."

"I'll be . . . fine," Preacher told him. "Just need to . . . rest up a mite more."

"I'm sure you're right," Roland said with a nod. "You'll be glad to know, too, that your horse and your dog are fine. They came into Garity's camp looking for you, and we've been taking care of them."

"I'm . . . obliged for that," Preacher said. Between what Lorenzo and then Roland had told him, he was pretty well up to date on what had happened since he blacked out . . . except for one thing.

"Where's . . . Casey?" he asked.

The smile vanished from Roland's face and was replaced with a bleak expression. "We don't know," he said grimly. "We never found Garity, either. I think he got away, Preacher . . . and he took Casey with him."

Chapter 24

Two days later, Preacher sat on a crate inside the front of the lead wagon in the caravan. The canvas flaps had been tied back so he could get some air and see where they were going. He felt much stronger. Rest and food had done wonders for him, along with his own sturdy constitution. He had always been fast to recover from injury. He would have thought everything was going to be all right . . . if he hadn't been consumed with worry about Casey.

He and Roland had spent a lot of time talking about that bloody night when the grizzly bear had come rampaging into the outlaw camp. The last Preacher had seen anything of Garity, he had kicked the man underneath the wagon where Casey was tied to one of the wheels. Garity's right arm had been broken, but other than that he was all right.

It was possible, they had decided, that while all eyes were on Preacher's epic battle with the bear, Garity had gotten hold of a knife with his left hand

and cut the ropes holding Casey to the wheel. If he had acted quickly enough, he could have then clamped his good hand over her mouth to keep her from crying out and dragged her under the wagon with him. If that was what happened, he had probably knocked her out to keep her from struggling and crawled away from the wagons into the darkness, dragging Casey with him.

Where Garity had gone from there, no one knew. After Lorenzo and the other men arrived to set the prisoners free, Roland had searched frantically all around the site of the outlaw camp. He had found some horse tracks and surmised that Garity had left Casey hidden somewhere while he snuck back and stole one of the outlaws' mounts. From there, they could have gone anywhere.

But the only destination that really made sense, Roland thought—and Preacher agreed with him—was Santa Fe.

Garity could have forced Casey to splint and bind up his broken arm, but he would need real medical attention sooner or later, and Santa Fe was the closest place he could get it. He obviously had friends there—he'd mentioned knowing a man who ran a whorehouse and probably planned to hole up there while he recovered, as well as going ahead with his plan to sell Casey to the proprietor of the place. If Garity could do that, he would salvage what had otherwise been a disaster.

Since Santa Fe was the closest outpost of civilization, the wagons had to proceed there as planned, anyway, but now there was another goal.

Find Casey. Settle the score with Garity. Those were the thoughts that burned in Preacher's brain.

Being forced to double up on some of the wagons and teams had slowed the caravan, but two more days would bring them to Santa Fe. Preacher was looking forward to it. He could have used more like two weeks to recover from the ordeal, but a full recuperation would have to wait. By the time they reached the settlement, he would be ready to do whatever needed to be done. Anything else wasn't an option.

They had plenty of horses again, since they had recovered the mounts belonging to the dead outlaws. Roland kept two outriders scouting ahead and behind the wagons. He didn't have the manpower to do any more. He was usually one of them, and as Preacher watched, the young man rode back toward the wagons after a foray ahead.

"Everything still looks clear," Roland reported as he swung the horse around and fell in alongside the lead wagon. "I think we've already had our share of trouble on this trip, and more besides."

"Don't say things like that," Preacher warned. "You'll jinx us."

He hoped Roland was right, though. They were past the area where the worst danger of Indian attacks lay, and since the bear was finally dead, its great shaggy carcass far behind them, the only real threat was that they might run into another gang of outlaws. If that didn't happen, likely they would make it to Santa Fe without any more problems.

"I can't stop thinking about Casey," Roland said with a sigh. "Do you really think we'll find her, Preacher?"

"Damn right we'll find her. Santa Fe ain't *that* big a place. I know some people there. Somebody will have seen her and Garity and can tell us where to find them."

"But what if Garity didn't take her to Santa Fe?"

Preacher's jaw tightened. "Where else would he go? But if he didn't, as soon as I'm in better shape, I'll head back to the spot where he grabbed her and pick up their trail."

"After all that time?" Roland sounded dubious.

"I'll find 'em," Preacher said. "If it takes a year, or two, or however long, I'll find 'em. And then Garity'll pay for what he done."

The wagons rolled into Santa Fe's broad plaza late in the afternoon. With Lorenzo's help, Preacher climbed down from the vehicle where he had been riding. The mountain man wore boots, whipcord trousers, a linsey-woolsey shirt, and a broad-brimmed brown hat, all of which came from the freight carried by the caravan. His buckskins had been too bloody and shredded to be saved, but he figured he could get another set of them in the settlement . . . once the rest of his business was done.

He was armed with a new knife, two pistols, and a rifle, also new. He had offered to owe Roland for them, but the young man wouldn't hear of it.

"We'd all be dead now if it weren't for you, Preacher," Roland had said. "I'll never finish paying that debt."

"You best be careful," Lorenzo warned as he and Preacher stood beside the wagon. "You may not be too steady on your feet yet."

"I'll be fine," Preacher said.

Roland came over to join them. "Where's this place you're going?" he asked Preacher.

The mountain man pointed. "A block down that side street over yonder. It's called Juanita's. Ask folks if you can't find it. They can tell you where to go."

Roland nodded. "I'll see you later, then, after I've made arrangements for the freight and the wagons."

"Good luck with that," Preacher said.

"Don't worry about that," Roland said with a smile. "Despite the fact that he didn't know anything about the frontier, my father was a pretty canny businessman, and I learned from him. I'll be able to strike a good deal."

Preacher clapped a hand on the young man's shoulder. "I'm sure you will. Go do your pa proud."

He and Lorenzo walked across the plaza, not in any hurry. Preacher felt fairly steady, but he didn't want to rush things. They went down the side street to a square adobe building where the strains of guitar music drifted out through the open front door. The cool dimness inside felt good when they walked in.

The cantina had a hard-packed dirt floor, a scattering of rough-hewn tables and chairs, and an actual hardwood bar across the back. Old Esteban, who had owned the place, had paid a pretty penny to have the bar brought up from Mexico City ten years earlier. Unfortunately for him, he had come down with a fever and died before it ever arrived. His widow Juanita, who was considerably younger than her late husband, had continued running the cantina.

Preacher had met her a few years later during one of his previous visits to Santa Fe and had heard the story of Esteban and the bar from Juanita while they were in bed together, basking in the afterglow of some vigorous lovemaking. Luckily for Preacher, the earthy, voluptuous widow had been finished with her mourning by the time he came along, and the two of them had hit it off splendidly.

She was behind the bar when Preacher and Lorenzo came in. The air was thick with the smells of pipe smoke and burning hemp, tequila and beer, perfume and unwashed human flesh. Men laughed and talked, and the pretty girls who carried drinks to the tables let out the occasional yelp as the customers got a little too friendly. In the low-cut peasant blouses and long, embroidered skirts, the nubile young women put plenty of lecherous ideas in the minds of the patrons.

Juanita set a bucket of beer on the bar to be delivered to one of the tables, then glanced at the two newcomers. Her head jerked sharply as she looked again. Her eyes widened in recognition, and a big smile appeared on her face as she hurried out from behind the bar and practically ran across the room to greet the mountain man.

"Preacher!" she said as she threw her arms around him. "*Dios mio!* I almost didn't recognize you, dressed like a civilized person instead of a wild Indian! What are you doing—" Juanita stopped short and frowned as she looked into Preacher's gaunt, haggard face. "Preacher, are you all right? You look sick!"

"Nope, I ain't sick," he assured her. "Just beat up

and wore out. Reckon we could find an empty table and sit down?"

"Of course." She held on to his arm and led him to one of the tables. As the three of them sat down, she nodded toward Lorenzo and asked, "Who is your amigo?"

"I ain't his slave, if that's what you're thinkin'," Lorenzo said.

Juanita shook her head. "Preacher is not the sort of man who would keep another in bondage. I can tell the two of you are friends."

"His name's Lorenzo," Preacher said. "He's kind of a cantankerous old codger, but he's handy to have around ever' now and then."

Lorenzo snorted. "Saved your bacon more'n once, I seem to recall."

Preacher didn't argue about that. Instead he turned to Juanita and said, "You're lookin' as pretty as ever, darlin'." His compliments still had the power to make her blush with pleasure, he noted.

She said, "Of course I'm glad to see you, Preacher, but what brings you to Santa Fe?"

"I need a place to stay, Juanita."

"With me," she replied instantly. "Do not even think about arguing."

Preacher chuckled. "I wasn't intendin' to. Reckon you can find a bed for Lorenzo, too?"

"Of course. You can both stay as long as you like. At least a month. It will take that long for my cooking to fatten you up and make you healthy again."

Preacher's mouth watered a little at the memory of all the savory vittles Juanita had fixed for him in the past. Beans and tortillas, strips of beef, and the peppers . . . Lord, the peppers! There was nothing like them to get a man's vital juices stirring. Juanita was right. A month of her cooking would put him back on his feet again, good and proper. Washed down with plenty of tequila, of course.

"I can't tell you how good that sounds, darlin'," he said, "but there's something else I need to take care of first."

She heard the edge in his voice. She frowned again as she said, "Trouble. That's what you mean."

"You're right," Preacher admitted. "I'm lookin' for an hombre."

"A man you intend to kill."

Juanita's words were a statement, not a question, but Preacher inclined his head in agreement anyway.

She looked at Lorenzo and asked, "If you're his friend, have you not told him that he is no shape to be seeking a battle?"

"I reckon you've knowed him longer'n I have, ma'am," Lorenzo said. "You think it does any good to tell Preacher anything?"

She sighed. "Not really. Not once his mind is made up." She looked at Preacher again. "So tell me, who is this evil man whose life you wish to end?"

"How do you know he's evil?" Preacher asked.

"Because if he wasn't, you would not want to kill him. Despite all the rough edges, you are a good man, Arturo."

Lorenzo looked across the table and raised his eyebrows as he repeated, "Arturo?"

"Never you mind about that," Preacher snapped. He had told Juanita the name he'd been born with—Arthur—and sometimes she called him Arturo in bed. It was the first time she had used it anywhere else. He went on, "The fella I'm lookin' for is named Garity. I never heard his first name."

He went on to describe the outlaw while Juanita nodded slowly. He told her about how Garity and the other thieves had attacked the wagon train twice, how they had tortured him, how Garity had escaped during the battle with the bear and evidently taken Casey with him. Juanita's eyes widened in amazement as she listened.

"Dios mio, Preacher," she said when he was finished, "how can one man get into so much trouble?"

"That's what I been askin' myself for a long time now," Preacher growled. "Seems like some of us are just born to it."

"And now you want my help finding this man Garity and the woman he has with him? Who is this Casey to you?"

"A friend," Preacher replied honestly. She had been more than that to him for a while. That was over, but he still cared for her, and wanted to help her. "She's been through a lot in her life, and whatever's happenin' to her now, she don't deserve it."

Juanita thought about it for a moment and then nodded. "You say Garity might have taken her to a house of ill repute?"

"More than likely. He's probably stayin' there himself while that busted arm of his heals up."

"I don't know every whorehouse in Santa Fe, you know. I run a respectable establishment here."

Calling that cantina respectable was stretching the definition a mite, Preacher thought, but he didn't say it. Instead, he said, "You know a lot of people, though. I figured you could put the word out, quiet-like. Let folks know you're interested in findin' out if an hombre with a busted wing and a pretty young blonde has showed up in town lately, and if they have, you want to know where they're stayin'. Don't say anything except to people you trust. I don't want word gettin' back to Garity that I'm lookin' for him. He don't need to know I'm in Santa Fe . . . until I'm ready for him to know."

Juanita nodded. "I will help you, Preacher," she said. "But then you have to let me take care of you until you are well again."

"It's a deal," Preacher said. "If I'm still alive."

Juanita glared at him. "You had damned well better be!"

CHAPTER 25

Preacher knew it might take a few days for Juanita's quest for information about Casey and Garity to pay off. He spent that time taking it easy, recovering from everything he had been through. Every minute that passed while he didn't know where Casey was gnawed at his nerves.

He forced himself to relax. Juanita fed him well, as she had promised, and each day he felt a little stronger. She deemed him still too weak for any exercise in the bedroom, and although he might have argued that point, he didn't make an issue of it. If they got the chance, they would make up for lost time later, he figured.

Roland paid several visits to the cantina. When they located Casey and mounted a rescue attempt, he wanted to be part of it. Preacher was inclined to go along with that. Roland had grown up some during the journey from Missouri. That plan he had hatched to get Preacher and Casey away from Garity hadn't been too bad. It hadn't actually worked, of course, but nobody's plans worked all the time, not even Preacher's.

"How'd you fare with sellin' that freight?" Preacher asked the young man as they sat at a secluded table in a corner of the cantina with Lorenzo and Juanita.

"I'm working on it," Roland replied. He had been letting his beard grow, and with the dark tan his skin had acquired during the journey over the Santa Fe Trail, he was starting to look a little like one of the *Nuevo Mexicanos*. "The deal has turned out to be more complicated than I expected, but I'm confident I'll come to a suitable arrangement soon." He took a sip from the cup of tequila he held. "Anyway, I'm in no hurry to leave Santa Fe. I won't be going anywhere until we have Casey back safe and sound."

Preacher had a hunch Casey was still alive—the girl had proven herself to be a survivor, after all—but they had no guarantees that was true. Taking care of Garity might come down to avenging Casey's death rather than rescuing her, Preacher knew. Roland ought to be prepared for that possibility.

Before he could say anything, the old man who played the guitar in the cantina during the evenings came into the place and looked around. Spotting them at the table, he headed across the room toward them with an excited look on his white-bearded face. His sombrero was thumbed back on his mostly bald head, and his guitar was slung by its strap on his back.

He tugged the broad-brimmed, steeple-crowned straw hat off and held it in front of him respectfully as he stopped beside the table and said, "Señora."

"What is it, Pepé?" Juanita asked.

"I have news of the man and the woman you seek," the old man said.

Preacher, Roland, and Lorenzo all leaned forward in anticipation. They had been waiting for that moment, and they hoped it turned out to be true.

"Go ahead, Pepé," Juanita told him. "What have you discovered?"

"I have been talking to my nephew Pablo. He came into town yesterday with a mule train from Mexico City. Well, you know Pablo . . . The first thing he had to do when he arrived was to find a pretty señorita with whom to spend some time. The boy is my sister's *niño*, and I love him, but like all young men, he thinks of little else but romance."

Preacher felt a surge of impatience. He wanted to tell the old man to hurry up and get to what they wanted to know, but he reined in the impulse. Trying to hurry Pepé might result in slowing him down even more.

"Yes, go ahead," Juanita gently prodded. She knew how to handle him.

"He mentioned that he went to the house of ill repute owned by Egan Powell."

Juanita's eyes widened, and Preacher asked, "Who's Egan Powell?"

"A very bad man," Juanita replied. "An American, as you can tell by the name. He came here several years ago and became a Mexican citizen, saying that he never wanted to go back to the United States. You can probably guess why."

"He was a wanted man there," Preacher drawled. "The law probably made it too hot for him."

Juanita nodded. "That is the rumor, although no

one knows for certain. What I do know is that Powell has killed several men since he has been in Santa Fe, each of them with his bare hands."

Lorenzo asked, "They let fellas get away with murder in this town?"

"Those killings were not murder. In each case, the man got drunk and caused trouble in Powell's business. They were all armed with guns or knives. Powell took their weapons away and beat them to death."

"Sounds like a pretty bad hombre, all right," Preacher said. "Just the sort of gent who'd be friends with a lowdown skunk like Garity."

Pepé's head bobbed up and down. "Sí, señor. Pablo said he saw a man, an American, at Powell's with his arm in a, how you say it, a sling, like this young gentleman here wore when he first came to Santa Fe."

Pepé pointed to Roland, who had discarded his sling the day before as his wounded shoulder continued to heal.

"The arm had splints on it," Pepé added.

"There can't be more than one American in Santa Fe with a broken arm right now," Roland said excitedly.

"You can't be sure of that," Preacher pointed out, "but I admit, it ain't likely. What else did your nephew say, Pepé? Did he notice a blond American girl there?"

Pepé shook his head. "No, señor. But he was not looking for one. He only recalled the man with the sling when I asked him about such an hombre just now. He might not have remembered even then had not Señor Powell gotten angry with the man and told him to stay upstairs."

Roland looked over at Preacher and asked, "Why would Powell want Garity to stay upstairs?"

"He's keepin' him out of sight for some reason," Preacher guessed. "He don't want anybody to know that Garity's there."

"Why would he care about that?" Juanita asked.

Preacher shrugged. "Maybe Garity told him about the run-ins he had with me, and Powell don't want me findin' him there. I hadn't heard of Powell, but that don't mean he ain't heard of me." The mountain man smiled. "I know that's a mite immodest, but I got a little reputation in some circles."

"A reputation as a dangerous man," Juanita said. "*Un hombre muy malo.*" She nodded. "Yes, Powell might know of you. Even if Garity told him the bear killed you, Powell would not want to take the chance that you would come looking for him."

"Which is exactly what I've done," Preacher pointed out.

"I wish Pablo had seen Casey, too," Roland said with a worried look on his face. "I'd like to know for sure that she's still alive. What if she's not there?"

"Then Garity can tell us where she is," Preacher said. "We'll make damn sure he don't die until he does."

Lorenzo said, "If this fella Powell is as bad as the señora says he is, we can't just go bustin' in and expect to kill Garity and take Casey outta there. Powell's liable to have some men workin' there that are almost as bad as he is."

Juanita nodded. "I was just about to say that. There are always three or four men around who are experts with knives and guns, keeping order in the place when Powell isn't there or is busy with something else."

"I have eight bullwhackers who will go in there with us if I ask them to," Roland said. "I think we'll be more than a match for Powell and his bully boys."

Preacher shook his head. "Those fellas are tough as hell, but in close quarters like that, they wouldn't be any match for Powell and his men, not to mention Garity. He may have a busted arm, but I reckon he's still as dangerous as a rattlesnake. He proved that the way he snatched Casey away."

"Then what *can* we do?" Roland asked. "Now that we know where she is—where she *probably* is—we can't just do nothing!"

"Somebody needs to go in there and scout around a mite. Make sure Casey's really there. I can't do it, because somebody'd be likely to recognize me."

"And I can't do it," Lorenzo said. "I'd draw too much attention, bein' black and all."

"Not to mention you're way too old have any use for a whore," Preacher said.

"What the hell you talkin' about?" Lorenzo demanded. "Why, I'll have you know I can still—"

Preacher held up a hand to stop him and looked at Roland. "Reckon that leaves it up to you. You'll have to be mighty careful. If Garity sees you, he'll recognize you, sure as shootin'. You up to the job?"

"Of course I am," Roland said without hesitation. "If it means getting Casey back, I am. What do I do?"

They all leaned forward as Preacher said, "You'll

go to Powell's place tonight. I reckon Juanita can get some Mex duds for you."

She nodded to indicate that she could.

"Keep the brim of your sombrero pulled down," Preacher went on. "Dressed like that, and with that beard, there's a chance Garity might not recognize you right off, even if he does see you. When you tell 'em you want a gal, they'll likely ask if you've got anything special in mind. Tell 'em you're lookin' for a gal with yeller hair, especially if she's an American."

Roland's features hardened into a grim mask. Preacher knew what he was thinking. In the time that Casey had been at the whorehouse in Santa Fe, there had probably been quite a few men who had asked for her. But if Roland had been willing to accept what he knew about her past in St. Louis, he ought to be willing to accept that, too, Preacher thought. It sure as hell wasn't Casey's fault.

"If she's there, what do I do?" Roland asked.

"Take her upstairs," Preacher said. "Look for a back way out. I'd like to get Casey clear before we deal with Garity."

As long as Casey was safe, Preacher didn't care all that much what happened to him. He had long since accepted the fact that he would never die in bed with a bunch of grandkids and great grandkids around him. Like that grizzly bear, when he reached the end of his trail it would be a violent one, but that was all right. Preacher was just fine with that as long as he got to put a pistol ball or a knife into Garity first, or even choke the life out of the son of a bitch with his own hands. He couldn't think of a better way to go than while killing a skunk like that.

"We'll be waitin' at different spots around the buildin'," Preacher went on. "Once you and Casey are safe, I'll go in and deal with Garity."

"By yourself?" Lorenzo shook his head. "You wouldn't stand a chance, Preacher. Powell and his men will protect him."

"Well . . ." Preacher grinned slyly. "We might ought to have a little distraction to keep Powell and his bunch occupied while I'm seein' to Garity. Like, say, if some of them bullwhackers were to go in there and start a brawl."

Roland nodded eagerly. "I'm sure they'd be willing to do that."

"It's liable to be dangerous," Preacher warned. "Some of 'em might get hurt, even killed."

"They'll know that. They won't care, if it means settling the score with Garity. I wasn't the only man who lost someone out there on the trail. They lost some good friends as well."

"All right, then, it's settled. Be back here a little after dark, Roland, and bring any of the bullwhackers who want to give us a hand with you." Preacher looked around at the others. "With any luck, this'll be over tonight."

In a felt sombrero with a fancy band, a charro jacket with embroidered decorations on it, a frilly shirt, and tight pants, Roland looked like a well-to-do young Mexican. He wouldn't pass a close inspection, more than likely, but Preacher thought he ought to be able to keep up the deception long enough in a dim, smoky brothel to get upstairs.

"What if they try to give me some other girl besides Casey?" Roland asked nervously as he and Preacher stood in an alley across the street from the two-story frame building that housed Egan Powell's place of business. Heavy curtains were drawn across all the windows, and yellow light showed dimly through the narrow cracks around the drapes.

"If they admit they got a girl like that there, chances are it's her. Tell 'em you'll wait for her if she's busy with another customer. Nurse a drink at the bar for a while."

Roland nodded in the shadows. "All right."

"Remember, I'll be right here," Preacher told him. "If you need me in a hurry, stick your head out a window and holler. I'll come a-runnin."

"Are you sure *you're* all right, Preacher? You went through so much on the way here."

Preacher grinned. "I bounce back pretty quick-like. Don't worry about me."

"Fine. Preacher—"

Preacher had had more than enough of Roland thanking him for everything he'd done. He said, "Lorenzo's around back of the place, and those bullwhackers are down yonder in the next block waitin' for my signal. Let us know as soon as you get out of there with Casey."

"I will." Roland took a deep breath and squared his shoulders. "I guess I'm ready."

"I think so," Preacher said.

The young man shot him an appreciative glance, then stepped out of the alley. Strolling like he didn't have a care in the world, he walked across the street and opened the door to go into the whorehouse. For a second he was silhouetted against the light inside, and then he was gone.

Over the years Preacher had learned how to wait patiently. Many times, that ability had saved his life. But just because he could stand or sit motionless for hours at a time didn't mean he liked doing it. His mind always roamed. The older he got, the more his memories intruded on his thinking. He remembered his family—vaguely—and he remembered the friends he had made during the long, adventurous years since he had left home. For all the vastness of the frontier, in some ways it was a small place. Almost anywhere he went west of the Mississippi, sooner or later he was likely to run into someone who knew him. It was why he had decided against going into Powell's. Even if Powell didn't recognize him, somebody else might, and holler out something like, "Why, Preacher, you old son of a bitch, what are you doin' here?" That would have ruined—

The sudden sound of a shot from across the street made Preacher's head jerk up in alarm.

Chapter 26

Preacher's first impulse was to yank the pistol from behind his belt, run across the street, and charge into the whorehouse ready to start shooting.

With an effort, he controlled that urge. Trouble broke out in those places all the time, and the gunshot he had heard didn't necessarily have anything to do with Roland and Casey. Even if it did, if he rushed in it might get them killed.

Still, he couldn't just wait in the dark, not knowing what was going on over there. He was going to have to risk going in.

He tugged his hat brim down low over his face and stepped out of the alley. As he started across the street, he saw several of the bullwhackers approaching the whorehouse as well. They had heard the shot and gotten worried about Roland. Preacher caught the eye of one of the men and waved him back. The man passed along the order, and they all stopped and began to withdraw with obvious reluctance.

There had only been the single shot, but Preacher didn't know if that was a good thing or a bad one.

Maybe a single shot was all it had taken to kill Roland Bartlett.

He was only about halfway across the street when a man carrying a rifle stepped out the front doorway of the whorehouse. Instinct sent Preacher diving to the side as the rifle barrel came up. Orange flame geysered from the muzzle. Preacher heard the heavy lead ball hum past him as he went to one knee. He had his pistol in his hand, snapped it up, and fired. The rifleman ducked back inside as Preacher's shot chewed splinters from one of the porch posts.

Preacher ran for a parked wagon nearby. He didn't know what the hell was going on, but it couldn't be anything good. He took cover behind the wagon and reloaded his pistol.

A man's deep, gravelly voice boomed out through the open door of the whorehouse. "Preacher! Preacher, can you hear me?"

A frown creased the mountain man's forehead. He didn't recognize the voice.

"I hear you!" he called back harshly. There didn't seem to be any point in denying who he was. "Who are you, mister, and what do you want?"

"It's more a matter of what *you* want," the man replied. "I've got Roland Bartlett and the girl called Casey in here!"

Preacher bit back a curse. Obviously, Roland's disguise hadn't worked at all. Garity must have known somehow that they were in Santa Fe and had been watching for Roland or Preacher, waiting for them to show up looking for Casey.

Well, that wasn't a complete surprise, he mused. They hadn't kept the arrival of the wagons a secret. A man like Egan Powell probably had sources of information all over the settlement. He could have been told the Bartlett wagon train had rolled into Santa Fe several days earlier. If he'd passed that on to Garity, the two of them could have set up a trap, with Casey for the bait—

"Preacher! You'd better listen to me if you ever want to see those two youngsters alive again!"

Preacher had no doubt the gravelly voice belonged to Powell. "I'm listenin'!" Preacher shouted. The pistol was reloaded, and his hand wrapped tensely around the butt.

"A friend of mine's got a score to settle with you! He's willing to let Bartlett and Casey go if you'll turn yourself over to him."

"We're talkin' about Garity?"

"That's right. How about it, Preacher? Is your life worth the two of theirs?"

Preacher didn't believe for a second that if he walked into that whorehouse and surrendered, Garity would let Roland and Casey go unharmed. The outlaw was a natural-born double-crosser. He would kill all three of them and be done with it.

Or rather, he would kill Preacher and Roland. Casey would likely continue to suffer whatever degradations she had already been through, and more.

Preacher took a deep breath. "Now, you listen to me!" he shouted. "Here's how this is gonna work. You and Garity bring Roland and Casey to the west side of the plaza tomorrow mornin' at dawn. Just the two of you! I see anybody else and the deal's off. I'll be on the east side, unarmed. I'll start across at the same time you start Roland and Casey walkin' toward me. Once they're clear, Garity can do whatever the hell he wants to me."

"Do you really think we're stupid enough to fall for a trick like that?"

"It's the only deal you're gonna get from me!" Preacher said. "I've risked life and limb for those two over and over again, and I'm gettin' sick of it! I swear, Powell, I'll just ride away, and Garity can have 'em!"

That wasn't true, of course, but Powell and Garity couldn't be sure of that. Preacher was convinced that Garity was probably right inside the building, listening to the conversation. He wondered if Powell had cleared all the customers out the back and sent the soiled doves up to their rooms as soon as they grabbed Roland.

The whorehouse remained dark and silent for several moments, no doubt while Powell conferred with Garity. Finally, Powell called, "All right, Preacher, you got a deal! The plaza at dawn! But you'd better not try anything funny, or those two will be a long time dying!"

The front door banged shut.

A sound behind Preacher made the mountain man whirl around and level the pistol at a dark shape his keen eyes picked out of the shadows.

"Don't shoot!" Lorenzo yelped. "Land's sake, Preacher, it's just me!"

Preacher lowered the gun and took a deep breath. "Damn it, Lorenzo, I almost blowed your fool head off."

"It's a good thing you didn't," the old-timer said, "'cause I come to warn you. They's some men sneakin' around the alleys right now tryin' to get behind you."

Powell's hired killers, Preacher thought. He stepped over to Lorenzo, took hold of the old man's arm, and said, "Let's get out of here."

"That's just what I was thinkin'!"

They ran across the street. Preacher knew the bullwhackers would still be watching from the next block. He waved for them to withdraw. If anything had gone wrong with their plans, they were supposed to rendezvous back at Juanita's.

Well, things had gone wrong, Preacher thought . . . about as wrong as they possibly could.

But Roland and Casey were still alive. At least he hoped so. He just had to come up with some idea to keep them that way.

Preacher and Lorenzo gave Powell's men the slip without much difficulty. They were accustomed to handling drunken, lecherous fools in close quarters, not capturing a fella who knew how to move through the shadows like a night wind. If not for what it might mean to Roland and Casey, Preacher would have waited for them and turned the hunters into the hunted. He probably could have killed all of them before he was done.

But if he did that, Garity and Powell might abandon the bargain and kill Roland. Besides, Preacher had Lorenzo with him, and he wanted to keep the old-timer safe, too.

As they walked back to Juanita's, Preacher said, "I reckon you heard that shot inside the whorehouse."

"Yeah, and I seen a bunch o' sheepish-lookin'

fellas come out the back door a minute later," Lorenzo replied, confirming Preacher's hunch about what Powell had done with the house's customers. "Then I heard some more shootin', and you yellin' out in front of the place, so I figured the whole plan was blowed to hell."

"You got that right," Preacher muttered. "They must've spotted Roland as soon as he walked in there. They were probably waitin' for him."

"That varmint Garity's smarter than we done give him credit for."

"Bein' a lowdown skunk don't keep a man from bein' smart. I should've remembered that."

"Anyway, I knew I'd better find you and see what was goin' on. That was when I spotted them fellas skulkin' around like red Injuns."

Preacher nodded. "You done good, Lorenzo. I'm obliged to you."

When they reached the cantina, Juanita met them and said in a low voice, "The men who left with you got here a few minutes ago. I put them in the back room. They said things went wrong."

Preacher nodded. "That they did. Come with us. We got to hash it all out."

The three of them joined the bullwhackers in the back room. The men were sitting at a table, passing around a jug. The burly Cliff Fawcett, acting as spokesman for the group, stood up and asked, "What the hell happened, Preacher?"

"Garity and Powell grabbed Roland," Preacher explained. "They plan on tradin' him and Casey . . . for me."

Fawcett and the others stared at him. "Are you goin' through with it?" Fawcett asked.

"I don't have much choice. They'll kill Roland if I don't, and if Casey's lucky, they'll kill her, too. But they probably won't."

The grim expressions on the rough, bearded faces of the men grew even more bleak.

"Dios mio, Preacher, you can't go through with it," Juanita said. "It's a trick. They will kill you, and the others, as well."

Preacher nodded. "I reckon they'll try."

He took the jug when Fawcett offered it to him, tipped it back, and let some of the fiery tequila slide down his throat and set off a blaze in his belly. When he passed the jug on to Lorenzo, one of the bullwhackers opened his mouth as if he were about to say something about sharing the liquor with a black man, then shrugged and let it go.

Preacher wiped the back of his hand across his mouth, then asked Juanita, "Ain't there any law in this settlement? I know Powell's place ain't in a very good part of town, but there were three shots and nobody came to see what was goin' on."

Juanita's shrug was eloquent. "There is an army garrison, but they have little to do with civil matters unless there is an insurrection. The constables seldom venture into that area, and anyway, Powell pays them to ignore the things that go on in his house. We cannot look to the law for help, Preacher."

The mountain man snorted. "I wasn't plannin' to, just a mite curious is all. I been my own law, most of my life."

"So what are you goin' to do?" Fawcett asked.

Preacher laid out the setup for them. Lorenzo asked, "If you start across that plaza unarmed, what's to stop Garity and Powell from shootin' you right then and there?"

"Nothin' . . . except I think that'd be too easy for Garity. You didn't see him when he had me and the others prisoner. He's got a real mean streak in him. I think he's plannin' on torturin' me to death and makin' it last a long time."

"So you're figurin' if they let Roland and Casey go, then we'll come after you and rescue you before Garity can finish killin' you?"

"We can storm that whorehouse," Fawcett said. "I'd like to see 'em try to keep us out."

Preacher shook his head. "They won't let Casey and Roland go. I suspect they'll have some sharp-shooters with their sights lined on the two of 'em, ready to blow their lights out as soon as Powell gives the signal. But we'll have some sharpshooters of our own." He looked around the table at the bull-whackers. "Who's the best with a rifle?"

After some discussion, they settled on two men named Newcomb and Tobin as the best shots in the bunch. "You two will set your sights on Garity and Powell. I'll see to it they know if they don't go through with the bargain, they won't leave the plaza alive."

"So what it comes down to is you'll be tryin' to outbluff 'em and make 'em let go of Casey and Roland," Lorenzo said.

Preacher nodded. "Yep."

"There's just one problem with that," Lorenzo said.

"That leaves you in the hands of those awful men!" Juanita finished.

"I'll take my chances," Preacher said, grinning around at those gathered in the cantina's back room. "You may have noticed, I'm a mite hard to kill."

At that altitude, the nights were quite cool even in the summer. Wisps of fog floated ghostlike in the plaza in the predawn light. Santa Fe slumbered. The streets were deserted, and so was the plaza with its low-walled well in the center. The settlement was quiet.

Preacher waited with Lorenzo, Fawcett, Newcomb, and Tobin behind a wagon parked on the east side of the plaza. The other five bullwhackers were in a nearby alley, holding rifles in case they were needed.

The mountain man had rounded up a set of buckskins. He wanted to be back in his normal duds for the showdown. If it was to be the day he died, he didn't want to be wearing town clothes. He was bareheaded, and he didn't have rifle, pistol, or knife. He had told Powell he would be unarmed, and he was a man of his word, even when he gave it to no-good snakes.

He hadn't slept any, and weariness set deep in his bones. He knew he wasn't in good enough shape yet. Circumstances didn't leave him much choice, though. He had fortified himself with some of Juanita's frijoles and a few slugs of tequila before leaving the cantina.

Juanita had given him something besides the

frijoles. She had drawn him to her and kissed him hard on the mouth, pulling back and telling him, "Come back to me, Preacher. If you die, the angels who greet you in heaven will not be nearly as pretty as I am."

"I reckon you're a mite mixed up about which direction I'll be goin' when I cross the divide," he had told her with a grin, "but you're right about bein' prettier'n any angel."

"I am right about the other, too," she had whispered as she hugged him.

As pleasant as the memory of that moment was, he put it aside and turned his head to look at the eastern sky. The time had almost come. The sky was growing lighter by the minute as the sun climbed from behind the mountains. Streaks of red and gold shot through the purpling vault above the earth.

Preacher nodded to Lorenzo and the other three men. "Don't forget what we talked about," he told them.

"Ain't no chance o' that," Lorenzo assured him.

As the sun peeked above the mountains, Egan Powell called from the other side of the plaza, "Preacher! Are you there?"

"I'm here, Powell!" Preacher shouted. "Step out where I can see you!"

"You first!"

Counting on the fact that Garity wanted something more satisfying than just having him shot down from ambush, Preacher moved out from behind the wagon into clear view of anyone watching from the other side of the broad, open plaza. He held his hands out at his sides and called, "Here

I am, just like I said I would be! You can see for yourself I ain't got no guns!"

"Turn around!" Powell ordered.

Still holding his hands out, Preacher turned slowly, revealing that he didn't have a pistol stuck in his belt behind his back. When he was facing across the plaza again, he said, "All right, I kept my part of the bargain! Let's see Roland and Casey!"

From the narrow alley between impressive-looking buildings across the way, Roland Bartlett stepped into view. He still wore the Mexican duds, but not the sombrero. A brawny, bald-headed man followed him. It was Preacher's first good look at the expatriate American whoremonger, Egan Powell.

Holding a pistol pointed at Roland, Powell called, "You try anything fancy, and I'll kill this boy, Preacher!"

"*You* try anything fancy, and you're a dead man!" Preacher shot back. "There's a rifle pointin' at you right now!"

"Same for you! It looks to me like this is a stand-off, so we may as well go through with it!"

Preacher frowned. "Wait just a damned minute! Where's Garity and the girl?"

"They're not coming," Powell replied with a laugh. "Trading two for one isn't fair, Preacher. You get the boy back. The girl stays with me."

Preacher wanted to lash out angrily. The deception didn't take him completely by surprise. He had expected some sort of trickery from his enemies.

"How about it?" Powell prodded. "You can still save the kid's life."

Preacher took a deep breath. "Send him over here."

"You start this way!"

Preacher glanced behind the wagon. Newcomb and Tobin had their long-barreled rifles trained on Powell. Lorenzo looked worried, as usual. Preacher flicked a quick grin at the old-timer to tell him it would be all right, then stepped farther into the plaza, walking toward the other side with a firm step.

Up ahead, Roland stumbled slightly as he started out. Powell kept his pistol trained on the young man's back, speaking quietly. Preacher couldn't make out the words, but he knew they had to be a warning not to try anything.

Time seemed to drag as Preacher and Roland stumbled toward each other. Preacher didn't get in any hurry. Behind him, the sun rose higher above the mountains.

And he saw what he hoped to see, the glint of sunlight reflecting off rifle barrels in a pair of windows in one of the buildings across the plaza. Newcomb and Tobin knew to look for those same reflections, and the two bullwhackers ought to be shifting their aim away from Powell and toward the man's hired killers. Preacher knew their orders were to shoot Roland down just before he reached safety, when Preacher would be too close to the other side of the plaza to escape.

Preacher didn't intend to let things get that far.

He veered a little to his left to go around the well. Roland moved to his right to do the same. The young man's face was pale and stricken, and as he came within hearing, he said, "Preacher, I'm so sorry—"

"Forget it," Preacher said. "This ain't over. Stumble a little."

"What?"

"Slow down!" The timing was almost right, almost . . .

"Kill the boy!" Powell bellowed suddenly as he caught on to what Preacher was doing. "Kill him now!"

CHAPTER 27

Preacher dived forward and to the side, tackling Roland Bartlett and driving the boy off his feet. From the corner of his eye, he saw powdersmoke erupt from the windows of the building across the plaza. He and Roland hit the ground behind the well, and the rifle balls hummed past harmlessly to thud into the hard-packed dirt.

Two shots boomed from the wagon behind them. That would be Newcomb and Tobin, Preacher knew. He risked a glance over the low wall that ran around the well and saw one man toppling from a window, obviously fatally wounded. He couldn't tell if the bullwhackers had gotten the other man.

Preacher turned his head toward the wagon and shouted, "Cliff!"

Fawcett stepped out from behind the vehicle for a second. His powerful arm went back and then flashed forward. The knife he had thrown spun glitteringly in the early morning sunlight.

The throw was accurate. The knife blade dug

into the ground only a few feet from Preacher. He reached out and grabbed the handle.

More guns began to boom. Other men who worked for the whorehouse owner must have been nearby, as Preacher suspected, and Powell called them into action.

The bullwhackers poured out of the alley where they had been hiding and returned the fire. Preacher and Roland kept their heads down as rifle balls crisscrossed the plaza in a deadly storm of lead.

"Preacher, we have to get out of here!" Roland gasped. "Garity's still got Casey!"

"I know. Did you see her?"

Roland nodded. "Just for a minute. She looked like she was all right." He grimaced. "I'm sorry I couldn't pull it off. A couple of men jumped me as soon as I went in there last night. It was like they were waiting for me!"

"They were," Preacher said. "Garity must have heard we were in town and figured we'd try somethin'. He was probably spyin' from upstairs and gave Powell's men the high sign as soon as he recognized you. Was that you who fired the pistol?"

Roland nodded. "Yes, but I didn't hit anything except the wall. One of the men had already grabbed me from behind." He paused as the rifles continued to roar on both sides of the plaza. "You knew Garity and Powell were going to double-cross you, didn't you?"

"Figured it was pretty damn likely," the mountain man acknowledged with a nod.

"So you set things up to double-cross them right back."

Preacher grinned. "Let's just say I was ready for trouble."

The shots died away then, and a moment later Cliff Fawcett called, "Hey, Preacher, I think we got 'em all!"

"What about Powell?"

"Sorry! He ducked back out of sight before anybody could draw a bead on him."

"That means he'll go back to the whorehouse and tell Garity what happened," Roland said. He clutched Preacher's arm. "They're liable to kill Casey! We have to stop them!"

Preacher knew the young man was right. "You ready to risk it?" he asked.

"Anything!"

"Then come on."

Holding the knife, Preacher stood up and ran toward the far side of the plaza. Roland was right behind him.

One of Powell's men wasn't dead after all, only wounded. He reared up and thrust a pistol at them. The weapon blasted, but the ball cut through the air between Preacher and Roland. A second later, several rifles roared as the bullwhackers returned the fire, and the would-be killer was thrown backward by the impact of several lead balls slamming into his body.

Preacher and Roland reached the alley where Powell had disappeared. Preacher knew that Lorenzo, Fawcett, and the rest of the men would follow them, but there was no time to wait for their allies. He and Roland had to reach the whorehouse just as fast as they could if they were going to be in time to save

Casey. Garity might kill her, or he might decide to try to escape and take her with him.

Santa Fe was honeycombed with streets and alleys that twisted crazily and sometimes abruptly came to unexpected dead ends. Preacher had to rely on his uncanny sense of direction in order to guide him and Roland through the squalid maze. He wasn't sure if every turn they made was the right one, but suddenly he recognized a landmark and knew Powell's place was down the street they had just entered.

Preacher grabbed Roland's arm and pulled him back around the corner. "What are you doing?" the young man demanded frantically. "We've got to find Casey!"

"If we go chargin' up to the front of the place, they'll be waitin' for us and gun us down," Preacher said. "We'll circle and come in from behind."

He was keenly aware they had only a knife between them as far as weapons were concerned. He hadn't wanted to take the time to get anything else, but that also meant they would have to be careful. He led Roland on a circuitous route that took them to the alley running behind the whorehouse.

There was a buggy parked there with a couple horses already hitched to it. As Preacher and Roland paused at the corner of a shed, Egan Powell emerged from the back door of the building and headed for the buggy, carrying a valise. Probably stuffed with money, Preacher thought. Powell was heading for the tall and uncut while the getting was good. The question was whether Garity and Casey would go with him.

The answer wasn't long in coming. Garity appeared in the back door, dragging a struggling Casey with him. He was having trouble controlling her because he had only one good arm. As she let out an angry cry and almost broke away from him, Garity yelled, "You bitch!" and let go of her to slam a punch into her face, stunning her.

That was more than Roland could stand. Moving too fast for Preacher to grab him, he broke out from behind the shed, shouted, "Bastard!" and raced toward the building.

Powell was placing the valise in the back of the buggy when Roland emerged from cover. He jerked around, grated a curse, and pulled a pistol from under his coat. As he eared back the hammer, Preacher stepped into view and threw the knife.

The expert throw had the weapon revolving once before the blade buried itself deep in Powell's chest. The man staggered back a step as he pulled the trigger. The shot went into the air over Roland's head.

Garity saw Roland coming and thrust Casey's limp body away from him. He pulled a knife from his belt and slashed at Roland with it. Even left-handed, he was swift and deadly with a knife. Roland tried to twist away, but the blade raked across his midsection, slicing his shirt open and drawing blood. He ducked the backhanded slash that Garity swung at him, but he couldn't avoid the kick that Garity drove into his chest. It sent him sprawling into the alley.

Powell had dropped his empty pistol and fallen to his knees. He pawed futilely at the handle of the knife in his chest. Preacher ripped the blade free as he dashed past. Blood welled from one corner of Powell's open mouth as he swayed there for a second longer, then toppled forward on his face.

"Garity!" Preacher yelled.

The outlaw swung to face him as Preacher leaped and swung the knife. Sparks flew in the air as steel clashed. The men collided, went down, broke apart and rolled away from each other. Garity reached his feet a second earlier than Preacher did and charged the mountain man, swiping his knife through the air with such ferocity that Preacher had to back up as he barely parried thrust after thrust.

Preacher heard Powell groan behind him. The man might be dying, but he wasn't dead yet. Powell heaved himself up from the ground and tackled Preacher, wrapping his arms around the mountain's man knees. With his legs jerked out from under him, Preacher went over backward.

Garity raised the knife high, ready to plunge the blade into Preacher's chest. Before the blow could fall, Roland hit him from behind. They fell, and all four men tangled on the ground.

Powell got his hands around Preacher's throat. Looking into the man's glaring, murderous eyes from only inches away, Preacher saw Powell's strength fading. Only a few more moments of life remained in the whorehouse owner, but that might be enough for him to choke the life out of the mountain man.

Preacher still had the knife in his hand, and he drove it upward into Powell's throat, unleashing a flood of crimson. Powell let out a grotesque, bubbling cry and slumped sideways as his grip on

Preacher's throat slid away. Preacher shoved clear of the corpse and rolled to his feet again.

A few feet away, Garity was on top of Roland, trying to stab him. Roland jerked his head aside. The blade gashed the side of his neck.

"Garity!" Casey cried.

Preacher watched as Garity looked up. He saw the outlaw's eyes widen as Garity peered at Casey, who stood a couple feet away with a pistol gripped tightly in both hands, aimed directly at his face. Before Garity could do more than open his mouth to yell a protest that went unvoiced, Casey pulled the trigger.

The pistol boomed. Smoke gushed from the barrel and engulfed Garity's head. The outlaw flew backward and landed with his back against the buggy's wheel. His head slumped forward. As the smoke cleared, Preacher saw that the pistol ball had smashed Garity's skull and blown out the back of his head. It was a grisly mess.

Lorenzo had come running up along with Fawcett and the other bullwhackers during Preacher's struggle with Powell. He had been so busy fighting for his life that he hadn't noticed their arrival. "She took my pistol," the old-timer said. "I figured she had it comin'."

Casey slowly lowered the pistol. A strand of gray smoke still curled from its barrel. "Come back from that, you son of a bitch," she whispered at Garity.

Then she dropped the gun and would have collapsed if Roland, bleeding from several wounds, hadn't been there to pull her into his arms and support her.

"It's over," he told her as she started to sob. "It's really over this time."

Preacher looked at Lorenzo and nodded. "You done good givin' her your gun that way. If anybody had the right to blow that varmint's brains out, it was her."

"That's what I figured," Lorenzo agreed. "You all right, Preacher?"

"Yeah. A mite tired, that's all." In fact, when he tried to take a step, he staggered and almost fell. Fawcett gripped his arm to steady him.

"We need to get you back to Juanita's place," Lorenzo said. "I got a hunch that after a few weeks of the señora takin' care of you, you'll be just fine."

"I expect you're right about that," Preacher said with a grin.

Roland and Casey came to see him at the cantina a week later. They had been staying at one of the hotels in town. They had some healing up of their own to do, so Preacher didn't worry when he didn't see them for a while.

He was feeling a lot better himself. Plenty of sleep and good food—along with nobody trying to kill him—worked wonders for his health. He was sitting at the table in the corner with Juanita and Lorenzo when the two young people came in and started across the room toward them.

Preacher raised a hand in greeting. "You two look like you're doin' a mite better than the last time I saw you," he commented.

Roland still had a bandage on the gash on his neck, and Preacher could tell from the way he moved that his torso was probably bandaged where Garity had slashed him. But he had a big grin on his face.

Casey was smiling, too. As the two of them sat down at the table, she said, "We came to issue an invitation."

"Oh?" Preacher said with a twinkle in his eyes. "Somethin' special about to happen?"

"We're getting married," Roland burst out as if he could no longer contain himself.

"Well, congratulations," Lorenzo said. "Can't say as I'm surprised, though."

"I was surprised when Roland asked me," Casey said. "I didn't figure any man would ever want me after everything that—"

Roland stopped her by laying a hand on hers and squeezing.

Preacher drawled, "It's a wise man who knows that today and tomorrow are a hell of a lot more important than yesterday. Somebody said that once, but I don't remember who."

"Let's just call it the wisdom of Preacher," Juanita suggested.

"Let's not," he said dryly. He changed the subject by asking Casey, "So, I reckon this means you'll be headin' to St. Louis with Roland when he starts back with the wagons?"

"I'm not going back to St. Louis," Roland replied before Casey could say anything.

Preacher raised his shaggy eyebrows. "You ain't? What're you gonna do with those wagons and ox teams?"

"I've already done it. I sold them to one of the

other freight outfits. Cliff and the other bullwhackers will be going with them."

"So what do you plan on doin' with yourself if you ain't in the freight business no more?"

"I was negotiating with a man who owns a store here in Santa Fe, trying to sell him the goods we brought out here," Roland explained. "But when he mentioned that he wanted to sell out, *I* just bought the store from *him* instead. It'll be well-stocked with all the goods we had in the wagons."

"And I'll help him run it," Casey said.

Preacher smiled and nodded slowly. For Casey, remaining here in Santa Fe would be a lot better than going back to St. Louis. The odds of anyone recognizing her or knowing anything about her past were a lot smaller.

"Sounds like things have worked out just fine for you."

"Thanks to you, Preacher," Roland said. "I'm not sure I'd ever want to go back over the Santa Fe Trail without you."

"And we ain't goin' that way when we leave here," Lorenzo said. "Preacher's done promised to show me the mountains."

"But you can't leave before the wedding," Casey protested.

Juanita reached over and took Preacher's hand. "He's not going anywhere," she said firmly. "He still has a lot of recuperating to do, and I intend to see that he does it."

Preacher chuckled. "You don't hear me arguin', do you?"

But he knew the time would come when the call of the wild and lonesome country would be too strong for him to resist. When that day arrived, he would have to bid a fond farewell to Juanita and answer that summons, even though she would be sad to see him go.

The trail of Preacher's life was a long and winding one, and he hadn't reached the end of it just yet.

Turn the page for an exciting preview of

MATT JENSEN, THE LAST MOUNTAIN MAN:
DAKOTA AMBUSH

by

William W. Johnstone
with J. A. Johnstone

Coming in February 2011
Wherever books are sold

CHAPTER 1

When Matt Jensen rode into Swan, Wyoming, few who knew him would have recognized him. He had a heavy beard, his hair was uncommonly long, and he looked every bit the part of a man who had not been under a roof for two months. He had said good-bye to Smoke Jensen in Fort Collins, Colorado, arranging to meet him in Swan eight weeks later. Not since then had Matt seen civilization, having spent the entire two months in the mountains prospecting for gold.

The success of Matt's two months of isolation was manifested by a canvas bag he had hanging from the saddle horn. The bag was full of color-showing ore. Prospecting wasn't new to Matt. He had learned the trade under the tutelage of his mentor, Smoke Jensen, so he knew the color in the ore was genuine. But exactly how successful he had been would depend upon the assayer's report.

Swan was a fly-blown little settlement, not served by any railroad, though there was stagecoach service to Rawlings where one could connect with the

Union Pacific. The town had a single street that was lined on both sides by unpainted, rip-sawed, false-fronted buildings. It could have been any of several hundred towns in a dozen western states. As Matt rode down the street, a couple scantily dressed soiled doves stood on a balcony and called down to him.

"Hey, cowboy, you're new to town, ain't you?" one of them shouted.

"You gotta be new 'cause I don't know you," the other one added. "And I reckon I *know* just about ever' man in town if you get my drift," she added in a ribald tone of voice.

Matt smiled, nodded, and touched the brim of his hat by way of returning their greeting.

"Come on up and keep us company. We'll give you a good welcome," the first one shouted down to him.

"Ladies, until I get a bath, I'm not even fit company for my horse," Matt called up to the two women as he rode underneath the overhanging balcony where the two women were standing.

The second soiled dove pinched her nose and, exaggerating, made a waving motion with her hand. "Oh, honey, you've got that right," she teased.

Laughing, Matt rode on down the street until he reached a small building at the far end. A sign in front of the building read, J.A. MONTGOMERY, ASSAYER.

Matt swung down from his saddle and tied his horse at the hitching rail. Hefting the canvas bag over one shoulder, he stepped inside where he was greeted by a small, thin man.

"Can I help you?" the little man asked.

"Are you the assayer?"

"I am."

Matt set the canvas bag on the counter, then took out a handful of rocks and laid them alongside the bag.

"I need you to take a look at this," Matt said.

Montgomery chuckled. "You want me to tell you if it is gold or pyrite, right?"

"No, mister," Matt said. "I know it's gold. What I want you to do is tell me how much money all this is worth."

The assayer picked up a couple rocks and looked at them casually, before putting them back down. Then, taking a second look at one of them, he picked it up again, and examined it through a magnifying glass.

"What do you think?" Matt asked.

"You're right," Montgomery said. "It is gold."

"You have any idea as to the value?"

"Do all the rocks have this much color?"

"I wouldn't have bothered carrying them in if they didn't," Matt replied.

"Well, then I would say you have two or three hundred dollars here. In fact, I'll give you three hundred dollars for the entire bag, right now."

Matt put the rocks back in the bag. "Would you now?"

"In cash," Montgomery said.

"You always cheat your customers like that?" Matt asked.

"What are you talking about?"

"What I have here is worth two thousand dollars if it is worth a cent," he said. "Thank you, Mr.

Montgomery, but I believe I'll take my business somewhere else."

"I'm the only assayer in town."

"Perhaps. But Swan isn't the only town," Matt said as he left the office.

Up the street from the assayer's office Matt saw a sign that read HAIRCUTS, SHAVES, BATHS.

"Tell you what, Spirit, you've had to put up with my stink long enough," Matt said, speaking to his horse. "I think I'll get myself cleaned up before I go looking for Smoke."

Dismounting in front of the building, Matt lifted his bag of ore from the horse, then went inside. Fifteen minutes later he was sitting in a tub of warm water, scrubbing himself with a big piece of lye soap.

"Don't know if there is enough lye soap in all of Wyoming to get that carcass clean," a voice teased.

"Smoke!" Matt said, a big smile spreading across his face. He started to stand.

"No, no need to stand," Smoke said, holding his hand out, palm forward, to stop him. "You think I want to see that?"

Matt laughed. "How did you know I was in here?"

"We did say we were going to meet in Swan today, didn't we?"

"Yeah."

"I saw Spirit tied up out front. Did you think I wouldn't recognize him? He used to be my horse, remember?"

"I remember," Matt said.

"How did you do?" Smoke asked.

"See that bag there? It's full of ore. At least two thousand dollars worth, I would guess."

Smoke whistled. "That is good," he said.

"Tell you what, I'll be finished here in a bit. What do you say we go get us a beer? I haven't had a beer in two months."

"Sounds good to me. I'll go get us a table, and I'll even let you buy the beer, seein' as you had such a good outing," Smoke said.

A few minutes after Smoke left, Matt was out of the tub, had his shirt and trousers on, and had just strapped on his gun belt when three men burst, un-expectedly, into the room. All three had pistols in their hands.

"We'll take that bag of ore, mister," one of them shouted.

"Who are you?" Matt asked.

"We're the folks you're goin' to give that bag of ore to," one of the three said, and they all laughed.

While the three men were laughing, Matt was drawing his pistol, and while they were reacting to him drawing his pistol, Matt was shooting.

The pistol shots sounded exceptionally loud in the closed room as Matt and the three men ex-changed gunfire. When the shooting stopped Matt had not a scratch, but the three would-be robbers lay dead on the floor.

Matt was examining the bodies when four more men came bursting into the room. Three of them were carrying sawed-off shotguns. They were also wearing badges.

The fourth man with them was the assayer.

"There he is, Sheriff! He is the one who stole the bag of ore!" Montgomery shouted, pointing at Matt.

"What?" Matt asked. "What are you talking about? I didn't steal any ore from you!"

"He come into the office a little while ago," Montgomery said. "He had a bag of worthless rocks, usin' it as a way o' getting my attention. While I was looking at his rocks, he stole a bag of genuine ore. I didn't have no choice but to send my brother and two cousins to get the ore back. Didn't know it would come to this, though."

Montgomery looked down at the three dead bodies, then shook his head sadly. "If I had known they was goin' to be murdered like this, I never woulda sent 'em over here. A bag plumb full of gold nuggets isn't worth getting three good men killed."

"Come along, mister," the sheriff said, waving his shotgun menacingly at Matt. "You are about to learn that folks don't come into my town to steal and murder and get away with it."

"Sheriff, this man is lying," Matt said. "I brought some ore in for him to assay. He tried to cheat me out of it so I told him I would go somewhere else. You think I would stop to take a bath if I stole anything in this town?"

"I don't know what you would do, mister," the sheriff said. "But the thing is, I know Montgomery and I don't know you. So I reckon we'll let the judge sort it all out."

Matt looked at the three shotguns leveled at him. He was holding a pistol and he had a notion, but declined. He might be able to kill the sheriff and both his deputies before they realized what was happening, but then, he might not, either. They were carrying shotguns, which gave them an advantage. It would also mean killing innocent men and he couldn't bring himself to do that.

Matt turned the pistol around and handed it, handle first, to the sheriff.

"You are making a mistake, Sheriff," Matt said.

"You let me worry about that."

Montgomery reached for the sack of gold ore.

"Leave it," the sheriff said.

"Why should I leave it, Sheriff? This is the self-same sack of ore he stole."

"Leave it," the sheriff said again. "We'll let the judge decide whether or not that gold ore is yours."

Montgomery glared at the sheriff, then looked over at Matt. "I'll be standin' in the crowd, watchin' you hang," Montgomery said.

"Let's go, mister," the sheriff said to Matt with a wave of his shotgun. "I got a nice jail cell for you until the judge gets here."

Matt had been in jail for three days awaiting the arrival of the circuit judge so he could be tried. Smoke sat outside his cell visiting with him.

"I shouldn't have left you," Smoke said.

"Why not? If you had stayed, you would be in jail with me right now," Matt said. "What good would that do?"

"I guess you have a point. I couldn't help you any if I were in there with you. At least, by being out here, if you can't convince the judge you are innocent, I'll take matters into my own hands. I'll get you out of here, no matter what I have to do."

Matt was about to answer when he looked up to see the sheriff coming into the jailhouse, leading Montgomery. Montgomery was in shackles.

"What is it?" Matt asked. "What is going on?"

"You're free to go," the sheriff said as he opened the door to the cell. "Mr. Montgomery here will be taking your place."

"Sheriff, I have to hand it to you for doing your job," Matt said. "You've had a good three days of investigating."

"It wasn't me," the sheriff said. "It was John Bryce."

"Who?"

"John Bryce," the sheriff repeated. "Mr. Bryce is a newspaper writer for the *Swan Journal*, and he has been doing some, he calls it, investigative journalism. Here, read this," he said, handing Matt a newspaper.

An Innocent Man in Jail!

J. A. MONTGOMERY A CROOK
SHOULD BE CALLED TO ACCOUNT

We are under obligation to report to the public in general and to Sheriff Daniels in particular, the criminal activities of J. A. Montgomery who has set himself up in Swan as an assayer. Montgomery is no such thing. Although he has hanging on the wall of his office a degree from Colorado School of Mines, this newspaper is in receipt of a letter from that institution claiming that no such person as J. A. Montgomery graduated, nor was ever a student there.

Further investigation has disclosed that Montgomery is wanted by the sheriff of Madison County, Montana, where, also fraudulently passing himself off as an assayer, he murdered and robbed a prospector. The circumstances of that event are so similar to the recent event between J. A. Montgomery, his brother Clyde, two cousins, Drake and Birch, and a recent visitor to our town, Matt Jensen, that this newspaper believes Mr. Jensen, who is currently incarcerated, is innocent.

Should Matt Jensen be any longer detained, it would be a gross miscarriage of justice. Subjecting the county to a trial to establish his innocence would be a waste of time and taxpayers' money. The writer of this piece, John Bryce, is willing to stake his reputation upon the accuracy of this report, and urges Sheriff Daniels to act quickly to correct this error.

"After the paper come out I sent a telegram to the sheriff of Madison County Montana, and he answered that Montgomery was wanted for murder, just like the newspaper article said. I went over to talk to Montgomery and found that he was tryin' to leave town."

"So I am free to go?" Matt asked.

"Yes, sir, you are free as a bird."

"Is this fella, John Bryce in town?" Matt asked.

"Yes, sir, he's over at the newspaper office right now," Sheriff Daniels said.

"I think I'll go look him up."

"Do you own this paper?" Matt asked when he and Smoke found John Bryce hard at work in the newspaper office.

"Oh, heaven's no. It takes a lot of money to own

and operate your own newspaper," John said. "I just work here for Mr. Peabody as one of his journalists. Someday I expect to own my own paper, though," he said.

Matt, who had had the ore returned to him, reached down into his canvas bag and pulled out four pretty good sized rocks. "Here," Matt said, handing the rocks to the newspaper man. "Cash these in and you may have your paper sooner than you realize. If there is ever anything I can do for you, just let me know."

"Bless you, Mr. Jensen," John said, accepting the gold with a broad smile. "I'll never forget you for this."

Chapter 2

Fullerton, Dakota Territory, twelve years later

A brick had been thrown through the front window, and great jagged spears of the glass reached out from all corners of the frame. Two months earlier John Bryce had paid a professional painter to come over from Bismarck to paint the window.

Fullerton Defender

John Bryce—*Publisher*
Millie Bryce—*Office Manager*

The letters were broad and black, outlined in white and gold. That sign, once a source of pride, was now no more than a few discordant letters on the remaining shards of glass.

LLE	ON	F	DER
J	y		*lisher*

Not one letter of Millie's name remained.

At the moment John was standing inside the office of the *Fullerton Defender*, surveying the damage. The perpetrators had done more than just break his front window, they had also trashed the office. His arm was around his wife, and he held her close to him as she sobbed quietly. Type had been scattered about the room, newsprint had been ripped and spread around, the Washington Hand Press, by which John put out his weekly paper, was lying on its side.

They had come to the newspaper office directly from their breakfast table, after City Marshal Tipton told of the break-in. More than a dozen citizens of the town had already been drawn to the scene of the crime by the time John and Millie arrived. The group stood in a little cluster on the boardwalk in front of the building.

The perpetrators had left a note.

*Don't be writting no more bad artacles about
Lord Denbigh or we will kum back and do
more damige to you nex time.*

"Who would do such a thing?" Millie asked between sobs.

"It's fairly apparent, isn't it?" John replied. "Denbigh did it."

"We don't know that," Marshal Tipton said.

"The note doesn't suggest that to you, Marshal?" John asked.

"Just the opposite," Tipton said. "Denbigh is an educated man. Now, I'm not as smart as you are, but even I know how to spell the words *come*, and *damage*."

"I don't mean Denbigh did it himself," John said. "I mean he had it done."

"Maybe there are just some people in town who got upset with you because you've been coming down pretty hard on Denbigh in your stories. Denbigh has done a lot of good for this town."

"Really? What good has he done?"

"Let's just say he does a lot of business with the town."

"Yes, by allowing only the businesses he wants to stay, and squeezing out the others. He's killing this town, Marshal Tipton. And the people in town know it, only they are too frightened to do anything about it."

"So you plan to mount a one person campaign do you, Bryce?"

"If I am the only one willing to do anything about it, then yes, I will mount a one person campaign."

"Uh—huh," Tipton said, stroking his jaw as he surveyed the shambles of the newspaper office. "And look what it got you."

"It has set me back a bit, I'll admit," John said. "But it won't stop me. It'll take me a day to clean up. I'll have the paper out this Thursday, just as I do every Thursday."

"I'll help you pick up all the type, Mr. Bryce," a young boy of about twelve said.

"Thank you, Kenny."

"I can go get Jimmy to help too, if you want me to."

"That would be nice," John said. He turned

toward the group of people still standing outside the office, and seeing Ernie Westpheling, called out to him.

"Ernie, would you help me set the printing press back up?"

"Sure thing." Ernie, who had been a colonel during the Civil War, was a local businessman who owned a gun store.

A couple other men also volunteered to help, and within a few minutes the printing press had been righted and was once again in its proper place. John surveyed it for a moment or two, then patted the press with a big smile.

"Not a scratch," he said. "It takes more than a few of Denbigh's hooligans to put ole George out of business."

"George? I thought your name was John," one of the men who had helped him said.

"It is. George is the name of my printing press."

"You've named your press?"

"Sure. It's not only a part of this newspaper, it is the heart of the newspaper."

"What are you going to do about your window?" Ernie asked.

"I'll have to order a new glass from Bismarck," John said. "In the meantime I guess I'll just board that side up."

"What are you going to do about this, Marshal?" Ernie asked.

"I'll look into it, see if I can find out who did it," Tipton replied. "But if I don't come up with any witnesses, I don't know what I can do."

"There has to be a witness somewhere," Millie

said. "It had to make a lot of noise when they broke out the window."

"You live no more than a couple blocks from here, Mrs. Bryce. Did you hear anything?" Tipton asked.

"No."

"The newspaper belongs to you and your husband, so you would be even more attentive, I would think. You heard nothing, but you expect others in the town did?" Tipton shook his head. "No ma'am, I don't expect I'm going to find anything."

"That's because you aren't looking in the right place," John said. "You and I both know who is behind this."

Tipton glared at John, but he said nothing.

Central Colorado

"Is the son of a bitch still following?" Cyrus Hayes asked Emmet Cruise. The two men had stopped for a moment in order for Hayes to relieve himself, and Cruise crawled up onto a rock to look back along the trail.

"Yeah, he's there," Cruise said.

"What the hell? Are we leaving bread crumbs or something?" Hayes asked as he buttoned his trousers. "Who the hell is that, and how is he staying on our trail?"

"I don't know who he is, but he's good," Cruise said.

"Yeah, well, let's go," Hayes said. "The more distance we can put between us and him, the better I will feel."

* * *

Earlier that morning, Hayes and Cruise had robbed the Rocky Mountain Bank and Trust in Pueblo, Colorado, and, during the robbery, had shot down in cold blood, a teller and two customers. The two customers, a man and his pregnant wife, had been friends of Matt Jensen. Because of that, even before the state got around to offering a reward for two bank robbers and murderers, Matt went after them.

Knowing they would be pursued, the two outlaws took great pains to cover their true trail, while leaving false trails for anyone who would follow. Reaching a stream, they rode right down the middle of it, confident they were erasing any sign that could possibly be followed.

For most trackers that might work, but not for Matt. He had learned his tracking expertise from Smoke Jensen, who had learned his own skills from an old mountain man named Preacher, arguably, the best tracker who had ever lived. Because that know-how had been passed down, Matt was almost as accomplished as Smoke or Preacher. He could follow a trail through the water by paying attention to such things as rocks dislodged against the flow of water, or silt disturbed by horse's hooves, leaving a little pattern in the water for several minutes afterward.

He was tracking down the streambed when a rifle boomed and a .44-40 bullet cracked through the air no more than an inch from his head.

He leaped from his horse and ran though the stream, his feet churning up silver sheets of spray as he ran. The rifle barked again. Right on top of that he heard the flatter sound of a pistol shot. Almost simultaneously two bullets plunged into the water close by.

Reaching the bank on the opposite side of the stream, Matt dived to the ground then worked his way toward a nearby outcropping of rocks. He sat with his back against the biggest of the rocks while he took a few deep breaths.

"Who are you?" one of the men called out to him.

"My name is Jensen," Matt called back.

"Jensen? Matt Jensen? Son of a bitch!" The outlaw had obviously recognized Matt's name. There was fear in his voice.

"Which one are you?" Matt called back. "Are you Hayes or Cruise?"

"What? I'm Hayes. How did you know our names?"

"Half the town saw you two boys riding away from the bank, and half the ones who saw you, knew who you were."

"What are you after us for, Jensen?" Hayes called. "I've heard of you, but I ain't never heard that you was someone who would chase a fella down for the reward. Is that why you are chasin' us?"

"I'm not after the reward."

"Then if you ain't after the reward, what the hell are you comin' after us for?"

"It seems the thing to do," Matt said without being specific as to his reasons.

"Well, mister, you made a big mistake," Hayes shouted. "'Cause all you're goin' to do now is get yourself kilt!"

Hayes and Cruise fired again, and once more the bullets whistled by harmlessly.

"You still there?" Hayes called.

"I'm still here."

"I tell you what, mister. Me and my partner here just talked it over, and we got us an idée. We have got us near 'bout five thousand dollars that we taken from the bank. A thousand of it is your'n if'n you'll just go away," Hayes called.

"No deal."

There was a beat of silence, then Hayes called out again. "All right, how 'bout two thousand? We'll give you two thousand and all you got to do is let us ride away."

"You expect me to believe you two are willing to give me nearly half of what you took from the bank?"

"Why not? It's no big deal, we can always rob another bank," Hayes shouted back. "Two thousand dollars. You don't come across money like that very often, do you?"

"Not very often," Matt agreed.

"So, what do you think? You going to take us up on the offer?"

"Let me think about it," Matt said.

"You do that."

Matt had no intention of taking the two men up on their offer, but he responded in such a way as to enable him to stall for time until he figured out how best to handle the situation. He picked up a stick about two feet long, put his hat on top of the stick, then raised it slightly above the rock.

A rifle boomed, and the hat flew off the end of the stick.

"Ha! You got 'im, Cruise!" Hayes shouted.

"Whoa, I guess you two boys weren't really serious

about giving me all that money, were you?" Matt called out.

"Son of a bitch, I missed!" Cruise said.

"Mister, you know what I said about givin' you that money? Well you can forget about it. We ain't goin' to give you nothin'," Hayes said. "Except maybe a bullet right between your eyes." His shout was punctuated with another rifle shot hitting the top of the rock, then whining off into the valley.

After that there was silence.

The silence stretched into several long minutes.

"Hayes? Cruise? You still up there?" Matt called.

Another rifle shot hit the rock just to the right of him. The one with the rifle had improved his position. As Matt scooted around to put the rock between himself and the shooter, there was a second shot.

Matt saw the puff of smoke from the rifle, so he aimed at the spot and waited. Seconds later he was rewarded by seeing Cruise's face raise up.

Matt pulled the trigger, and Cruise fell forward, sliding belly down until his face ended up in the stream. Matt watched for a moment longer to make certain Cruise was dead when suddenly he heard the sound of horse's hooves. Looking around he saw that Hayes had used the opportunity to get mounted and was galloping toward him. Hayes had his pistol in his hand, firing at Matt as he rode.

Matt fired back. A puff of dust rose from Hayes' vest, followed by a tiny spray of dust and blood. Hayes pitched backward out of his saddle but one foot hung up in the stirrup. His horse continued to run, raising a plume of water as the outlaw was dragged through the stream. When the horse reached the other side of the stream and started up the bank, Hayes' foot disconnected from the stirrup and he lay motionless, half in the water and half out, not more than ten feet from where the body of his partner lay.

Matt ran over to them, his gun still drawn, but the gun wasn't necessary. Both men were dead.

CHAPTER 3

Hayes and Cruise were not the first outlaws Matt had ever tracked down. He was neither a lawman nor someone who hunted other men for any reward the government paid, but he was always on the side of law and order. Sometimes, going after an outlaw just seemed to be the right thing to do.

He never sought trouble but, somehow, trouble had a way of finding him. As a result, Matt Jensen was one of a select company of men in the West whose very name evoked fear among the outlaws and evil doers.

Matt took the bag of bank money from Hayes' saddle, and started back to Pueblo, but just after noon, his horse stepped into an unseen prairie dog hole. The horse broke a leg and Matt had to shoot him. It was a hard thing to do; Spirit was only the second horse he had ever owned. Indeed, that horse had carried with him the spirit of his first horse, who was also named, not coincidentally, Spirit. There was nothing Matt could do but take shanks mare, so, throwing his saddle, saddle bags, and the money bag over his shoulder, he began walking.

Matt Jensen dropped his saddle with a sigh of relief, then climbed up the berm to stand on the ballast between the railroad tracks. Before him the clear tracks of the Denver and New Orleans lay like twin black ribbons across the landscape, stretching north to south from horizon to horizon. For the moment they were as cold and empty as the barren sand, rocks, and mountains that surrounded him, but Matt knew a train would pass through there sometime before sundown.

Since putting his horse down, Matt had walked for two hours, carrying his saddle with him. At the moment, he was standing alongside the railroad tracks some thirty miles south of Pueblo. All that was left for him to do was catch the train, so, using his saddle as a pillow, he lay down beside the tracks to wait. As he waited, he thought of the horse he had just put down. In order to combat the grief that threatened to consume him, he turned his thoughts to his first horse named Spirit, and how he had come by him.

Right after the war, while still a boy named Matt Cavanaugh, the man known as Matt Jensen made the trip west from Missouri with his father, mother, and sister. On the trail west, their wagon was attacked by outlaws, and all were killed but Matt. He escaped, managing to kill one of the outlaws in the process. The incident left Matt an orphan and shortly thereafter he wound up in the Soda Springs Home for Wayward Boys and Girls. Rather than providing a refuge, the orphanage was so evilly run that eventually Matt escaped from the home.

A few days later Matt, nearly dead from hunger and the cold, was found in the mountains by the legendary Smoke Jensen. Smoke took the boy in and raised him to adulthood. Out of respect and appreciation, Matt Cavanaugh changed his name to Matt Jensen and though there was no blood relationship between the two men, they regarded each other as brothers. When it was time for Matt to go out on his own, Smoke had surprised him with an offer.

"Why don't you go out to the corral and pick out your horse?" Smoke had asked.

"My horse?"

"Yeah, your horse. A man's got to have a horse."

"Which horse is mine?" Matt asked.

"Why don't you take the best one?" Smoke replied. "Except for that one," he added, pointing to an appaloosa in one corner of the corral. "That one is mine."

"Which horse is the best?" Matt asked.

"Uh-uh," Smoke replied, shaking his head. "I'm willing to give you the best horse in my string, but as to which horse that might be, well, you're just going to have to figure that out for yourself."

Matt walked out to the small corral that Smoke had built and, leaning on the split-rail fence, looked at the string of seven horses from which he could choose.

After looking them over very carefully, Matt smiled, and nodded.

"You've made your choice?" Smoke asked.

"Yes."

"Which one?"

"I want that one," Matt said, pointing to a bay.

"Why not the chestnut?" Smoke asked. "He looks stronger."

"Look at the chestnut's front feet," Matt said. "They are splayed. The bay's feet are just right."

"What about the black one over there?"

"Uh-uh," Matt said. "His back legs are set too far back. I want the bay."

Smoke reached out and ran his hand through Matt's hair.

"You're learning, kid, you're learning," he said. "The bay is yours."

Matt's grin spread from ear to ear. "I've never had a horse of my own before," he said. He jumped down from the rail fence and started toward the horse.

"That's all right, he's never had a rider before," Smoke said.

"What?" Matt asked, jerking around in surprise as he stared at Smoke. "Did you say he's never been ridden?"

"He's as spirited as he was the day we brought him in."

"How'm I going to ride him, if he has never been ridden?"

"Well, I reckon you are just going to have to break him," Smoke said, passing the words off as easily as if he had just suggested that Matt should wear a hat.

"Break him? I can't break a horse!"

"Sure you can. It'll be fun," Smoke suggested.

Smoke showed Matt how to saddle the horse, and gave him some pointers on riding it.

"Now, you don't want to break the horse's spirit," Smoke said. *"What you want to do is make him your partner."*

"How do I do that?"

"Walk him around for a bit so he gets used to his saddle, and to you. Then get on."

"He won't throw me then?"

"Oh, he'll still throw you a few times," Smoke said with a little laugh. *"But at least he'll know how serious you are."*

To Matt's happy surprise, he wasn't thrown even once. The horse did buck a few times, coming down on stiff legs, then sunfishing and, finally galloping at full speed around the corral. But, after a few minutes he stopped fighting and Matt leaned over to pat him gently on the neck.

"Good job, Matt," Smoke said, clapping his hands quietly. *"You've got a real touch with horses. You didn't break him, you trained him, and that's real good. He's not mean, but he still has spirit."*

"Smoke, can I name him?"

"Sure, he's your horse, you can name him anything you want." Matt continued to pat the horse on the neck as he thought of a name.

"That's it," he said, smiling broadly. *"I've come up with a name."*

"What are you going to call him?"

"Spirit."

As Matt lay alongside the track he continued to think about his two horses named Spirit. He had given them good lives, treated them well, always making certain they were well fed and cared for, but in the end, both had died before their time. By being his horses, they had been subjected to more danger than most.

He thought about the expression in Spirit II's eyes, just before he had pulled the trigger. It was as if Spirit II knew what was about to happen to him. Was he blaming Matt? Was he telling Matt he understood it had to be done?

Before he could sink any deeper into the morass of melancholy, he heard a distant whistle. Pushing the gloomy thoughts away, he got up from his impromptu bed and looked south, toward the train. When first he saw it, it seemed to be creeping along, though Matt knew it was doing at least twenty miles per hour. It was the distance that made it appear as if the train was going much slower. That same distance also made the train seem very small. Even the smoke pouring from its stack seemed but a tiny wisp against a sky which had been made gold by the setting sun.

Matt could hear the reverberation of the puffing engine, sounding louder than one might think, given the distance. When the train came close enough for him to be seen, Matt stepped onto the track and began waving. After a few waves, he heard the train braking so he knew the engineer had spotted him and was going to stop. The train which had appeared so tiny before, appeared huge. It ground to a squeaking, clanking halt with black smoke pouring from its stack. Tendrils of white steam, escaping from the drive cylinders and limned in gold by the rays of the setting sun, wreathed the huge wheels.

The engineer's face appeared in the window. "What do you want, mister? Why'd you stop us?" he called down to Matt, raising his voice over the rhythmic sound of venting steam.

"My horse stepped in a prairie dog hole and I had to put him down," Matt said. "I need a ride."

The engineer stroked his chin for a moment, studying Matt as if trying to decide whether or not he should pick him up.

"What's going on here? Why did we stop?" another man asked, approaching the engine quickly and importantly from somewhere back in the train. The man was wearing the uniform of a conductor.

"This fella needs a ride," the engineer said. "His horse went down on him."

"I'm not in the habit of giving charity rides to indigents," the conductor said.

"I can pay," Matt said. "I need to get to Pueblo."

"You can pay, can you? Well let me ask you this. Does this place look like a depot to you? Do you think you can just flag down a train and board it anywhere you wish?" the conductor asked in a self-important and sarcastic voice.

"I don't know about you, Mr. Gordon, but I wouldn't feel right just leavin' him out here," the engineer said. "I mean, him losin' his horse and all, kind of makes it like an emergency, don't it?"

The conductor stroked his chin and spent a long moment studying Matt. All the while the pressure relief valve continued to vent steam, giving the engine the illusion of some great beast of burden, breathing heavily from its exertions. Some distance away a coyote barked, and closer in, a crow called.

"Hey! What's going on? Why have we stopped?" a passenger called, walking toward the engine.

"Get back in the cars, sir!" the conductor shouted. "You've got a trainload of people wondering why we stopped. We've got a right to know what is going on," the passenger said.

"Please, sir, get back in the cars," the conductor repeated. "I will take care of the situation." The conductor waited until the passenger re-boarded the train, then he looked up at the engineer.

"All right, Cephus, have it your way," the conductor said. He turned to Matt. "I don't like unscheduled stops like this, but I don't want it said that I left you stranded out here. It is going to cost you two dollars to go to Pueblo."

"Thanks," Matt said, taking two dollars from the poke in his saddle bag and handing it to the conductor.

"Sorry about your horse, mister," the engineer called down from the cab window.

"Yes, he was a good horse."

In an elaborate gesture, the conductor pulled a watch from his vest pocket, popped open the cover, and examined the face. The silver watch was attached to a gold chain making a shallow U across his chest.

"Cephus, we are due in Pueblo exactly one hour and twenty-seven minutes from right now," the conductor said to the engineer as he snapped the watch closed and returned it to his vest pocket. "I do not plan to be late. That means I expect you to make up the time we have lost by this stop."

"Yes, sir, Mr. Gordon, don't worry. If Doodle keeps the steam up, we'll be there on time."

"Don't you be worryin' none about the steam," Doodle, the fireman said, stepping onto the platform that extended just behind the engine. "You'll have all the steam you need."

"Come along," the conductor said to Matt. "You can ride in any car. There are seats in all three of them. They are all day coaches."

"I'd rather ride in the express car, if you don't mind," Matt said.

"No, I'm sorry, I can't let you in there," the conductor replied.

"Maybe you haven't heard," Matt said, "but the bank in Pueblo was robbed this morning."

"Yes, I heard. What does that have to do with anything?"

Matt held up the canvas bag he had taken from Cyrus Hayes' body. "This is the money that was taken from the bank."

"What? What the hell, mister? Are you telling me you are the one who held up the bank?"

"No," Matt said. "I'm the one who is taking the money back to the bank. I would just as soon not be riding in one of the passenger cars, while I'm carrying this."

"Oh," the conductor said.

At that moment the door to the express car slid open, and the express messenger looked down on them. "He can ride in here with me, Mr. Gordon. It will be all right."

"I'll let him in there, but remember, it was your idea, not mine," Gordon replied.

"I'll remember. Hi, Matt," the messenger said.

Matt smiled up at a friend with whom he had played cards many times. "Hi, Jerry," he greeted.